THE
PARADISE
Inn

JOHN CHARLES GIFFORD

THE PARADISE INN

iUniverse books may be ordered through booksellers or by contacting:

iUniverse
1663 Liberty Drive
Bloomington, IN 47403
www.iuniverse.com
844-349-9409

ISBN: 978-1-6632-1059-3 (sc)
ISBN: 978-1-6632-0993-1 (e)

Library of Congress Control Number: 2020919469

Print information available on the last page.

iUniverse rev. date: 11/05/2020

Come, all ye people, to dis tropical isle.
We will dance and sing and beguile you with style.
Forget your cares; forget that old rat race.
Enjoy da sun, enjoy a drink or two, but just in case,
we have many more things for you
in dis romantic, mystical rendezvous.

Movie stars! Nightclubs! Gambling abounds!
Havana at night is your personal playground!
But you must start off first at a small hotel
where the Hannigans and Hunter and Sammy as well
will guide you gently through this city of sin.
Oh, come, all ye people, to the Paradise Inn.

1

Under the Stars

New Year's Eve 1956

Dig it.

Ash Hunter threw back the last of his mojito and asked for another. He sat at the bar of the Bajo las Estrellas and looked behind him over his shoulder, glassy-eyed. The tables were filling up, and the partygoers were still filing into the Tropicana. They wore tuxedos and evening gowns and brought mucho dinero. A mambo sizzled from the orchestra; most of the guests were either dancing or eating a four-course dinner served on china bearing the famous Tropicana emblem: a figure of a ballerina. A few men were standing in groups of two or three in shadowed corners, talking in hushed voices, with their eyes darting here and there and cigars clamped firmly in their jaws. Cigar smoke wafted through the humid air amid aromas of pork, black beans, and alcohol and the balmy lushness of the flowers and palm trees in the outdoor cabaret.

The night was electrifying.

Hunter turned his head again in time to see the barman's hand draw back as a fresh mojito appeared in front of him—crushed mint sprigs, sugar soaked in rum, gassy water, and ice cubes in a tall glass

1

sweating on the outside. Something cold for the hot Havana night. He tamped his Dunhill Lovat briar pipe, relit it with a match, and sent a stream of smoke in front of him.

His eyes followed the smoke as it rose in front of him and dissipated, revealing his image in the mirror behind the bar. He wasn't particularly vain, at least not any more so than the average fellow, but he liked what he saw. The rented white tuxedo looked classy on him; the blue carnation in his lapel added a little vitality and pizzazz. His black hair, combed back, glistened with Brylcreem: "Just a little dab will do ya!"

Cadillacs and Lincolns had been inching their way forward on Truffin Avenue toward the entrance for the last four hours. The parking valets were working overtime. Hunter had taken a taxi— with the radio tuned to CMQ with Pérez Prado, Celia Cruz, and Benny Moré all the way—to the point where the convoy started to back up, and then he'd walked the rest of the way. He'd arrived early, so he'd lit his pipe and stood in the grassy patch opposite the carport and entrance to the cabaret, near the Fountain of the Muses and its eight life-size nude nymphs having a great time splashing water at each other, and watched the carnival of people arriving, trying to find a familiar face in the crowd. He was in no rush. He had an invite—a reserved seat, the best in the house for the main stage show. His seat guaranteed perfume scents, skimpy costumes, long legs, and a lot of flesh up close. Hunter grinned. Sometimes the anticipation of an event turned out to be better than the event itself. That wasn't going to be the case that night. He was certain of it.

Hunter glanced at his watch and then picked up his drink and made his way toward the stage with his pipe firmly secured between his teeth. The show would begin soon. A friend, jive-talking Havana radioman Mario Lavin, had invited him to sit at his table while he broadcast his show live. Hunter found his seat four down from Lavin at a long table set nearly flush to where the stage would be when it suddenly appeared like magic. Lavin, leaning over and speaking into the mic, his eyes dancing to his left, caught Hunter's movements and winked. Hunter was the only American at the table. The others, all Cuban, had rum drinks in front of them, with little Cuban and American flags on toothpicks stuck in pieces of fruit.

Tiny white lights had been strung overhead between the catwalks and the palm trees. Candles in glass brandy-snifter-shaped vases lined the tables and flickered as warm breezes swept over them.

At ten thirty, the orchestra stopped playing, and the dance floor slowly elevated and then mutated into a stage. Hunter sipped his drink and puffed on his pipe, waiting with the others—who probably numbered more than a thousand at that point—for the show to begin. He had seen shows at the Tropicana before, and they all had been incredibly staged, but he never had viewed one from this close. He twisted in his seat to have a look behind him. Two tables to his left, Ava Gardner, leaning to her side with her hands cupped, was whispering something into the ear of Marlon Brando, who then turned to his left at the next table and repeated it to Ernest Hemingway. They threw their heads back and laughed. *Havana— you gotta love it*, Hunter thought.

The lights dimmed. Hushed whispers faded into silence as the handsome, pencil-mustachioed young master of ceremonies, wearing a white tuxedo, made his way to the dark stage. *Flash!* The spotlights glared down on him. "Ladies and gentlemen," he said in a resounding voice, "the Tropicana cabaret is proud to present"—he paused for theatrical effect—"*Omelen-ko!*"

A Cubana Airways aircraft landing on a runway was projected onto an overhead curtain. As it touched down, the bandleader raised his baton, and the orchestra began to play George Gershwin's "Cuban Overture." The curtain then drew back, exposing a painted full-size wooden mock-up of an airplane. The side door opened, and out came the female chorus, dressed as stewardesses, followed by a group dressed as American tourists. They were met by the male chorus—the baggage handlers. They gathered together center stage and, as the orchestra segued into the next song, sang, "Volar por Cubana de Aviación. ¡Qué emoción!"

3

The performers did some cutesy stuff for the tourists sitting in front of them. There was thunderous applause.

Hunter clapped too. Although he had seen this routine before, he was still impressed by its glamour. But he wasn't there to see Cubans pretending to be Americans; he was there to see *Omelen-ko*. He took a sip of mojito as the lights dimmed again to near blackness. Lavin, with his head bent slightly forward and to his left, whispered into his mic to people at home in front of their radios, describing every minute detail of what he was witnessing with restrained excitement. There was organized rushing onstage; a new set appeared, and then there was silence.

Then came drums, drums, and more drums. Pounding Yoruba drums. Pounding batá Santería drums. The pounding reverberated throughout Bajo las Estrellas. Okónkolo drums, Iyá drums, and Itótele drums pounded and pounded in a frenzy of Lucumi polyrhythmic beating. Hunter could feel the vibrations on his table, in his hand that held his drink, in his bones, and in his blood.

Bajo las Estrellas trembled. Bajo las Estrellas shivered. The audience, surrounded by lush tropical vegetation in the outdoor cabaret, was mesmerized by the primeval African sounds. In the dim lights, pigeons, goats, and roosters abounded, awaiting their mock sacrifices to the Yoruban gods. The drums beat on and on. The stage—no, the entire cabaret—had transformed into a primordial jungle.

Dig it!

The lights slowly came on again. It was a balmy night. No one looked up at the stars; their eyes were fixated on the stage.

The drums beat on and on.

Pairs of skimpily clad dancers contorted their bodies to the drumbeats in their ritual-praise summons for the Yoruban saints, their *santos*. First summoned was Elegguá, the orisha of birth and death, who opened and closed the paths of life. The dancer wore Elegguá's red and black colors. Next summoned was Ochún, seductive and sensual, the female ideal, who held the power of love and sex in her hands. The dancer representing her wore yellow. On and on it went—drums beating; performers dancing; bare-chested men stomping out the rhythm; the chorus singing in Yoruba; the audience watching, nearly hypnotized; and Hunter's mojito vibrating on the table with the pounding of the African drums.

A woman who sat a few tables to the left of Hunter in the front row wore a sleek black evening dress and fox furs draped over her shoulders. Hunter could tell she couldn't resist the primal rhythms coming from the stage; he could see that she was unable to restrain herself. He watched her body shiver slightly as she sat transfixed in an eye-glazing stupor with her full attention on the Yoruban ritual onstage. The shivers intensified, and her movements became more exaggerated. She was held captive by the drums, the music, and the dancing.

Suddenly, without warning, she got up, leaped forward, flung herself onto the stage with the others, and began shaking and shivering, throwing her arms up and out uncontrollably, dancing with the dancers, a blonde white woman among black Africans. Hunter watched in amazement as the woman in a black evening dress and furs danced and danced like a woman possessed by the devil.

Dig it now!

She grabbed her dress in the middle, just under her breasts, and flung her arms up and to the sides, ripping the dress, furs and all, off her body, revealing a scantily fringed undergarment. She continued to dance the way the others were dancing—frenzied, trancelike, magnificent. This continued for a few minutes, until Death, bare-chested, his skin dark and glistening, pointed at a twenty-foot geometric metal sculpture looming up and around the stage, dotted with tiny white lights. "Climb!" boomed Death.

She climbed.

The woman ascended the sculpture as if under an African spell, grasping the metal tubes like a circus performer—skilled, lithe, dazzling. Below her, drums beat, dancers danced, and animals raced

5

about. Once at the top, with all eyes glued on her, she stood erect with her arms high over her shoulders and Death twenty feet below her. The audience was mesmerized. Hunter was mesmerized. Then she dived down headfirst, swanlike, with arms extended and was caught by a double line of men. Everyone, relieved this was part of the show, stood and frantically clapped for several minutes for Chiquita, the woman who had started out as part of the audience and had defied Death.

The show continued until a minute before midnight, at which point the lights brightened, and the master of ceremonies came out and stood in the middle of the stage, as he had done at the beginning of the show. The cast formed a crescent moon behind him, along with the animals, to show that they had not, in fact, been sacrificed to the gods. He said a few words and began the countdown for the birth of a new year. All joined in: "¡Diez, nueve, ocho, siete, seis, cinco, cuatro, tres, dos, uno! ¡Feliz Año! ¡Muchas felicidades! ¡Feliz 1957!"

Chiquita released twelve good-luck doves into the air. Confetti rained down. Champagne flowed. There were embraces, kisses, and noisemakers. Hunter hugged the strangers around him, both male and female. Succulent grapes had been laid out on the tables for the guests to partake in. Eating twelve of them brought good fortune in the coming year. A mistake had been made, and only eleven were in Hunter's bowl in front of him.

Hunter was glad he had come. He was glad he was starting out the year at the Tropicana. Among the gaiety and festivities, however, neither Hunter nor the other guests that night could have anticipated what was to come.

An hour later, at the bar of Bajo las Estrellas, someone tapped Hunter on the shoulder.

Swiveling around on his stool, Hunter said, "Alfonso. Happy New Year!"

"To you as well, my friend. I don't want to spoil your night, but can I see you in my office? I have a grave problem. If there is a way to solve it, I think you can do it."

Grave problem? Hunter thought. This was highly uncharacteristic of Alfonso. He always put pleasantries before business or concerns. It must be serious, on this of all nights.

Hunter followed Alfonso Gomez around the bar, and they shouldered their way through the hordes of well-dressed partiers to a narrow hallway and, finally, to small office at the end. Once they were inside with the door closed, the silence was deafening.

"Sit, please," Alfonso said, gesturing with his hand. He went to the side of his desk to a cart with an assortment of liquor bottles and glasses. He poured brandy into two snifters and handed one to Hunter. Next to the cart, on its own pedestal, was a sculpture of a woman without arms and without legs below the knees. Hunter had seen it before, a Rita Longa, and never liked it. What was so beautiful about a woman with no arms?

"¡Salud!" they both said at the same time, clinking glasses.

Leaning against the edge of his desk, Alfonso got right to the point. "I want to hire you for a job. The police must be kept out of it."

Alfonso Gomez was old enough to be Hunter's father, although he was in good physical condition and looked much younger. His combed-back hair was graying but still mostly black. He had a thick mustache under a Roman nose and wore thick black-framed glasses. To Hunter, he looked more like a lawyer or politician than a casino manager.

The basis of the friendship between the two men was personal. The casino there at the Tropicana was one of Hunter's favorite places to gamble. He and Alfonso had struck up a friendship several years ago. Alfonso had always been impressed that Hunter was a private

7

investigator, but he never had had need of his services—that was, until now.

Hunter emptied the dottle from his pipe into an ashtray and filled the pipe with his blend again, waiting for Alfonso to explain. He could see by Alfonso's expression that he was trying to organize his thoughts and was having a difficult time.

"Ah, where to start?" he finally said. "I suppose at the beginning; that's always the best place. Last night, an Argentinian who is vacationing here from Madrid was playing baccarat and lost badly. Of course, we were concerned because he told us he had no money to pay his debt. He had been also playing some other games. My people made the mistake of allowing him to continue because, well, he looked wealthy. I invited him to my office to discuss that matter. He sat where you're sitting right now." He pointed. "I was a little confused because he didn't seem upset, you know, the way one would expect someone in his situation to be. To gamble and not to be able to pay your debt is serious. Think if he had won and we hadn't given him what he earned!"

Alfonso went on to say that the man had told him he had been Eva Perón's personal secretary before she died. It had taken all Alfonso had to control himself. He'd wanted to laugh. Alfonso had thought the man was joking, but his face had told a different story. As if that story weren't ridiculous enough, the man had proceeded to tell him that he had inherited some jewels from Perón and that they were in the safe at the hotel he was staying at.

Alfonso paused to sip his brandy and then said, "This man— his name is Ignacio Navarro—had been living in Madrid, and he stopped in Havana to vacation before returning to Buenos Aires to live permanently again. He wanted me to hold the jewels until his bank wired him the money to pay his debt. Then we could return the jewels to him. It sounded like a big con game to me. I've managed this casino for many years, so I've heard hundreds of stories about why people cannot pay their gambling debts. This one was the best—ingenious in many ways yet completely absurd.

8

"As it happens, I know someone in Mexico City who served in the Perón government. He comes to the Tropicana several times a year. If Navarro was telling me the truth, I figured my friend should be able to verify it."

"And?" said Hunter.

"And he did. What Navarro had told me was the truth. My friend also said that Navarro was a fine, upstanding man."

Hunter lit his pipe and sent a cloud of smoke into the room.

Alfonso said he'd had someone from the casino go with Navarro to get the jewels he had locked up in the hotel safe. His man had inventoried them, as Alfonso had told him to do—a set of diamond earrings, two diamond rings, and a diamond tiara—and he'd given Navarro a receipt for them.

"On his way here, a car ran him off the road, and two men got out. They had guns and demanded he hand over the jewels. Somehow, they knew about them. Of course, my man had no choice but to do as he was told. He drove back immediately and told me what had happened."

"How well do you trust your man?" Hunter asked, calmly puffing on his pipe.

"He's my nephew. I've known him since he was born. He would never steal from us. He's completely trustworthy."

Hunter was skeptical but hoped his face didn't show it. "And you're sure the jewels were real?"

"My nephew was an apprentice to a jeweler for several years before coming to the casino to work for me. That's why I sent him. He examined the jewels carefully. He knows his diamonds. They're real."

"Then the only other answer is that Navarro had set this up beforehand with these two men in case he lost. Because the club lost his jewels, he will expect the Tropicana to forgive the debt. He'll consider the club negligent for not securing the transportation of the jewels better. He might even hammer you for a lot of money for the stolen jewels, holding the Tropicana responsible. A small fortune no doubt. He'll say it was your fault. He'll have you running around yourself in a tizzy. It's a solid scam if you ask me."

"Actually, that's exactly what he did say. And he was correct about that. I should have sent more men—armed, of course." Alfonso pushed himself away from the desk and plopped down in a chair beside Hunter. "I don't know what to think. According to my friend, Navarro is a sincere man with a good reputation. Could such a man be also a—how do you say it in America?"

"A con artist," Hunter said with a snicker.

"Yes, a con artist." After a long minute, he added, "Of course, he plans on staying in Havana until this matter is resolved. Word could get around, however. The reputation of the Tropicana is at stake. If we don't have our reputation, then we have nothing. Navarro assured me he would keep this to himself, but he does want this resolved. That's why we want you to look into this matter for us. We don't want you to strong-arm him. It's got to be done delicately. If he thinks we're playing hard, he might start spreading the word. Once it's out, regardless of who's at fault, it cannot be undone. That's why I'm asking you. If we involved the police, the whole of Cuba would know about it in an hour. Besides, if they found the jewels, they'd simply take them and lie about it. I know you will find this hard to believe, but you can find *gangsterismo* within the National Police as well." He smiled.

Hunter laughed. "Did your nephew get a good look at the men? Or the car?"

"Not a good look, no. It was dark, and their faces were shadowed. But he said one man was large, very fat. The other was of average size. Both wore hats pulled down to their eyes and dark suits. The fat one told him to get down on the floor of the car until they were gone. He did as he was told, until he could no longer hear the car driving away."

"So what exactly do you want me to do? Run interference?"

"That and more. I want you to find the jewels."

"Okay, Alfonso," Hunter said, "you've always been square with me, so I'll be square with you. I don't like it, not one bit. There are too many people involved, with too many possible angles. If I take on this case, you'd have to step aside and let me do what I think is right. I'll run the interference, not you. Either someone's lying, or it went down the way you were told. Everyone involved, from Navarro to your nephew to the two men, is a rotten egg until I prove otherwise. Those are my terms."

"I accept them," Alfonso said with a glimmer of hope in his eyes. "I will give you a thousand US dollars to begin with. If you need more, just ask."

"Okay then. I'll do my best, but I can't make any promises, and it won't be easy. We'll talk about my fees later. See what I come up with first. Maybe you won't want to pay me nuttin'."

They both laughed.

"That's unlikely to happen, hombre. I'd feel guilty since the casino has taken so much of your money already."

"Just keep the lid on my involvement. Remember, I don't have a license to snoop in Cuba. As far as the authorities know, I'm just a part owner of an economy tourist inn for Americans and anyone else gutsy enough to stay there and nothing more. I want to keep it that way."

"The Paradise Inn is a fine hotel. I've recommended it to my friends visiting Havana."

"Yeah, the ones you don't especially like." Hunter looked down at his pipe and tamped the ash down.

"Don't do a disservice to your establishment, Ash Hunter. You are providing a very necessary service to the Cuban economy. And yes, I remember that you are working without the necessary credentials. I am a man with many secrets. We all have our *mundos secretos*, our secret worlds."

"By the way, where's Navarro staying?"

"At the Hotel Sevilla-Biltmore."

"He's got expensive taste. Maybe he's planning on using the casino's money to pay his bill."

"Maybe, but just keep an open mind that Navarro might be an innocent victim. He was a well-dressed gentleman who seemed to have class and style. I detected nothing of the con artist in him."

"Oh yeah? That's what we thought about *el presidente* too."

"Yes, of course. I see what you mean. Gangsterismo is also found in the government, but don't tell anyone I said that. I will vociferously deny it."

With that, they laughed, finished their brandies, and shook hands.

"I should have something in a few days," Hunter said as he opened the door. "But I'm not going to throw you any angles. If I think it's a lost cause, I'll tell you up front. See you then."

He walked down the hallway and passed through the casino on his way to the outdoor cabaret. It was still crowded with partiers and would remain so until the sun came up.

As he approached the bar at the Bajo las Estrellas, he noticed a beautiful young woman walking past the stool he had sat on when Alfonso approached him. She had Spanish looks, with black hair and fair skin—a wonderful contrast to her red dress. She was Cuban no doubt. Hunter stopped briefly to admire her. A purse hung off her right shoulder, and her hand grasped the long strap. She walked with confidence, almost arrogance, with her head held high. Hunter's eyes were glued on her. Maybe there was a handsome young man waiting for her somewhere in the crowd. Just his luck.

As she got to the end of the bar, there was a terrible explosion that momentarily blinded Hunter. By the force of the blast, or perhaps by his own instincts, he found himself on the floor. He took a handkerchief out of his pocket and wiped his eyes. They were tearing badly and stung, so he wiped them again. He could hear shouts and screaming. When he looked over at the bar, the smoke and dust were thick but began to settle. Through the haze, little by little, he could see the young woman with the red dress lying on her left side. Her right arm, which had been ripped off at the elbow, lay on the marble floor next to her.

2

The Start of a Good Year

"Take two Alka-Seltzer and go back to bed, Hannigan," Babs said
to her husband, who sat next to her. She gazed at the print hanging
on the wall in front of them. "You look like one of those surrealist
melting watches of Dalí's. If you can't make it to bed, I could drape
you over a limb on the tree outside, like in the painting."

Hannigan looked up, stared at the painting for a moment, ran
his fingers over his bristled chin as if he were deliberating on her
proposal, and said, "More java." Then he grunted and shook his
head.

"Get the man some more coffee, Sammy," Babs said. "I think
he said he's not going anywhere. I think he said he's fine and dandy.
The man is surreal, Sammy." Looking back at him, she asked, "Are
you fine and dandy, Hannigan?"

He let out another grunt.

Sammy got up, took Hannigan's cup to the coffee nook, and
filled it. He slid the cup in front of him. "Mr. Slane, you want I
should help you to your room?"

Hannigan managed an awkward grin. "As the lady said, Sammy,
I'm fine and dandy."

"Actually, you're not in bad shape, considering you had a dozen daiquiris from eight last night until four this morning," Babs said. "I thought we were going to run out of rum. I'm glad our guests leaned more toward gin and tonic. No sympathy with your morning coffee for you today."

"We have plenty of rum," Hannigan growled. "Can't a guy enjoy New Year's Eve with paying guests without his wife barking at him the next day?"

"A guy can indeed," Babs said. "Can't a guy, Sammy?"

"*Oui*, a guy surely can!" Sammy said cautiously. "But as we like to say in Haiti, 'A rock in the water does not know the pain of the rock in the sun.'"

"See, Babs?" Hannigan said, jabbing a finger at her but missing the mark. "Sammy says you're not sympathizing with me." He gulped down some coffee.

"Sammy, did you put a little brandy in the man's coffee?" Babs asked. "Seems like he's got some Dutch courage all of a sudden."

"But you have to admit we threw a great party," Hannigan said. "Half our guests stayed here to celebrate instead of going out. We took in more money than we did last New Year's Eve."

"I haven't counted the receipts yet, but I think you're right," Babs said. "Who knows where that'll lead? Maybe the Paradise Inn will start getting a good reputation."

Hannigan leaned back in his chair with a confident grin on his face. "My dear old aunt Sofie. She knew I'd make it big someday."

"You don't have an aunt Sofie."

"If I did, she'd have known."

This time, it was Babs who grunted.

A few of the inn guests entered the café and seated themselves. A man and woman who looked to be retirement age, wearing matching Hawaiian shirts, sat down in a booth. A tall, thin woman in her forties, a bespectacled librarian-type with short gray hair and a guidebook cradled in her arm, took a table at the far end. A stout couple wearing cowboy hats and boots entered, stopped, and then looked around the café. The husband pointed his cigar at a table, and they waddled over to it. The Paradise's morning specialty was an American breakfast with all the works, just like home. Grits were included if requested.

Guests had been filtering in and out for most of the morning. Babs got up and greeted them and handed out menus. Sammy went into the kitchen, filling in for the cook, who was off that day. Hannigan picked up his coffee, took it to the small lobby nearby, and went behind the reception desk. He opened a folder that contained yesterday's receipts and grunted a few more times as he tried to peruse them. He knuckled his eyes and then decided it was useless to engage in bookkeeping at the moment and put the folder on his desk behind him. He went to the employees' washroom behind the desk and took two Alka-Seltzer. Babs would be pleased.

When he got back to the reception desk, a man in a white suit and panama hat was waiting there. He had the demeanor of a doctor, lawyer, accountant, or mobster. Hannigan had had too many daiquiris last night to figure out which.

"Are you Slane Hannigan?" the man asked.

"That's what people tell me. How can I help you?"

"I heard you have a boat for charter."

Excitement sopped up the alcohol in his system, leaving him with a sharp mind. "She ain't a boat, my friend, but you heard right. The Valiant Queen—she's a wood-hulled, twin-engine, standard sedan motor yacht built in 1939 by the Matthews Boat Company and designed for short- or long-term cruising. Forty feet in length, from bow to stern. Sleeps six in comfort. All the usual amenities and more. What did you say your name was?" Few things besides Babs could excite Hannigan as much as talking about the Valiant Queen. He had forgotten his hangover.

"I didn't, but it's Harry Smith." The man reached over, and they shook hands.

Hannigan couldn't help but notice Smith's eyes. He couldn't pinpoint it, but somehow, they belied his friendly demeanor. It was just a gut feeling, so he decided to ignore it. The guy was a possible paying customer. "Whaddaya have in mind, Harry Smith? Fishing in the bay? A jaunt to Key West? Sightseeing the coast?"

"No, nothing like that," Smith said. "I'd like you to pick up a package from a freighter in the Straits of Florida this evening. I can give you the exact coordinates the boat will be at."

Hannigan narrowed his eyes and cracked his knuckles. He didn't like what he was hearing.

"I guarantee you, Mr. Hannigan," Smith said, nonplussed, "this is all on the up and up." He threw his hands up, showing his open palms as evidence. "It's all very clean—nothing illegal."

"I'm glad you threw that in, Mr. Smith, because the Valiant Queen is my pride and joy, and I wouldn't want her to be confiscated by the Cuban police, and I wouldn't want to be thrown in the hoosegow and have my work visa revoked and be sent back to Minnesota. I run a clean business here in Havana and make a half-decent living. I like Havana. I like her a lot. Havana's my home, at least for the time being. I think she likes me back. I'd like to stick around. Besides, a freighter isn't a boat, and a yacht isn't a boat. A boat's a boat."

"You speak of Havana as if it were your mistress; it's only a city. But I certainly understand your sentiments. As I said, this is all legal. The package contains something of value that I don't want to bring here by conventional means. The value, you know? It's insured, but that's not the point. It's a one-of-a-kind object that can't be replaced."

"So once it's in my hands, I become responsible for this object of value. Is that it, Mr. Smith? A lawsuit in the making? Nix on that. Or are you coming along for the ride?"

"I'm not able to be here with you this evening, but I will sign a statement releasing you of any responsibility for it. Listen, you're making this into something that it's not. All you have to do is get the package, bring it back here, and put it in your safe. You do have a safe here, right?"

"I have a safe here."

"Good then. I can pick it up tomorrow morning. Do we have a deal? I'll pay you three times what you're going to ask."

That, more than anything, caught Hannigan's attention. "Why don't you come around the counter here and sit down at my desk? We'll work out the details. It's all copacetic." Hannigan put his arm around Smith's shoulders as he squeezed through behind the front desk. "You say you have the coordinates?"

An hour later, the guests had finished their breakfast and left to see the sights of the city. Babs and Sammy were sitting in one of the booths, talking over coffee, taking a break before the noon-hour crowd came in for lunch. Generally, during the tourist season, the guests staying at the inn were out and about in the city after having breakfast, so lunchtime was usually light.

Ash Hunter appeared at the entrance to the café. He stopped and stretched, yawning into his fist. Babs looked over at him.

"It's about time you got up," she said. "Half the day is gone already. You must have had a helluva night."

Hunter slid into the seat next to her.

"It serves you right for abandoning us on New Year's Eve," she added.

Hunter was a third partner, along with Hannigan and Babs, and shared the responsibility of the inn. He also ran a detective service on the side for extra revenue. It was strictly a word-of-mouth operation, as he couldn't get a license to practice in Cuba.

"Let me get you something to eat, Mr. Ash," Sammy said, getting up.

"Just toast and hot chocolate, Sammy," Hunter said. "Thanks." He looked at Babs. "I had a wonderful night at the Tropicana. I got to see a woman's arm—"

Both of them shifted their gaze toward the reception area and saw Hannigan shaking the hand of someone in a white suit. Hannigan showed the man out and came over to them.

"We've got a date this evening, Babs, with the Valiant Queen. A little errand job that will take a few hours. A Mr. Smith paid five hundred smackers upfront."

"Mr. Smith, hmm?" Babs said. "Sounds fishy to me. Does he want to go fishing, this Mr. Smith?"

"Nope. Just wants us to pick up a package—that's all. I'll explain later. It's all on the up and up; it's all copacetic."

"The more you talk, the fishier it sounds. I smell something rotten in the air."

"It'll be fine, Babs. The guy's above board. He was wearing Florsheim shoes."

"Well, that certainly settles the matter."

Shifting his gaze toward Hunter, Hannigan said, "You look worse than me, kid."

Hannigan sat down, and Hunter told them about the bombing at the Tropicana.

Babs said it was probably the rebels. They had taken up a little hobby in the last few years of planting bombs across the country and blowing up people. "Poor girl, having her arm blown off like that."

"You're right," Hunter said. "I stuck around for the police. That's why I got back so late. After eyeing the area where the bomb went off, they were convinced it was the girl herself who had the bomb in her purse. They thought it was one of those homemade jobs, and it went off prematurely. It was a small one. Only a few people around her were hurt, but it did a number on one of the bars."

"Just the same," Babs said, "the poor girl. I wonder what the rebels told her to get her to do something like that."

Hannigan jumped in. "I'm sure they promised her the moon and the stars if they took power. They'd get all the politicians, hustlers, whores, grifters, and low-rent hoods off the streets and turn Cuba into a workers' utopia. Then they'd go after the Domino Sugar executives and the United Fruit bigwigs. After that, they'd chase Batista out of the country and close down the casinos. What's an arm worth if she gets to live in heaven on earth?" He looked around the café, as if rebel spies were somehow there. "If that happens, I'll guarantee you the American corporations will leave, and the money will dry up because there won't be any tourists. We'll be back in Saint Paul, broke, singing in the streets, trying to hustle a living."

"You're a cynic, Hannigan," Babs said.

"No, I don't think that's going to happen. I'm just telling you the line the rebels probably gave her. What if that had been a bigger bomb? Dozens of people could have been killed. Maybe a lot more. They had to tell her something like that to get her to do what she did."

"Anyway," Hunter said, "that's not going to happen. Batista's going to squeeze them out of the mountains and lock them all up, and their support in the cities will dwindle down to a few fanatics. It's only a matter of time."

Sammy returned with Hunter's toast and hot chocolate and set them in front of him.

"All that aside," Hunter said, "I got a job last night from the Tropicana."

"Let me guess," Babs said. "You're going to be the new dishwasher."

"It's too early for jokes, Babs," Hannigan said. "Let the man talk."

Hunter explained the situation in detail, going over the Argentinian, the jewels once belonging to Eva Perón (Babs oohed and aahed as Hunter described the jewels), the two men who stole them, and Alfonso Gomez's nephew.

"I think I'll get a nice slice of the pie if I can find them," Hunter added. "More revenue for the Paradise." He stuffed a piece of the toast into his mouth, followed by a gulp of the hot chocolate.

"What are your chances of finding them?" Hannigan asked. "There are a lot of crooks in Havana, and they all look alike."

"Not good," Hunter said. "It's a long shot. The Tropicana knows that, but they're still willing to lay out the cash. Alfonzo offered me a grand to start the ball rolling. I told him to hang on to it. If I don't find the jewels, I'll get at least that; if I find them, I'll probably get a lot more."

Babs looked at her husband. "Did you hear that, Hannigan? Ash turned down a grand. What's the world coming to?"

"The world has always been an uncertain place. Let the man finish."

Hunter looked at Babs. "Relax. The grand is a sure thing. My point is this: if I find the jewels, we could be looking at five or ten thousand dollars. I have a feeling the jewels are worth a hundred thousand or more. Ten percent is a fair fee for finding them."

"Yeah," Babs said, "*if* you find them."

"Now who's the cynic?" her husband asked. "You've got to think positive!"

Sammy, who had been listening to the conversation, picked up his guitar. "I believe I have something to say about all this."

"Sing away, Sammy," Babs said. "Enlighten us! Clear the air!"

He began singing and strumming out a calypso tune, making up the lyrics on the spot:

> In dis uncertain world, where things go awry,
> you cannot sit back and ask, "Why, oh, why?"
> Listen to your heart and a man called Ash.
> He's a rascal and tricky, and he'll bring you hard cash.
> Evita is dead, and her jewels are gone,
> so just listen to this man, and see the bright new dawn.

"See, Babs?" Hannigan said. "Sammy knows the score. Hooray for Sammy!"

They all clapped, hooted, and shouted. Sammy stood up and took a bow.

"Okay, okay," Babs said lightheartedly. "I'll stop being a cynic, and I'll start listening to my heart and wait for our dear, lovely home-bred snoop Ashton Hunter to bring the hard cash on home to Mama."

They all had a good laugh at that.

Hunter finished his hot chocolate and then got up. "I'm off," he said. "Thank you, Sammy, for the vote of confidence. Right now, I gotta see a man about an interview."

"Don't forget, Ash," Babs said to Hunter's back as he walked toward the main entrance. "Mama will be waiting here to see tomorrow's bright new dawn—and all that cash!"

A short time after Hunter left, Slane Hannigan crossed the road near the inn and went down to the bay in front of the Paradise, at the tip of Havana Centro, leaving Babs and Sammy to watch things on the home front. The sun was out, the sky was clear blue, and it was windy. The ocean waves crashed against the seawall that rimmed the northern edge of the city. They splashed upward, spraying a fine mist onto the people sitting on benches or walking along the Malecón, the waterfront esplanade. It was a lazy day for all. They were, after all, recovering from the celebrations of last night.

Hannigan sat on a stone wall and looked around him. The mist felt good against the heat of the sun. Lovers strolled hand in hand. Old men stood with their canes while their wives rested on the wall, all staring out into the sea, perhaps recalling their youth. Children with their parents threw around huge balls, skipped rope, or bought bits of candy from street vendors. American tourists in weird clothing clicked their Brownies, living out their fantasies on their once-in-a-lifetime trip to the tropics. The Malecón had been built initially to protect Havana from flooding and from Los

Nortes, but it had become much more than that. Now it harbored a multitude of dreams and passions, hopes and desires.

Hannigan shifted his gaze out to sea. Just like the Cubans, he had his own hopes and dreams. He had come 1,600 hundred miles to realize them. That had been nearly ten years ago. He had worked hard back in Saint Paul, saved his money, and earned more from investments. So had Babs and Ash. It hadn't been a fortune but had been enough to make a down payment on the Paradise and the motor yacht. It had been his dream, and it later had become theirs as well.

He had understood well enough the risks. For six of the ten years, they'd struggled—they almost had gone bankrupt. Then the American tourists had started to flock in, as Hannigan had predicted they would, and things had changed for the better. They suddenly had had enough money to make renovations to the inn and upgrade the Valiant Queen with new engines.

It was a good day, this first day of January—a good day to begin the new year. The Paradise was full to capacity, Hannigan and Babs had a profitable charter for the Valiant Queen, and Ash Hunter had a new client with the possibility of earning a nice chunk of cash—all money funneled back into the Paradise Inn. Indeed, the new year was starting off with a bang.

What could possibly go wrong?

3

The Cabaret in the Sky

The owner of the Tropicana cabaret, Martín Fox, had been a gambling man ever since his early days in Ciego de Ávila, a city in the central part of Cuba, where he'd lost his middle finger in a lathe accident. He'd been forced to look for another way to make a living. That one incident not only changed his life forever but did so miraculously. After considering his options—there had been few open to him at that time, as he was uneducated and unskilled in anything but being a machinist, which he could no longer do—he had decided it was only right and proper to indulge his passions by taking bets for the illegal, off-the-record lottery called La Bolita. Of course, that had been years ago, when he was a young man. He often joked that he'd had to cut off his finger to become a rich man, but he hadn't been using it much anyway. Now youth was only something for him to reminisce about.

Presently, his doctors at Peter Bent Brigham Hospital in Boston were telling him he would have to slow down; his health was at stake. He seemed to be managing his diabetes well, but his pace was too fast. He wouldn't be able to go on as he had without serious complications.

They were right to tell him that. He rarely relaxed; his body seemed in perpetual motion; and he had a business to run, to say nothing of living up to the image he had created for himself. He was one of the wealthiest men in Cuba, a relentless businessman who wielded influence across the landscape of politicians; other businessmen, both Cuban and American; the higher echelons of the police and military; and the general population of Cuba as a whole. If that hadn't created enough of the high level of stress in his life, he also had a multitude of people who counted on him for a variety of reasons: his wife, his extended family, his partners, and his four hundred employees—the dancers, models, singers, waiters, croupiers, cooks, musicians, busboys, bartenders, cigarette girls, seamstresses, makeup artists, and dishwashers. In short, the cabaret couldn't function the way it did without him.

"Martín, you're not getting any younger," his doctors had warned him. "You've got to slow down."

Martín Fox considered their advice, but …

After the escape hatches were secured and the tail wheel was unlocked, the pilot and first officer of the Lockheed Constellation proceeded to the before-start-up checklist. They set the parking brakes, pulled the throttles back to idle, set the magneto starter switches to off, turned the four generators to on, set and confirmed that the landing gear was locked, and opened the cowl flaps for all four engines. They checked the weather and set the altimeter, transponder, and altitude.

Without skipping a beat, they moved to the start-up checklist. After the entry and cargo doors were secured and the engine areas were cleared, the flight engineer gradually opened the throttle to 10 percent. With the booster pump on, engine number three, starboard side, was primed and started—the propeller turned slowly, smoke billowed out of the exhaust, the propeller turned faster, and the booster pump turned off. They did the same for engine four and then for engines two and one, portside. With the navigation lights on and the radios set, the pilot requested taxi clearance. While he waited, he set the heading indicator to take off.

"We are clear on the left," the pilot said. "Are we clear on the right?" he asked the first officer.

"We are clear on the right."

With the landing lights on, the pilot released the parking brakes and began taxiing the aircraft.

At the end of the runway at Miami International Airport, the pilot set the parking brakes; pulled back the throttles to idle; set the propeller pitch to high revolutions per minute; with all booster pumps on, checked the engine instruments, set the radio, and set the avionics for departure; and then requested takeoff clearance.

Once clearance was granted, he released the parking brakes and pushed the throttles forward. The aircraft slowly moved down the runway, gradually gaining momentum to takeoff speed. The pilot then eased the yoke back, and the aircraft lifted off.

Once a positive rate of climb was established, he retracted the landing gear, pulled the flaps up, and trimmed the aircraft. Connie, as the aircraft was affectionately called, was in the air, heading for Havana, Cuba.

Martín Fox considered his doctors' advice, but he had other things in mind. He still wanted to turn the Tropicana into the most glamorous cabaret in the world, and he was heading in the right direction. Paris had the Folies Bergère, Crazy Horse, and Moulin Rouge. New York, of course, had many smaller, elegant cabarets, along with Broadway and fine restaurants. But neither city had one venue that brought everything all together if one threw gambling into the mix.

Havana, however, had the Tropicana, which had it all. Notwithstanding, he had to make sure there was a steady flow of customers, not just the local Havana crowd. He couldn't do that from his bed or on the golf course. So he'd thanked his doctors for their concerns and proceeded with his plan with Cubana Airlines to convert a Lockheed Constellation into a cabaret in the sky, bringing American tourists to Havana from Miami and giving them a little taste of the Tropicana in the process. He would call it the *Tropicana Special.*

Connie made a wide turn and then straightened out. The pilot reset his heading and throttled back the engines. They responded smoothly and quietly. He then looked back over his shoulder at the chief stewardess, who had just appeared inside the flight deck. The pilot was a man in his forties with an Errol Flynn mustache and smile who had flown Grumman F6F Hellcats off of aircraft carries during the war. He had shot down nine Japanese Mitsubishi A6M Zeros in the Pacific before the war's end.

"Let the show begin, sweetheart!" he said to her. "And don't forget to bring us some daiquiris!"

Flying Connie to Havana was going to be a piece of cake.

With the *Tropicana Special* aircraft, Martín Fox planned to offer a weekly charter, an all-inclusive package deal that bundled the flight, dinner and drinks at the Tropicana, a room at the Hotel Nacional, and breakfast the next morning. At $68.80 US dollars per person, he would realize a small profit, but he counted on two things to make it all worthwhile: the Americans would surely gamble, and they would tell their friends back home.

But he was not content to wait until the tourists arrived in Havana. He would prime them on the plane on the way there. He had some front seats taken out of his chartered aircraft and, in their place, installed a six-foot stage with an overhead arch—a much smaller version of his main stage at the Tropicana, the Arcos de Cristal. He also had a specially designed sixty-six-key piano installed. The entertainment would be delivered by some of the musicians and dancers from the Tropicana. He wanted all forty-six passengers well lubed and ready to part with their cash by the time they arrived.

By the time the plane got over the Florida Keys, the sun had set, and the lights attached to the arch over the small stage came on. The in-flight festivities were about to begin. The stewardesses welcomed the passengers with pink frozen daiquiris as a quintet in white ruffle-sleeved shirts played away on a trumpet, a piano, drums, a guitar, and maracas. From the onset, the passengers realized this would be a different kind of flight, something they had never experienced before. Martín Fox had made sure of that.

Mrs. Bradford Maddox of 454 Crestview Drive, Tampa, Florida, whose given name was Elizabeth—her friends called her Lizzy— leaned over and said something to her husband, who sat next to her. Bradford —never Brad—had been eyeing one of the females from the Tropicana crowd handing out drinks in the front of the cabin and didn't hear what she said.

"What's that, Elizabeth?"

"I said this is so exciting!"

"Yes, dear," he said, his eyes still fixed on a pair of long legs.

After the drinks were handed out and the passengers were absorbing a taste of Cuban culture, the conjunto, situated near the bulkhead, segued from a cha-cha to a mambo. Ana Gloria and Roland, headliners at the cabaret, suddenly appeared and danced to the music. After a few minutes of fancy footwork, they mamboed down the aisle, with Ana Gloria mussing the hair of several male passengers and patting the cheeks of others along the way, her hips swaying into their shoulders gracefully as not to disturb the drinks in their hands. The music was loud and infectious, and the movements of the dancers, appearing exotic to the tourists, were smooth and controlled.

The atmosphere in the cabin was electrifying. Connie had been in the air barely twenty minutes, and already the Americans were experiencing Cuba. The pair of dancers had invited some of the passengers into the aisle and were giving them lessons. Ana Gloria leaned back at one point in one of her sensational moves and asked Bradford, "Choo want to dance?"

Bradford, slightly embarrassed, sipped his pink drink and stayed in his seat.

"Go ahead, sugar plum," Elizabeth said, leaning into him. "I won't be jealous."

"I think she asked both of us, dear."

With that, Mr. and Mrs. Bradford Maddox of 454 Crestview Drive, Tampa, Florida, got up and mamboed in the aisle along with the others. Lizzy was a slight middle-aged woman of five feet, two inches in height. She was a peroxide blonde with a long, sharp nose. Her makeup was just at the precipice of being distasteful, hanging precariously off the edge but not toppling over. Bradford was six foot two, five years older than Lizzy, and in good physical condition but with a middle-aged spread. His face was nondescript. He was a better listener than talker most of the time. He spent a great deal of his time listening to his wife.

They eventually joined in a conga line, occasionally glancing at either Ana Gloria or Rolando for the correct moves, nearly forgetting they were on a plane. They easily could have been in a small club in Havana, having the time of their lives.

If Martín Fox had been on the flight, he would have been pleased.

After fifteen minutes, they were both exhausted. Being in their fifties wasn't easy for either of them. Taking their seats again, they saw that their daiquiris had been refreshed. Elizabeth took a sip from hers and then looked over at her husband. "Do you think we're doing the right thing?"

"We've talked about this a thousand times already," he said, grimacing, with an undertone of impatience. "Well, you have anyway. I thought we arrived at the same conclusion—that we have no choice. He left us no alternative. Are you telling me you're having second thoughts?"

Elizabeth thought he sounded harsh, which was uncharacteristic of him. She was fine with their decision, but she was uncertain about him. What harm could she cause by testing him?

She grabbed his arm affectionately and leaned into him, smiling. "Well, just a little bit, my love. But now I'm fine."

"You're sure?" Bradford looked hopeful but worried.

"Oh yes. Self-doubt can be helpful sometimes. It can make your resolve even stronger."

"And how's your resolve now?" he asked with some hope.

"It's fine, Bradford. Just fine."

She meant it.

The plane dipped, and they looked out the port window over the wing at the same time and saw the twinkling lights of Havana below. "It's a large city," Bradford said. "So many people. We're going to have a difficult time finding him."

"Hmm," Elizabeth said. "He's down there somewhere. We'll find him."

The music stopped, and those left in the conga line went back to their seats. The seat-belt light went on, the performers sat down, everyone buckled his or her seat belt, and the plane vibrated slightly as the landing gear went down. The stewardesses checked to make sure everything was secured and then went back to their jump seats, and they too sat down.

"Thank you for flying the *Tropicana Special*," the former fighter pilot who had shot down nine Zeros in the Asian campaign said over the intercom. "We'll be landing shortly. The weather in Havana is a balmy ninety-five. Buses will be waiting for you once we land to take you to your hotel. On behalf of Cubana Airlines, *¡gracias a todos!*"

Mr. and Mrs. Maddox straightened the backs of their seats and then looked at each other.

Elizabeth could see in her husband's eyes that there was nothing wrong with his resolve either. *He's down there somewhere*, she said silently to herself. *We'll find him.*

4

The Interview

The Hotel Sevilla-Biltmore was located on the tree-lined Prado Promenade in Havana Centro, a block north of the flamboyant Presidential Palace and a stone's throw away from the Colón Quarter's brothel district to the northwest. They formed a triangle of sorts—easy access for foreign dignitaries and pleasure-seeking tourists alike. It had been called simply the Sevilla when it went up in 1908. It had changed hands in 1920 and been renamed by New York magnate John Bowman, who owned a chain of Biltmores. For more than a decade, it had been the swankest hotel in Havana. Then the Hotel Nacional had gone up in 1930, and amid the recent construction of high-end hotels, the Sevilla-Biltmore was still in the running but with much more competition.

Ash Hunter took the elevator to the eighth floor, walked halfway down the carpeted hallway, and knocked on the door of room 815. While he waited, he thought about what Alfonso Gomez at the Tropicana had told him about the man he was about to see: he had a sterling reputation and had worked as a secretary for Eva Perón. That didn't preclude him from being a con artist, though. Plenty of wealthy people with impeccable reputations turned out to be hustlers in the end. Did the guy have an angle? Who knew? It was best to consider him guilty until proven innocent. Hunter didn't usually assume someone was guilty of something before a complete investigation, but he could live with that.

A man in his midfifties opened the door. "You must be Mr. Hunter," he said. "Ignacio Navarro." He offered his hand.

"I am," Hunter said soberly, shaking it.

Ignacio Navarro was a tall, thin, professorial-looking man with slumped shoulders that made his suit coat seem ill-fitted. His hair was gray and turning white at the temples, and he had a thick mustache and eyebrows that were more black than gray. Although his face was lined, there was enough evidence to suggest he'd been a handsome man in his youth, but his eyes hinted that he must have had great responsibilities and suffered hardships. They were set in, hollow, and the skin underneath them was dark, with tiny brown moles dotted here and there. One look at them revealed the torrid history of mankind. Yet there seemed a certain incontrovertible dignity about him.

"Come in, and sit down, please," Navarro said, swinging an arm behind him in the direction of a small table and chairs next to a window. "If you'd like something to drink, I could order room service."

"That won't be necessary, Mr. Navarro," Hunter said. "I've got a lot of things to do today, so I'll get right to the point."

They sat down at the table, facing each other. Latins liked to engage in personal conversation before conducting business. By jumping into the water right away, perhaps Hunter could disrupt Navarro's sense of decorum, putting him at a disadvantage from the onset. The man's face would show it sooner or later if Hunter pressed him hard enough. He was good at peeling away at deception little by little until there was nothing left but the truth. He knew how to interpret little facial tics, darting eyes, teeth biting at the lips, palms rubbing the chin, and shifting body positions.

"Do you mind if I smoke my pipe?" Hunter asked.

Hunter had smoked a pipe since his time in the army, when he'd picked his first one out in a small tobacco shop in southern Italy during the war, and he greatly enjoyed it. He'd discovered early on in his career as a private dick back in Saint Paul that his pipe could also be used as a tool during interviews. Generally, at the start of an interview, he would pack his pipe full with a tobacco blend, singe the top with a match, tamp the ash down, and then relight it. He'd puff on it, reflect, and puff again, drawing out the time, making the person he was interviewing wonder what he was thinking. Sometimes it would send the interview off in another unanticipated direction. He hoped that might be the case that day. The unanticipated was usually a more interesting path.

"Please do. I'll join you with a cigar."

Hunter filled his pipe, eyeing Navarro as he pulled out a leather case from the inside of his suit coat, took one of the cigars from it, and lit up. Navarro's eyes were sad looking. They reminded Hunter of the pictures he'd seen of Franklin Roosevelt at the Yalta Conference with Churchill and Stalin a few months before he died. Sad, weary, used-up, defeated eyes—visions of the end that was soon coming. Did Navarro have visions too?

"Thanks for seeing me today," Hunter said, puffing out some smoke across the table.

"Sorry you had to come here on this of all days," Navarro said. Then, almost as an afterthought, he added, "Feliz Año." He said the last words with such a lack of spirit as to render them meaningless.

"Yes, happy New Year to you, but I'm sure you're not very happy."

"I've had better days."

Hunter looked down at his pipe, tamped the ash with a pipe tool, hesitated for a moment, and then, looking up and making eye contact, said, "So you like to gamble, eh?"

Good gamblers, he reminded himself, gloried in deception. It was a mark of honor, an essential part of their character. Rarely, if at all, did they know how to turn it off, especially with those closest

to them. It was a trait they had in common with spies—and private
eyes.

Navarro pulled on his cigar and leaned back in his chair, perhaps
a little too defensively. "We all have our vices." He sighed, relaxing a
bit. "I'm afraid gambling has been in my blood since I was ten years
old. I would bet on anything." He suppressed a laugh and looked
out the window and then back at Hunter. "I haven't changed in old
age. I would bet you right now I'll finish this panatela before you
finish your pipe." His mouth drew back with a hint of a smile. "But
if I lost, I'm afraid I couldn't pay up—at least not right now."

Hunter used the pipe as a pointer, waving the stem across the
table. "If you were smoking a perfecto, I might take the bet." He
paused to tamp and relight the pipe. "Let me ask you: Besides
Gomez at the Tropicana, who would have known that you had the
jewels at the hotel and that Gomez had sent someone to get them?"

"No one. Absolutely no one. I don't advertise I have them," he
said testily. "Senor Gomez and I talked privately in his office."

Hunter took the pipe out of his mouth. "That's impossible, Mr.
Navarro. They're gone. Someone stole them, so someone had to
have known." He tamped the ash down and relit the pipe, waiting
for a response.

Navarro stared at Hunter for a long moment with a surprised
look on his face and then nodded in agreement.

"How many pieces of jewelry are we talking about?" Hunter
knew the answer already but wanted to confirm it.

"Two diamond rings, a set of diamond earrings, and a diamond
tiara. I have no idea of the actual value, but I'd guess one or maybe
two million US dollars, considering they once belonged to Evita."

Hunter's brows shot up. *Two million dollars!* he thought. *Jesus,
Mary, and Joseph!*

"Their value is more personal than monetary. Evita left them to
me in her will. I was her personal secretary for years. We were very
close. They were all I had that belonged to her."

Close? Hunter wondered. *Just how close were they?* He decided to ask.

"I was her secretary, but she was more like a daughter to me." He glanced out the window again and sighed heavily. "Gone before her time, and here I sit, an old man, still breathing. Where is the justice in that, I ask you?" He shook his head and looked down. "She was only thirty-three when she died." He looked up at Hunter again. "She had a good heart, you know—a very good heart."

Navarro seemed sincere; notwithstanding, Hunter couldn't let that cloud his judgment. Again, he had to remind himself that Navarro was a veritable gambler, and deceit was part of his character. But was Hunter being too judgmental with him? Hunter was, after all, a private detective investigating a crime. It was his job to be judgmental. He'd heard hundreds of sob stories in his career by some of the best liars, and on the surface, they all seemed sincere. He'd leave the sympathetic responses, such as "Oh, I'm so sorry for your loss," to others. He was after one thing only: the truth.

"Where did you keep the jewels?"

"In the hotel's safe."

"Not the safe in your room?"

"No, not in the room."

"I want you to think carefully about that night at the Tropicana. Was there anyone showing particular interest in watching you gamble? Anyone following you around the casino?"

Navarro looked out the window again and narrowed his eyes for a long moment. "No, I don't think so." Then he suddenly turned to Hunter. "Wait! Yes, now that you mention it, I do remember." For the first time, Navarro became animated. "I'd been so wrapped up in the game. I was losing and became frustrated and disoriented, but I noticed that two particular men were watching the game— watching, not playing. There were others playing besides me, maybe five or six more. I don't know how many were just watching, but there were quite a few. I remembered those two specifically because I had seen them on my flight from Madrid. I had thought it was a coincidence at the time—just a thought that quickly flickered in my mind—but then I really started to lose and forgot about them. But thinking back, yes, they were definitely on my plane from Madrid."

"Describe them to me."

"I never really focused on them long enough to remember much, just a glance here and there. My mind was on the game; I was losing. You know how you can look at something, but your thoughts are elsewhere, so you don't see much? You're left with a general impression but nothing more. All I remember for certain is that one was tall and rather stout, and the other was average size but on the thin side. I think they both had mustaches. Yes, yes, they did have mustaches. That much stood out."

Hunter immediately recognized the similarity to the description given by Gomez's nephew of the two men who had robbed him of the jewels. "And you can't remember any details?"

"I can't. No."

"Do you have any idea where they might be staying?" Hunter doubted he did, but sometimes questions like that could draw a person out and make him think deeper and harder.

"No, sorry. I saw them only those two times—once on the plane and once again at the casino. Do you think they are the ones who stole the jewels?"

"I can't say, but it looks promising."

"Do you think you can find them?"

Hunter set his pipe down on the table for a moment and then picked it up again. He tamped the ash and relit the pipe. *A sad old man or a goddamn liar?* He puffed some smoke out and then said, "I'll be straight with you, Mr. Navarro. If they're the ones who have your jewels, they could be anywhere right now; they could be in Timbuktu for all I know. Even if they're still in Havana, it's going to be difficult to find them. Too bad you don't have a better description of the pair."

Navarro got up and paced the room for a short time as Hunter followed him with his eyes. Then he swung around to Hunter.

"Then let me hire you officially, Mr. Hunter. I have a money wire coming in a few days. I'll pay you what you want. Money isn't an issue."

"You know the Tropicana already hired me. I can't take your money for the same job."

He thought for a moment and then said, "Okay, but couldn't I give you a reward if you find the jewels? Certainly that wouldn't be unethical."

"If I find the jewels—and that's a big *if*—you can do anything you want."

"Then it's settled. I can't tell you what it would mean to me to get the jewels back. When Evita passed on and I found out she had left me the jewels in her will, I realized she had felt the same for me as I felt for her. She was a rather reserved woman with her feelings in private, but the father-daughter relationship we had was real, if left unspoken. But in our own ways, we acknowledged it. Please, Mr. Hunter, do what you can. Please find the jewels."

"I'll do what I can. I told Gomez, and I'll tell you: I can't make any promises. I'm a private detective, not a magician. Don't get your spirits up too high; the higher they go, the harder they fall if all this goes down the gutter." He looked at his pipe and then knocked a fine ash into the ashtray. He glanced up at Navarro, who was still puffing away on his cigar. "Had we made that bet, Mr. Navarro, you would have lost."

Hunter left the hotel feeling irritated with himself. He hadn't read Navarro well during the interview. He was no wiser about him now than he'd been when he got up that morning. He crossed Monserrate into Havana Vieja and made his way through the crowded, narrow streets near the docks and piers, where there were dozens of bars catering to sailors and stevedores, stopping only once at a street corner to buy a cone of roasted peanuts from a *manicero*, an old man with one leg who wore a tattered straw hat. The sky, a well-nigh perpetual flawless canvas, was somewhere between an unblemished azure and robin's-egg blue, fragile but clear. In Havana, though, that could change on a dime.

He sidled up to the bar at Dos Hermanos with his thoughts and ordered a Hatuey. In the front, near one of the high open windows, was a conjunto playing one of the heartbreaking Cuban folk songs he'd grown to love. In the back, a rowdy group of American sailors in uniform were having a good time, being entertained and looked after by three of the local ladies.

"You look down today," the barkeep said in Spanish. "Has the Paradise gone under?"

"No, we're doing just fine, Hector. Never been better."

Hector had a thick graying mustache and was nearly bald. His face was pleasant enough to look at, but he was built like a brick shithouse and often intimidated people who didn't know him. Those who did know him knew him as a gentleman and held him in high regard.

"Good! I'm taking my wife to your restaurant for a nice meal tomorrow night. It's the only place where we can find excellent food and peace and quiet at the same time in Havana."

"I'll tell Babs you're coming. She'll make sure the cook prepares something special for you two lovebirds."

"Yes, lovebirds! It's our thirtieth wedding anniversary, and we still act like young lovers!"

"Good for you, Hector—and good for Doris too!"

Hector left to serve another customer, leaving Hunter feeling gloomy again.

Ignacio Navarro. Hunter didn't know what to make of him. The guy was an inveterate gambler by his own admission. Hunter never trusted gamblers—a contradiction, as he himself was one—because if they were capable of deceiving their opponents in order to win, they were capable of deceiving anyone for any reason. He had known his fair share of gamblers back in Minnesota. Some he even liked. Some were wealthy, dressed well, and drove fancy cars. Some he even associated with. But he never trusted them, and he always had problems with the ones who were his clients. They invariably withheld some crucial information during a case, costing him time and money, and a couple of times, they nearly had gotten him crucified.

He picked up the cone of peanuts, popped a few into his mouth, and washed them down with the beer.

Was Navarro any different? Was he nothing but a shark trying to sink his teeth into the Tropicana? Was he handing Hunter just another song-and-dance routine, albeit an inventive one, to get out of paying his debt?

Hunter didn't know.

Navarro's story about being close to Eva Perón sounded feasible, but it was unverified, at least by Hunter. Navarro did seem sincere, and the melancholy that hung over him like a monsoon cloud appeared genuine. He seemed depressed, with a heavy weight on his shoulders. It was difficult but not impossible to feign that. However, if Navarro were a good enough liar—he was certainly old enough and had enough experience in life to be one—he could pull it off.

Hunter consumed more peanuts and more beer.

The sailors in the back became louder. The small band had changed the tempo of their music, and several sailors started dancing with the ladies.

Everyone had an angle. Hunter trusted his partners, Hannigan and Babs. He also trusted Sammy, although he hadn't known him as long. Outside of them, he hadn't trusted anyone since the war. As a private dick, it wasn't healthy to do so. What was Navarro's angle? He had to have one. Maybe Navarro had begun gambling at the Tropicana with no intention of cheating them. When he'd started to lose big, maybe he'd concocted his plan right then and there. Maybe that was all there was to it. He'd gotten hold of two of his buddies, and the scheme had been out of the starting gate.

Hunter had gone into the interview believing that Navarro might pull the wool over his eyes. But Navarro had said something to make him doubt himself: he had proposed to hire Hunter himself to find the jewels and then said he would pay Hunter a reward. Why would he offer a great deal of money to Hunter if he already had the jewels? Neither would have been necessary to pull off the scam. It wouldn't have been a reasonable thing to do. But gamblers, whether they win or lose, have never been known to be reasonable people. They lie and cheat in order to feed their addictive habit. The fact was, outside of the little he'd been told about Navarro, he didn't know the man at all. Hunter was back to square one: Navarro was guilty until proven otherwise.

Hunter glanced at the sailors, who were on the threshold of alcoholic insensibilities; laid some pesos on the bar; and shouted, "Have one on me, boys!" He popped some more peanuts into his mouth, took a last gulp of beer, and left Dos Hermanos, heading for the Paradise Inn for some peace and quiet. With him, he took a gnawing suspicion that guilty or not, Navarro had deliberately withheld something important from him.

He was determined to find out what.

5

It's Complicated

"I don't like it, Hannigan."

"What's not to like about five hundred smackers?"

"The money's fine," Babs said. "I like that. I like that a lot. What I don't like is the name Harry Smith."

"What did he ever do to you? Whaddaya got against Harry Smith?"

"Like I said, his name. It sounds phony to me."

"Dang it, he can call himself Elijah Hogwood Clutterbuck for all I care. The man paid up front—paid cold, hard cash!"

Hannigan and Babs had gotten the Valiant Queen fueled up and were loading their fishing equipment on board, even though the gear wouldn't be used. They were both wearing crepe-soled shoes so they wouldn't fall on the vessel.

"You gotta learn to trust people more, Babs," Hannigan said.

"What I trust are my instincts, and my instincts are saying something's fishy about Harry Smith."

"Aw, fiddlesticks," Hannigan said after securing the fishing rods in place. "You wanna take her out, or you want me to? I'd like to be back before it's too dark."

"I'll captain the vessel today. You got the coordinates?"

After Babs calculated the bearings, she pushed both shifters forward, and then she did the same with the two throttle controls, pushing them to one knot, steering the yacht out of the slip. When she cleared the dock, she eased the throttles forward a little more, increasing the speed to five knots. Once she was out of the harbor, she pushed both throttles forward until they couldn't go any farther. The Valiant Queen sped off at forty-three degrees and reached cruising speed in no time. The wind blew her hair, and the fine mist felt invigorating on her face.

The weather was on their side. Havana Bay was calm, with only a few fishing boats in sight. Hannigan emerged from the cabin with a thermos containing coffee and a little brandy. He poured two cups and gave one to Babs. She took a sip.

"You know, Hannigan," she said, raising her voice slightly so she could be heard over the engines, "when we retire, we should spend more time at sea. I just love it out here."

"By the time we're ready to retire, we'll both be in an old folks' home, hooked up to a lot of tubes and whatnot."

"Double beds side by side in a private room. How romantic! Ash could visit us—bring us flowers and chocolates."

"Not gonna happen. He'll be in the next room."

"All alone. How sad," she said, sipping her coffee. "We should play matchmaker and hook him up with some beautiful senorita. They could grow old together and have double beds side by side too!"

"Ash isn't that type of guy. He won't settle for one. He likes variety."

"Maybe he could get a larger room and squeeze a few beds into it."

Hannigan laughed. "He'd need an auditorium."

About thirty minutes later, Hannigan saw the huge freighter flying the Liberian flag.

"There it is," he said, pointing. "Pull alongside, and keep her steady, Babs. I'll go onto the deck."

Babs reduced the speed and maneuvered the Valiant Queen alongside the freighter. They were ready for the pickup. Hannigan motioned with his hands to the man above him to lower the basket tied by a rope on a pulley. It swung back and forth several times, but Hannigan managed to grab it on the third try. He took the package out of the basket and gave him the okay sign with his fingers. The man waved and hoisted the basket. Babs steered the yacht past the freighter, swung it around to the right, and then throttled forward.

"Let's head back," Hannigan said over the engines. "I'm getting hungry."

Halfway there, Hannigan noticed a speedboat coming toward them from the port side. It flew a Cuban flag on either end of the stern. On the hull, in big letters, was *National Police*. Babs pulled the throttles back to about five knots, and they hurried to get their lines in the water as if they were trolling. The speedboat went by them, and the men on board waved. Hannigan and Babs waved back and smiled. It was always good to be friendly to the police.

"That was close," Babs said.

"Close nothing. We didn't do anything illegal."

"No? At the very least, we have a package with unknown contents. Even if it's all on the up and up, as you said, they could get us for a customs violation."

"Fiddlesticks!"

Whenever Hannigan said that, the topic was dead—in this case, dead in the water.

After a moment, Babs said, "Maybe we should do a little fishing, Hannigan. We could add some swordfish or tuna to the menu for the next few days."

"Naw, we should get back and put the package in the safe, like I told Harry Smith I would. Besides, we can always buy fish at the market."

"Well, that's no fun. You're a party pooper, Hannigan."

"Fiddlesticks!"

"Would you like to extrapolate on that?" When he didn't say anything, she added, "Then how about on the package? Extrapolate away, honey; I'm all ears."

"Fiddlesticks!" he said again.

"Okay, I get it, but what if this Harry Smith was lying to us?" Babs asked. "What if this package contains something illegal? We could be risking our livelihood. And for what? Five hundred dollars?"

Hannigan thought about that for a long moment as he put the fishing rods back. "Crank her up. Let's get back before it's dark."

With the harbor in sight, Hannigan, sitting in the aft deck, noticed the wind had picked up. He got up and went to the cockpit. "Take her in straight, Babs. There's a helluva wind."

"Hey, who's the skipper here? Go back, and sit down. Put your feet up; relax. Have a whiskey. It'll calm your nerves."

"We can't afford any repair bills. Just go in straight."

She glanced back at her husband and stuck her tongue out at him. Then she looked at the flag onshore to gauge the wind. It was stronger than the current. She reduced the speed to one knot, and then she pulled the starboard throttle back to reverse, backing the yacht into the wind. The vessel slowly made its turn. Again, she glanced at her husband, who watched every little move she made, and made a face at him. Making some small corrections, she gave it a little more reverse and eased the yacht back between the dock and the pilings. Then she cut the engines.

Turning to Hannigan, she said, "There, o ye of little faith. And no repair bills."

They both climbed onto the dock and began tying the Valiant Queen down.

"You're right, Babs," Hannigan said. "It was an unnecessary risk."

45

"What was?" she asked. "Bringing the yacht in? I knew I could do it. You're the one who thought it was risky."

"No, the package. Let's put it in the safe. Harry Smith will pick it up tomorrow, and that'll be the end of it."

"Let's hope so, Hannigan. Let's hope you're right."

In front of the Paradise Inn was the Malecón, a board esplanade, roadway, and seawall that looked out into the Bay of Havana. Behind the inn was Havana Centro, and nearby was Havana Vieja. On the night of February 15, 1898, the USS *Maine*, an American armored cruiser, had exploded and sunk in the harbor. The cause remained the subject of endless debate. Nevertheless, the incident had contributed to the war with Spain two months later. Three months, three weeks, and two days after that, Spain had sued for peace: America had been in Cuba's front door. Fifty-nine years later, Slane Hannigan; his wife, Babs; and Ash Hunter sat on the veranda of the Paradise late at night, drinking gin and tonics, looking out into that same harbor.

"All it took was about an hour and a half of time and a bit of gas, and we earned five hundred bucks," Hannigan said to Hunter. "The year is starting off like a year should—with a bang!"

"Oh yeah? Remember the *Maine*. That was a bang too, and it started a war," Hunter said.

"That's what I'm afraid of," Babs said. "I don't like bangs."

"You're a cynic, Babs," Hannigan said. "You never used to be that way." He glanced at Hunter. "So are you."

"I never used to be a lot of things," Babs said. "A cynic is just one of them. I prefer to be called a realist."

"You're getting paranoid. You never used to be that either."

"What did you pick up?" Hunter asked, tamping his pipe.

"Whatever it is, I hope it doesn't go *bang*!" Babs said.

Hannigan looked at her and grimaced. Turning back to Hunter, he said, "A package about this big." He put his hands out, indicating the length and width. "And it was heavy. I put it in the safe."

"A man calling himself Harry Smith is picking it up tomorrow," Babs said. "Can you believe it? Harry Smith? You'd think he'd be more inventive." After a moment, she added, "He was good looking, though."

"My darling wife thinks it's some kind of scam—that this Smith guy has an angle."

"I'm only concerned that we could be an accomplice to whatever Harry Smith is up to." Babs looked at Hunter and then at Hannigan. "I'm serious. If it's something illegal, we could lose everything, including the Valiant Queen, and be deported. Or maybe jailed. Cuban prisons are no vacations. They give a new meaning to 'a spot in the sun.' You even said as much when we got back." She pointed a finger at her husband. "You said I was right—that it was an unnecessary risk."

"I take it back. Can't a guy take something back if he wants to, or is it illegal in Cuba?"

"Babs is right," Hunter said, blowing smoke into the air. "We should be more careful. We have a lot of money invested."

"You see, Hannigan? The man speaks the truth! Listen to him."

"You're ganging up on me," Hannigan said calmly, sipping his drink. "My own wife and best friend. Anyway, we'll be done with it tomorrow. How'd the interview go today?"

Hunter tamped his pipe and took some short puffs to get it going again. He laid out the gist of the interview, along with Ignacio Navarro's background.

As he did, Hannigan reached to his side and grabbed a wooden box of mixed cigars. He took a cigarillo out and gave it to Babs and grabbed a robusto for himself. They lit up and sipped their drinks.

Hunter said, "I had my doubts about Navarro at the beginning—I still do somewhat—but after talking to him for an hour and thinking about it, I decided he seems to be on the up and up. He was actually Eva Perón's secretary, if you can believe him. She left him the diamond jewelry, including a tiara, in her will. Could be worth up to a couple mill."

"You still think the two men stole them, or are you working a different angle?" Hannigan asked.

"That's what I'm trying to figure out. Maybe the nephew who picked them up is trying to pull a fast one. I still need to talk to him, but it's a sensitive issue. His uncle is Alfonso Gomez, and I don't want to insult Alfonso by going behind his back and talking to the kid. Gomez is a good man, and I don't think he'd lie to me."

"I bet those two jokers are Spanish," Hannigan said, "and they knew about the jewels in Madrid. They found out that Navarro was leaving Madrid for good and followed him to Havana, looking for the right time to steal the jewels. They saw what happened at the Tropicana and made their move."

Hunter thought for a moment and then said, "You might be right. I could check the flight manifest and cross-check the names against hotels in the city, but I might be at it for the next month. They're not going to stick around here. Maybe they're already gone." He thought some more and then added, "What I am going to do is check with the dicks in the high-end hotels, give them the descriptions, and hope for the best. I told both Gomez at the Tropicana and Navarro that it was going to be a long shot. I don't have any high hopes."

"What about your fee for services rendered, Ash?" Babs asked. "We can't forget that."

"That hasn't changed. If I don't find the jewels, I'll get a grand for my time. And if I find them, I'll negotiate a percentage of the value."

"The value of two million smackers." Hannigan said. "Whoop-de-do!"

"Jeez, we could pay off the *Valiant Queen*!" Babs said. "Maybe even the mortgage on the Paradise!"

Hannigan and Babs puffed on their cigars, while Hunter used his pipe tool to scrape the dottle out of his pipe and then refill the bowl. A fresh breeze blew off the coast. Sammy must have put an album on the record player, because Sinatra was singing in the background—something about getting under his skin.

Babs ran her fingers through her hair, brushing the strands away from her face. She took a dainty puff of the cigarillo and said, "Do you remember when we were all working at the Saint Paul Hotel? Jeez, that seems like light-years ago. Ash, you were doing a line with a lady. It was hot and heavy, as I remember it. We thought you were going to get hitched up. Then, all of a sudden, it was over. You never did tell us what happened. I remember asking you, but you said it was—"

"Complicated."

"That's the word you used," she said, snapping her fingers. "*Complicated*. What was her name again? Angie? Angela?"

"Angie Bellandini."

"Angie Bellandini," she said, drawing out the name. "Long black hair, cute, and petite. Bubbly. A lovely girl. Nice little meatballs. You want to uncomplicate it for us and tell us what happened, Ash? You said you'd tell us, but you never did. It's been twelve years at least."

"Babs, let the man be," Hannigan said. "It's none of our business. If he wanted to tell us, he would have already. Whatever happened to your scruples? They used to be just fine."

"My scruples were just fine until we got married. Now they tend to take a vacation once in a while."

"Fiddlesticks!"

The record went silent for a few seconds, and then Ole Blue Eyes began crooning "They Can't Take That Away from Me" in the background.

"No, that's okay, Slane," Hunter said. "I don't mind talking about it." He puffed on his pipe a few times. "Angie Bellandini. You were right, Babs. We almost got married. We were in love. I mean truly in love."

"The way your smile just beams," Sinatra sang.

"We were actually at the stage of making plans for the future. We both wanted a little house in the countryside east of Saint Paul but not too far out. White picket fence. Cottage. A little retreat away from the hustle-and-bustle of the city. We even drove out and visited a few of them with a real estate agent. Then one day she invited me to a big family gathering to meet her parents and relatives. That was when the tornado swept through our lives."

Sinatra broke in again. "The way you haunt my dreams."

"Her parents lived in this huge house, a mansion almost. It was a party. Must have been thirty people there. Most of them were from Chicago. The women were all dressed up in their best and stayed in a room to themselves. I circulated among the men in another room. They all looked like longshoremen, but they were dressed in fine light-colored linen suits and shiny shoes, smoking cigars. They were friendly, slapping me on the back, all smiles. Until I introduced myself as Ashton Hunter. Then the smiles stopped."

"The way we danced until three," Ole Blue Eyes sang.

"They wanted to know how much Italian blood I had in me. I told them that both sides of my family were from England. This was in the middle of July, but it suddenly felt like the middle of January. I excused myself and went over to the table spread out with tons of food. I looked over my shoulder at the group of men, and I could see that there was this big discussion going on, a serious discussion. Their hands were flying all over the place—you know how Italians talk. Angie's father was there too.

"I was about to grab a plate from the table, when one of the men—I think he was one of Angie's uncles—put his arm around my shoulders and led me to the front door and outside. I remember glancing back through the door and seeing Angie looking our way. She was standing with her mother near the kitchen. They both had this look on their faces that was hard to describe, but it was sad."

"The way you changed my life," Sinatra sang.

"Out on the front steps, the uncle, or whoever he was, didn't say much. He reached into his pocket, peeled off ten one-hundred-dollar bills, and stuck them in my jacket pocket, as if he were tipping a doorman. 'Find yourself another girl to marry, Mr. Hunter. Don't come back. Don't see Angie again. Don't call Angie again. Good luck with your life.' That was all he said before he shut the door in my face."

"That's terrible, Ash," Babs said. "Did you see her after that?"

"I called her the next day, but there was no answer. I tried calling for the next week. I even went over to her apartment. She never answered the phone or the door. I finally sent her a letter, but she never answered it."

"Those wops took her from you, plain and simple," Hannigan said angrily. "They snatched her out of your arms, the bastards. That's what they did. You'd think we lived in the Dark Ages."

"That they did—they took her from me. I never saw or heard from her again."

But they can't take the memories away, Hunter thought. *They can't take that away from me.*

There was a long moment of silence while they finished their drinks and looked out over the bay. Tiny lights were twinkling, and the faint sounds of car horns could be heard.

Hannigan broke the silence. He slapped his knees and said, "Okay, it's getting late. Sammy's on duty tonight, so what do you say, Babs, about getting some shut-eye?"

Hunter continued to sit and smoke his pipe after they went back inside the Paradise. He hadn't talked about Angie Bellandini in more than a decade. He wondered where she was that moment and what kind of life she was leading. In all likelihood, she was probably married and had a half dozen children by then—married to someone her family approved of, no doubt, which in that case meant mob approved. He hoped she was happy. The best philosophers in the world, from the ancients to the moderns, had said that time healed all pain.

Hunter was still waiting for that to happen.

6

Deception as a Pastime

Sammy Laurent was as black as a piece of coal.

His fourth set of great-grandparents had been kidnapped by an enemy tribe and sold into slavery on the coast of West Africa and then shipped off to the French colony of Saint-Domingue, where they'd labored under the sun in the sugarcane fields. From 1791 through 1804, they, along with other enslaved people and their allies, had rebelled and fought a protracted revolution to win their independence from France. They'd renamed the western part of the island Haiti, and the Laurents had been free ever since.

Sammy had lived a poor but good life there, but he was adventurous. One day he'd packed a suitcase and boarded a ship to Havana. On his first day there, while wandering around the Malecón, he'd seen a sign across the road on a small hill: Paradise Inn. There he'd met a man named Hannigan and asked him for a job. As the inn was being readied to open the following week, Hannigan had hired him on the spot.

That had been ten years ago. More precisely, it had been on March 23, 1947, at 2:09 p.m. As Hannigan always said, "Dates and time should matter to people. They tell you where you were at any given time on this big, revolving planet. People ought to know things like that."

Now, after cleaning the tables off in the café and washing the breakfast dishes, Sammy picked up his guitar and began playing. Hannigan was nearby at the front desk, sorting through receipts. His ears perked up.

Oh me, oh my, poor Eva Perón has died.
People—dey sad, askin' how to abide.
Bad enough, but now her jewels are gone.

"Hey, Sammy!" shouted Hannigan. "Sing something about Ash."

"I was just coming to that, Mr. Slane. Patience is a virtue; that is what we always say in Haiti."

A tragedy, injustice! But thereupon
steps up a man who will set things right.
Ashton Hunter with pluck—he will fight the good fight.
And if he does not get da money for da Paradise Inn,
we will all be livin' in da Paradise loony bin!

"Ah, that's a good one, Sammy!" Hannigan shouted. "Ash would be proud of you. But we're already living in a loony bin."

"I know that, Mr. Slane, but I did not want to be the one to say it."

"By the way, you worked all night. You should call it quits and get a little shut-eye."

"I have a few things to do first, but yes, shut-eye sounds good and is high on my list of things to do today."

The brass bell above the front door dinged as a man in a white suit and panama hat appeared.

"Ah, Mr. Smith," Hannigan said, jabbing a finger at the man. "Mr. Harry Smith, the man who said he'd be here in the morning to pick up his package, and dang it, if he wasn't true to his word.

You were true to your word—I like that! A man who says what he means is a rare commodity in today's crazy world."

"Good morning, Mr. Hannigan. I trust all went well."

"Your trust is well placed, yes indeedy, Mr. Smith."

Hannigan disappeared into the back room and, a minute later, reappeared. "There you go," he said, setting the package on the countertop. "One package delivered, as promised. Trust is what you wanted, and trust is what you got." He reached below the counter, produced a business card, and set it on top of the package. "If I can be of service again, please don't hesitate to phone or just come in. And be sure to tell your friends about us."

"I will indeed." Smith put the card in his pocket and picked up the package. "Indeed I will. No snags with the pickup?"

"Nary a one. Everything went as smooth as silk, just like you said it would. Copacetic, it was. Got time for breakfast? It's on me, one friend to another. Maybe just a little coffee?"

"I'm afraid I'm in a bit of a rush," Smith said, picking up the package. "Maybe next time."

"Next time is fine with me, Mr. Smith. Next time is not as good as right now, but next time is always fine with me. Fine indeedy!"

Harry Smith left, and Hannigan resumed sorting through yesterday's receipts. He hoped Smith would return with more business—the man was quite free with his money, and the prospect of having him as a regular client for the Valiant Queen appealed to Hannigan—but at the same time, he was relieved the package was gone. He remembered what Babs and Hunter had told him. If the package had been contraband and the authorities had found out, he and Babs could have been implicated, and the inn, along with the yacht, would have belonged to one of the ministries of the Cuban government, which, in practice, meant that some general would have owned both.

But maybe Babs and Hunter were being paranoid. Things had gone well with Mr. Harry Smith. The money he'd paid was much more than what Hannigan had planned to charge. If he became a regular client, who knew how much more money he would be willing to dish out? Hannigan would gladly be his errand boy if the price was right, and it was. He always said that life was a risk; the road was never straight and smooth. If you didn't take a little detour once in a while, you'd never get what you wanted. If it weren't for Hannigan, the Paradise Inn never would have existed in the first place, and he, Babs, and Ash would have been slaving away back in Saint Paul, making money for someone else. Paranoid—that was what Babs and Hunter were.

Just then, there was another ding at the door. Hannigan looked up and saw a middle-aged couple enter, pulling suitcases behind them. Tourists no doubt—tourists with vacation money to spend!

"Good morning, folks, or, as we say here, buenos días! Welcome to the Paradise Inn, and welcome to the tropical island of Cuba!"

The pair took a step forward and then stopped. The door closed behind them and dinged again. Their eyes cautiously gathered in the landscape of the small lobby. To Hannigan, they looked as if they had been suddenly thrust into the aftermath of a firebombed building somewhere in Europe fifteen years earlier and were searching for an escape route. The Paradise Inn was a clean, well-maintained economy hotel that tourists enjoyed staying at; however, the Hilton it was not.

The woman finally focused on Hannigan. "We just arrived here last night and stayed at a luxury hotel as part of a package deal. The hotel was for one night, and we decided we didn't want to spend the extra money for the time we're going to be here. Hotels in the city seem to be full." She looked around the lobby again. "We were wondering whether you had a room for the next week or so." She paused for a moment and cocked her head. "We're on a budget, you know."

"If you'da come last night, I'da said no," Hannigan said. "But a couple from Iowa checked out early this morning, so you're in luck! Budget is what you want; budget is what you'll get! I'll need to see your passports, and you can sign the registry here." He pushed the registry in front of her.

The couple inched up to the front desk. The woman signed in for herself and her companion. Hannigan wrote down their names, address, and passport numbers on an official government form, which was standard in Cuba.

"A friend of ours back home recommended the Paradise Inn to us. He said the accommodations were more than adequate, the staff were friendly, and the price was, well, within our budget."

"Your friend was correct, ma'am. Seven-fifty per night for a double bed and shower, with sheets and towels changed daily. Soap and hot water are included. Our café serves breakfast, lunch, and dinner from seven in the morning until ten at night, and our menu can compete with the best of them. We aim to please! How was your flight?"

Hannigan could tell the couple's expectations had been in doubt when they first entered, but upon hearing the price of the room, which was reasonable during high season, the woman, though perhaps not her companion, loosened up.

"Incredible! It was a package deal with the Tropicana. There was music and dancing, and the drinks were nonstop. All on the plane!"

"You can't beat the Tropicana, ma'am," Hannigan said, handing the passports back to the woman. "You can pay for seven nights. If you decide to leave early, we'll give you a refund. We'll take greenbacks if that's all you have."

The woman paid in US dollars.

Hannigan walked around the counter. "I'll take your luggage to your room, if you'll follow me. It's just around the corner there," he said, pointing.

"Yes, of course. But I have one question first."

Hannigan set the luggage back down.

"This trip of ours," she said, glancing at her companion next to her, who hadn't said a word since entering, "is a well-deserved vacation. We plan to see the sights and mingle with the natives, if you know what I mean. But while here, we wanted to look up an old friend of ours who moved here years ago. Unfortunately, we lost contact with him. We have absolutely no idea where to find him or how we would even begin. All we know is that he's somewhere in Havana. The city is bigger than we thought. Do you have any suggestions on how we can find him?"

"As I said, ma'am, we aim to please. I have just the man for you!"

Ten minutes later, Ash Hunter, now fully awake and alert, walked down the corridor from his room to the front desk. He was wearing a light tan linen suit with a white shirt and no tie and carried his hat in his hand, swinging his arms and humming a tune.

"Ash," Hannigan said, "this is Bradford and Elizabeth Maddox from Tampa." Looking at the Maddoxes, he said, "This is Ash Hunter." He turned back to Hunter. "They need to find someone." He looked back at the Maddoxes. "Why don't you all go in the café while I take your luggage to your room?"

They sat at a table at the far end, with a view of the waterfront promenade, the Malecón. The sun was off to the east, rising lazily, sending a ray of light across the table. Sammy brought coffee for each of them. The woman looked off to the horizon. Her husband dipped his pinkie into his cup and then stuck it in his mouth.

Hunter smiled at them. "So you're here on vacation," he said.

"Yes, our first trip to the topics," the woman said, swinging her head around to him. It was always the woman who did the talking. The man just sat and stared at Hunter. Elizabeth Maddox explained that they wanted to look up an old friend but didn't know where to start. "It's a big, crowded city, you know. Do you have any suggestions?"

"I used to own a detective agency back in Minnesota before I came here. Part of my work was to find missing persons, sometimes people who didn't want to be found. I was good at my job. Still am, but I'm not licensed in Cuba to do that kind of work. I might be able to help you, though, as a friend, but of course, I can't charge you anything,"

Bradford Maddox spoke up. "But we could show you our gratitude by leaving a big tip when we check out, eh? Like a couple hundred bucks?"

Hunter, still smiling, said, "To show us your appreciation for a good stay at the inn, of course. I think that would work out just fine."

Hunter was always cautious when dealing with new clients he didn't know. The government never had confronted him about his detective services. They had no reason to. As far as he knew, they knew nothing about it. He wanted to keep it that way. He did that by being overly cautious with strangers. The authorities were capable of hiring someone to trap him if they suspected he was running a little business out of the inn. Bradford and Elizabeth Maddox were strangers to him. He knew nothing about them. They looked legit, but sometimes looks were misleading. He'd chance it.

"If I were to run into your friend in town, how would I know him?"

"He's an American, of course," Elizabeth said. "His name is Shaw Armstrong. He's about six foot three, has dark brown hair, and dresses well but not flashy. Single. Handsome. Looks like Tyrone Power." She paused to sip her coffee, and Hunter did the same. "But it's been a few years since we've seen him. Perhaps he's gone native, grown a beard, and married." She paused again and looked out the window for a few moments. "I think not, though," she said, swinging her head around to Hunter again. "Shaw always did like expensive clothes and the clean look, so I'm guessing he looks pretty much the same. Like Tyrone Power—with a Cuban tan, of course."

"What are you looking for? An address?"

"Yes, just an address. If you do run across him, we'd appreciate it if you didn't talk to him. We want to surprise him. We haven't seen him in years—it'll be so much fun getting back together again with him."

"Can you tell me anything about his habits? Does he like to gamble? Go to bars? Pick up women? This is Havana, after all. There are plenty of all three."

"All of the above."

"Do you know what he does for a living?"

"Back in Tampa—you're not writing this down. You should be writing this down."

"I have a great memory. You want me to repeat what you just said in the last ten minutes? I could embellish a little too."

"Back in Tampa," she said, ignoring his question, "he worked for a life insurance company. Transamerica. I don't know whether he still does. Can he do that sort of thing here?"

"It's possible, but I'll look into it. Have you tried the phone book?"

"Oh yes. There was no listing."

"Okay then. Give me a couple of days. I'll ask around. See what I come up with."

"We so appreciate your help, Mr. Hunter. I can't tell you how much we look forward to seeing Shaw again." She reached into her purse to pay for the coffee.

"Coffee's on the house," Hunter said with a wink.

They all got up from the table. The Maddoxes went to their room, and Hunter went over to Sammy, who was wiping off the tables.

"Sammy, I'll be gone for most of the day. The night too. If anyone calls, take a message. Tell him I'll call back tomorrow. I probably won't get back until very late."

"And if the caller is of the female variety?"

"Tell her I'm at Sacred Heart Church, saying the stations of the cross. You've got to make the ladies think you're a saint."

"But there are fourteen stations, Mr. Ash."

"Tell her to be patient. Sainthood takes time. I'll call her when I get in."

"Ah, you're going to see if you can find the jewels, no? Ash Hunter, hunting for the treasure!"

"Put that in one of your songs, why don't you?"

"I'll see what I can do, Mr. Ash."

7

The Rude Strangers

Ash Hunter walked down Calle Monserrate, cursing Hannigan under his breath.

The sky was clear, and there was a pleasant breeze. Both meant little in Havana. The weather could change faster than one could change a bet on a horse race at Oriental Park. The street was crowded; Habaneros were still in a festive mood from the New Year's celebrations. Nevertheless, Hunter was irritated. The source of his aggravation was Hannigan again.

Hunter, Hannigan, and Babs had a great deal of money invested in the inn. The Paradise was a legit business. Sure, they bent the rules now and again, but when they did, it was always a calculated risk. Payoffs to various government officials kept it that way. Hunter always managed to keep his sideline—his detective agency—under the radar of the authorities. It brought in a nice revenue, which was then fed into the inn. He had been doing this for ten years successfully. But Hannigan was another kettle of fish.

Hannigan had no idea what the word *calculated* meant. He wasn't exactly reckless, but when there was enough money involved in something, he could be imprudent. Such was the case with one Harry Smith. Hannigan had no idea who this character was. That could be said of most of the people who walked through the door of the Paradise, but all they wanted was a room and sometimes a boat to fish or to sightsee from off the coast. None of them had ever made the same request as Smith: for Hannigan to collect a package from an offshore freighter in the evening. If Hannigan had gotten caught in the middle of a shady deal, the yacht and the inn—everything— would have been confiscated, and they'd all have ended up in the hoosegow or deported or both. Hannigan had skimmed over the calculated part of calculated risk.

Hunter had known Hannigan since elementary school, when they'd lived on the east side of Saint Paul, where they grew up. They'd attended junior high together, and together they'd graduated from Johnson High School. When the war had broken out, they had enlisted in the army and served with General Patton during the invasion of Sicily and, later, with the Fifth Army during the Italian campaign. War had been a risky business, and they both had done things they would not have otherwise done in civilian life, and they'd gotten away with it, but Hannigan didn't seem to have learned a lesson from that. He was judicious most of the time, but occasionally, he stepped into deep water without first checking the depth. In Havana, doing something illegal occasionally was all that was needed to destroy everything.

Hunter shook his head and took a deep breath; he hoped he'd still be part owner of the Paradise when he got back. He continued walking down Calle Monserrate until he got to 355. There was a sign overhead: "La Zaragozana Restaurante. *Establecido en* 1830." Located in Havana Vieja, it was the oldest restaurant on the island. Their specialty was Spanish cuisine, especially from the Zaragoza region of Spain. If the two men who had stolen the Perón jewels had followed Ignacio Navarro from Madrid, they might be Spanish, Hunter thought. If they were Spanish, they might have shown up there at some point. It was a long shot—in fact, the whole case was a long shot—but Hunter had no leads, and the only cost to him was time, which he had plenty of. He reasoned that the two thieves were probably back in Madrid, sitting in a bar on Calle Francisco Ricci, hashing out the details with a fence on the best way to get rid of the jewels. But in case they were still in Havana, La Zaragozana was as good a place as any to find them. He opened the door and walked in.

The restaurant was big inside, with square tables topped with white linen tablecloths and red candles in brandy snifters off to the right and a long, curvy bar to the left. The flags of Cuba and Spain hung over the bar, with football memorabilia plastered on the walls. There were a few people at the tables, eating and drinking. The barman was wiping glasses behind the bar. Hunter knew a lot of people in Havana, including many who served the public in bars, restaurants, shops, and government agencies. Information flowed from these people, and Hunter was in the business of gathering information.

"I don't believe my eyes," the barman said in English as Hunter sat down on a stool. "Senor Hunter! Is this truly you? I haven't seen you since last year! I have been so depressed that my wife suggested more than once that I should see the medico. How pleased I am to see you—pleased beyond belief!" He appeared to be milking his speech with enough drama to satisfy a large audience in an auditorium.

"You're a comedian, Juan. I was in just last week for a Spanish omelet."

"With a very charming woman at your side. But you see, that was last year, 1956. Now it is the next year, 1957!"

"You're clever, Juan. How 'bout a Hatuey?"

"Hatuey coming up." In a sweeping motion, he grabbed a bottle from the cooler, popped the cap, and set the beer in front of Hunter. "You have that look again on your face, my friend."

"You've picked up the pastime of reading faces?"

"Senor Hunter, I am a man who tends bar for my life's vocation. I can see into the soul of man through his face." He threw his hands up in front of him. "That is my great burden in life. Sometimes what I see is not pretty. Men cannot hide their deepest secrets from me."

He leaned into Hunter as if he were his confidant. "They try, but it is useless," he whispered. "Useless!"

"You're in the wrong business, Juan. You should have been a shrink."

"Such are the vicissitudes of life, my friend," he said, cocking his head. "That is a new word I learned this morning from an American customer. This is my first opportunity to use it. I did good, no?"

"You did good, Juan. And what does my face tell you?"

"That you're looking for someone."

"My aunt Gladys could have told me that."

"Ah yes, but your aunt Gladys could not have told you where to find that someone."

"I'm actually looking for two people. Strangers. One's fat and tall; the other's average size and on the thin side. Well dressed. Might be Spanish. Might have come in for some Spanish chow. Have you seen anyone like that in the last three or four days or so?" He took a long swig, tipping the bottle nearly vertically.

Juan, whose fortunes in life had led him to tending bar rather than being in a plush office with a couch and a chair, scrunched his face as if in deep thought. After a moment, he said, "Well ..." Then, after another moment, as if he were unclear on the meaning of *well*, he said it again. "Well ..."

Hunter reached into his pocket, pulled out some greenbacks, and laid them on the bar.

"Two men I had not seen before—one fat and tall and one average, as you say—came in today, two hours ago. They were wearing white suits and sat there," he said, pointing directly behind Hunter. "But by their accents, I surmised they were neither Spanish nor Cuban." He smiled, seemingly confident he had used the word *surmised* correctly.

"What nationality were they?"

"That I cannot say. I tried to start a conversation with them, but they were rude. They just wanted to eat and leave. Which they did. Maybe they were South American. Maybe from the States."

"Anything else?"

"*Lo siento*, no. Wait!" His hands flashed in front of his face again. "Both had mustaches and black hair, I think. They wore hats that they did not take off while they ate. They looked—how do you say?—seedy. Definitely mean. You want me to call you at the Paradise if they should come in again?"

"Do that, Juan. Leave a message if I'm not there."

Hunter paid for the beer, shook Juan's hand, left, and walked over a block and then turned north on the tree-lined Prado Promenade in Havana Centro, toward the Hotel Sevilla-Biltmore. If the two men who'd eaten at La Zaragozana were the same jokers who'd nabbed the jewels—and the evidence seemed to point in the right direction to make Hunter eager to believe they were—then they were still in town. But why? That didn't make sense. The jewels had been stolen three days ago. They could have taken a flight out of the country the next day, on New Year's Eve. But they hadn't. They'd stayed around. Why? Why risk being caught? The jewels were worth a fortune.

Unless they planned on doing something else. It would have to be something really big to warrant the risk of being arrested.

Once at the hotel, Hunter crossed the lobby to a small office. The door was open. He rapped his knuckles on the doorjamb.

Augusto Cesario Faustano Zapatero was sitting at his desk; he swiveled around. "Look at what the cat dragged in," he said with a big smile on his face. "My little American *chico*. Come in, come in. Sit."

Born in Cuba and educated in Texas, Zapatero had been the chief detective for the security of the hotel for the last nine years. Before that, he'd been with the Bureau for the Repression of Communist Activities, the Cuban secret police agency, and before that, he'd been a high-class thief. He'd specialized in relieving wealthy Cubans and Americans of the burden of worrying about the security of their jewels.

"Auggie," Hunter said as he sat in a chair next to the desk, "I see life has been good to you."

Zapatero, when standing, reached six foot five inches, and weighed every bit of two hundred, seventy pounds, most of it muscle. But he was approaching sixty years old now. Although his stature was beginning to diminish, his weight was not. He wore a drooping mustache, and both that and his hair were going gray. He reached into a desk drawer and pulled out two shot glasses and a bottle of Johnny Walker. He poured two fingers in each.

"Salud!" both men said.

After they downed the whiskey, Zapatero poured two more fingers. "Isabella asks about you from time to time. I always tell her you're a man of mystery. She likes that. I'm an open book to her. I think she's bored with that, so mystery men fascinate her."

"We all have our dark secrets, eh, Auggie?"

"I suppose," he said, running an index finger and thumb down his mustache. "Some more than others. You didn't come to chat, Ash. What's up? How can I help you?"

One of the secrets Zapatero knew about Hunter was that he was running a detective agency out of the Paradise without a license. He'd found out about it when he worked for the government. But he liked Hunter, and he'd kept his mouth shut. "Live and let live" was Zapatero's moto. From that moment, Hunter had been indebted to him. Now they were like brothers, or rather, they were like father and son. But did Hunter trust him? He had no other alternative.

Hunter told him the whole story about the stolen jewels.

Astonished, Zapatero said, "Never in my former career did I ever steal jewels worth that much! Don't get me wrong. I went after the expensive stuff all right—but never anything worth that much. The thieves were clever rascals, eh?"

"What I need to know is whether Ignacio Navarro used the hotel safe to secure the jewels."

"That's easy enough to find out." He reached over his desk for a clipboard and flipped through several pages. "Everyone who uses our safe is listed in this log. It is important to record when guests put their valuables in it and when they retrieve them; otherwise, we could be held liable for something missing. There is only one key per box, and if they lose it, they will have to pay to replace the entire lock. Now, let's see. Ignacio Navarro." He ran his fingers down the list of names. After going through several pages, he did it again. "I see no one by that name listed here. I can tell you with certainty that this Navarro did not use our safe during his stay with us."

During Hunter's interview with Navarro, Navarro had told him he kept the jewels in the hotel's safe. Hunter had clarified that point by specifically asking him whether he'd used the safe in his room. Navarro had confirmed he'd kept them in the hotel's safe.

"Do you mind if I use your phone?" Hunter asked.

"Not at all," Zapatero said, standing up. He towered over Hunter. "I have to do an errand. You can have privacy."

After Zapatero left, Hunter picked up the phone, dialed the operator, and gave her the number to the Tropicana. After talking to Alfonso Gomez and to his nephew, the person who had picked up the jewels from Navarro and from whom the jewels had been stolen, he hung up. The nephew had clearly stated that Navarro went into his bedroom and not downstairs to the hotel's safe to get the jewels.

Ignacio Navarro, former secretary to Eva Perón and longtime gambler, a person who was held in high esteem by his peers and who had become emotional when talking about Evita, had lied.

The question was, why?

And what else had he lied about?

8

El Barrio Chino

The Chinese had first arrived in Cuba in significant numbers during the great diaspora in the late 1850s to toil in Cuba's sugarcane fields. In Havana, they'd established Chinatown, which had grown to forty-four square blocks and once had been the largest such community in Latin America. They were an industrious lot and had not confined themselves to the fields. They'd opened shops, restaurants, and laundries and worked in factories.

Senor Yat-Sen Wong, whose ancestors had made that long journey one hundred years ago, was fully assimilated into Cuban society and spoke Spanish as well as he spoke Chinese. He had one foot firmly planted in each culture. Furthermore, for the last decade, he had been teaching himself English to better communicate with the flocks of American tourists who flew onto the island and fluttered their wings in his small gift shop on Calle Cuchillo. With each step forward, his fluency increased. As he interacted with more and more American tourists, he began piecing together the vast fabric of American culture and realized just how complex it was. An American from Dallas seemed to be from a different country than an American from New York. One from Mississippi bore no resemblance to one from Iowa. They spoke differently and acted differently. He was often baffled by this and found the whole thing rather bizarre.

Late that afternoon, a well-dressed man stepped into the shop. He was wearing a white linen suit and a panama hat. Resting in the crook of his arm was a package wrapped in light brown paper, secured by twine. He walked up to the front counter. He didn't look Cuban to Wong, yet he didn't appear to be the typical tourist who came into Wong's shop. Wong didn't want to offend the man in case he was Cuban, so he greeted him in Spanish.

"Buenas tardes. Bienvenido! ¿Cómo puedo ser de ayuda?"

The man looked at him for a moment. Wong thought he saw a slight grimace. It was nearly imperceptible, but it was there all right; he was sure of it. Had Wong offended him somehow? Wong went out of his way never to offend a customer—or any other person, for that matter. He had been brought up to treat all people with respect. Yet this man grimaced.

"Do you speakee English?" the man asked condescendingly and louder than necessary.

Better than you, Wong thought, smiling at the lug. *American no doubt.*

"Of course," Wong said. "How may I be of service to you? We have jade and gold jewelry; a wide variety of chopsticks, including lacquered ones; statues of all kinds; fans of various colors and designs; bookmarks; combs and brushes; and wooden spoons and other cooking utensils. Are you looking for anything in particular for yourself or perhaps as a gift?"

The man set the package on the glass countertop. "I have this statue here. I heard you make your own statues. I want to know if you can make a replica of this one. Like an exact one."

"I must see it first in order to make that determination, sir. Shall we open it?"

Wong reached into a drawer below the counter, took out a pair of scissors, and cut the twine; then he unwrapped the statue, revealing a Guan Yin. He knew it instantly. It depicted a young woman wearing a flowing robe with a necklace signifying Chinese royalty. In her left hand was a jar symbolically containing pure water, and the right one held a willow branch. The crown on her head had the image of Amitābha, the celestial Buddha known for his pure perception and deep awareness of life. Wong marveled at its beauty. It puzzled him that it was unpainted and very heavy. It was obviously made of plaster, but its weight was much heavier than it should have been.

"Do you know what this is?" asked Wong.

"Sure. It's a Chinese statue. Can you make one exactly like it?"

"It is a Guan Yin, the goddess of mercy. It is associated with compassion and venerated by Mahayana Buddhists."

"Yeah, yeah, I know all that. What I want to know is if you can make me another one. An exact copy of this, down to its weight and every little detail."

"This will not be a problem, sir."

"There's one issue, though: I need it right away. Like tomorrow."

"This too will not be a problem. It will be my honor. I can have it ready for you tomorrow by the end of the day. I use an ancient Chinese technique to make my statues. No one else on the island can make one faster and with more accuracy."

"That's good. That's very good. How much will it cost?"

Wong thought for a moment. "For you, there will be a special price. Twenty-five US dollars."

"Have it ready for me tomorrow, and there'll be a big bonus in it for you."

Wong bowed at the waist. He wore a traditional *changshan*, a long silk black tunic under a crimson *magua*, or riding jacket, with golden trim. On his head, he wore rounded black hat. His attire was a bit old-fashioned and worn by most for formal pictures, weddings, and other important events, but Wong usually wore it in the shop because locals as well as tourists seemed to believe that was the everyday dress of all Chinese men. That was what they expected to see in a Chinese gift shop. He did not want to offend them.

"It is my honor to do this, sir."

"But you need to keep this to yourself, if you know what I mean."

"Look to your left there," Wong said, holding out his hand. "See the statue of four wise monkeys? Confucius said many centuries ago, 'Look not at what is contrary to propriety; listen not to what is contrary to propriety; speak not what is contrary to propriety; make no movement which is contrary to propriety.' The first three monkeys are covering their eyes, ears, and mouth. The fourth monkey is covering his genitals. They all warn not to do anything evil."

The man looked at Wong with his face scrunched up in thought. He stayed that way for a long moment, and then he relaxed his face. "Yeah, that's good. That's very good," he said for the second time. "Okay, mister."

"Wong. Yat-Sen Wong."

"Okay, Mr. Wong, you don't say anything about this, and I'll be in tomorrow afternoon to pick them up."

"I'll be like the monkeys and observe the utmost propriety." He bowed again.

"You do that."

"And your name, please?"

"Smith. Harry Smith."

After Smith left, Wong flipped the sign on the glass door and locked up for the day. He picked up the statue and went through the curtains into the back room. *The weight is not right*, he thought. He had a lot of work to do. Something inside him buzzed with delight. He didn't exactly know what it was, but the buzz was there. He could feel it in his bones.

The room was long and narrow. In the front, to the left, was his work area, where he made statues for the local Chinese and tourist trade as well as for rich Cubans, who usually placed special orders. Between the shop and the statues, he made a good living. The rest of the room contained folding chairs set up in neat rows facing the width of the room. He reminded himself that there was an important meeting there that night. It would be packed with men of the Hip Sing Tong. He would do as much work as he could now before the start of the meeting, making a second statue for Mr. Smith, and when the meeting broke up, he would resume his work.

He couldn't get out of the meeting, not only because it was there in his shop but also because he was the leader of the tong, and as such, he had to present the agenda, which included exploring new methods of racketeering, prostitution, counterfeiting, robbery, extortion, illegal gambling, arms trafficking, money laundering, and drug smuggling. He knew he couldn't get through the agenda in one meeting, but he had to get the members thinking in a different way if they were going to hang on to their businesses. They had taken a beating in the last year. There was so much competition coming from the Italian gangsters those days that the tong had to regroup and formulate new strategies. That was vitally important if they were going to survive.

As leader of the tong in Havana and the nephew of Sai Wing Mock, a.k.a. Mock Duck, who had started the organization in New York City decades before, Yat-Sen Wong had a big responsibility to uphold tradition and standards.

He would be a busy man that night.

Harry Smith was flying high that day.

His plans were seamlessly coming together. In two or maybe three days, he'd hit a grand slam, and they'd be complete. Then he'd be ready to implement the final phase.

He hadn't told his girlfriend, Margot, yet. Maybe that was a mistake. Maybe he should have let her in on it from the beginning. In telling her now, he'd have to admit he'd kept it a secret from her. She wouldn't like that, he knew. Not one bit. But after he gave her the details, she'd throw her arms around him and jump for joy. At least he hoped she would. How could she not?

But knowing Margot the way he did, he knew he'd have to word his story just right. She'd have questions for him—plenty of them—so he'd have to think about how to handle that and sort out the answers beforehand. He might even have to rehearse telling her before breaking the news. Yes, he'd rehearse every word of it like an actor rehearsing before going onstage. He'd have to anticipate her questions and then memorize the answers. In the end, she'd be one happy gal.

This scheme of his, even though it wasn't yet completed, warranted a little celebration. He'd keep the celebration low-key, of course, just for himself. He had to be cautious and ever vigilant. His neck was on the line.

He grabbed a taxi and told the driver to go to Trader Vic's inside the Hilton. The restaurant had opened its doors just a few days before, and his friend Vic Bergeron owned it. Smith had wanted to go to the opening but had been tied up with business, so now he could congratulate his buddy and celebrate his good fortune at the same time.

Bergeron owned a chain of Polynesian-themed restaurants scattered on different continents, and the Havana restaurant was the latest one. He had invented the Mai Tai tiki drink, the Fog Cutter, and the Scorpion Bowl, which were now gaining popularity worldwide.

Fifteen minutes later, the taxi pulled up to the Hilton. Smith got out and found the restaurant inside. It was packed with Cubans and foreigners, many of them American businessmen and French and British tourists. He looked around. There were large-leafed potted plants and other greenery everywhere. Along the walls and on pillars made to look like rods of bamboo were tiki tribal masks and other artifacts he couldn't identify. Bergeron had spared no expense. *Good for him.* There was joy in the air; everyone looked happy. Guests were eating exotic food and drinking colorful drinks with fruit sticks on top.

Smith wasn't hungry, so he found an empty stool at the bar and sat down. As luck had it, Bergeron was behind the bar, serving up drinks. Smith caught his eye.

"Hey, Slick!" Bergeron said, going over to him and shaking hands. "Long time no see."

Slick. Smith hated that nickname. Ever since he could remember, Bergeron had called him that and never his true name. At first, he'd protested. But as their friendship had grown, Smith had decided the argument wasn't worth the effort.

"Hey, Vic. Sorry I didn't make the opening, but I see you're doing okay for yourself."

"Yeah, it's been this way since we opened the doors. Packing 'em in! Whaddya drinking? How 'bout a Mai Tai? No, wait," he said with a palm out toward Smith. "I've got just the drink for you. I've been working on it for the last six months in Hawaii. It's not on the menu here yet because I want a little feedback first. You up for a new drink?"

Being in a celebratory mood, Smith said, "Why not? But if it's rotgut, I might have to kick your ass."

"Hey," Bergeron said, chuckling, "without a little honesty now and again, you ain't got shit."

Bergeron hobbled to his left and right to get the ingredients for the drink. He then walked to the end of the bar to the refrigerator for an egg and returned. He started making the drink in front of Smith. "I want you to see exactly what's in it."

When Bergeron walked, he limped noticeably; he had a wooden leg. According to the story Smith had always heard, as a much younger man, Bergeron had been swimming somewhere in the South Pacific—the exact place changed with each retelling—when a hungry shark had ripped one of his legs off at the knee for a snack. Smith had always doubted the story, but Bergeron told it with such flare and gusto that he didn't mind if it was truthful or not. He always enjoyed listening to it, even though Bergeron modified the details a bit. The changes made it more exciting.

"So you take a little honey," Bergeron said, "and put it in the blender like this. Two teaspoons, to be exact. The measurements have to be exact. Then an ounce of lemon juice. Half an ounce of passion fruit syrup follows like this. Followed by an egg." He cracked an egg over the blender. "Two ounces of scotch and a scoop of crushed ice, and there you have it." He pressed the high-speed button on the blender for ten seconds. "I even have a special glass for the drink, Slick."

The glass was tall and light green, with a copper-colored bottom and a matching ring on the top. Along the sides were metallike vertical cords. "I had them made special for this drink. Designed it myself! I'm calling the drink the Starboard Light." He poured the drink into the glass, put a little fresh mint in it, and then laid a tiki pineapple stick across the top. He slid it over to Smith, looking like a proud papa. "You're the first person in Havana to have one."

Smith picked up the glass, took the pineapple stick off, dipped it into the drink once, and then drank, looking over the rim at Bergeron, who was staring at him with anticipation. He lowered the glass, ran his tongue over his lips, and declared, "Brilliant!"

"Ah, good! That's what the fellas in Honolulu said. Used the same word too. I think I'll add it to the menu next week." Bergeron looked to his left at the head bartender, who was pouring a pint. "Carlos, I've had enough standing for a while. I'm going to sit down. I'll be here to take up the slack if you need me."

Carlos nodded and continued pouring the beer.

Bergeron went around the bar, greeting people as he did, and finally sat down next to Smith. "So how's life going for you, Slick? Married yet? Kids?"

"Still seeing Margot. I think the time is right to pop the question."

"She's a good kid. You don't deserve her."

"I know I don't, but I hope she says yes anyway." He took a long swig of his drink, emptying half the glass.

"Still doing errands for that wop?"

"Santo? Yeah, I still work for him, but it's getting old now. The money's good, but I don't see a future in it. If Margot will have me, I'd like to go away somewhere, buy a little house in the country, and live in peace. Know what I mean?"

"You've got to follow your dreams, Slick, wherever they take you. If I hadn't, I wouldn't have what I've got now."

Smith was tempted to tell Bergeron his plans for the immediate future. Bergeron was wealthy and experienced, a self-made man. He was twenty years older than Smith. Smith wondered where he'd be in twenty years. Bergeron could probably give him some good advice, but what he was about to do was too risky to tell anyone besides Margot, even a trusted friend. It wasn't that he thought Bergeron would go around blabbing his mouth off. He wasn't that sort of guy. He could keep a secret. Yet sometimes things got out without the person being aware of it. If it got back to his boss, Smith would be a dead man.

"Yeah, just like the song says, you gotta follow your dreams."

"Well, the way I see it with these mob characters—and I've known quite a few of them over the years—it's all about power and money for themselves. Oh, there's loyalty, of course, but that only goes so far. It's power and money for themselves, first and last. If I ran my businesses the way they run theirs, sure, I might be more successful, but I wouldn't have any true friends, and I'd have to look over my shoulder constantly, if you know what I mean. I'd have employees who feared me. You can't live your life like that, having people around you afraid of you all the time. That's not true loyalty. This might sound a little selfish, but you have to look out for yourself and the people around you—genuinely respect them and treat them like real family. That's what it's all about."

In spite of himself, Smith had gotten a little advice from his friend—sound advice too. It made his resolve even stronger to go ahead with his plan.

Still, he had to tell Margot, and that wasn't going to be easy.

9

The Lady in the Bar

Calle Neptuno was crowded, as usual. Habaneros, men, women, and children—young and old; black, white, brown, yellow, and red; rich and poor; dressed in their finest or in rags—leisurely ambled the street in the tropical heat, sometimes stopping in small groups, standing on the sidewalk, or spilling into the street, chatting with one another. Wandering street vendors touted their wares in angelic voices: "Mangoes! Guayabas! Plantains! Papayas!" A couple of raggedy street urchins playing tag ran through and around groups of people, using them to hide behind, hoping to avoid or catch each other.

"Hey, you little shits!" a man called out, feigning anger. "Go play at home. You might trip someone, and then we'd have to call the police! You should be in school! Why aren't you in school?"

The kids paid no attention to him, zigzagging around the people. The man laughed and shook his head.

The day was sweltering; clothes stuck to sweaty bodies. But the Habaneros, perhaps more than most, knew the joys of living, whatever their fortunes in life were.

The scents that defined Havana all converged on Calle Neptuno. They exploded from storefront restaurants and floated from second-floor apartment windows above the street: arroz con frijoles, fried steaks, spicy chicken, baked breads, cigars, and coffee—always coffee. The aromas wafted through the air and became one with the sounds of singing peddlers; buses; rumbling American car engines; music from bars, restaurants, and passing cars; and the street-corner conjuntos, with their ever-present accordions, guitars, maracas, and bongo drums. The sounds and smells fused and danced proudly and defiantly, blissfully indifferent to the universe. Calle Neptuno wasn't so much a street as it was a living, breathing soul.

Ashton Hunter, who'd grown up in the frigid winters of Minnesota and fought in Italy in ice and snow during the war, loved every minute of it. He couldn't pinpoint exactly why he did. At first, he'd thought life there was going to be at a much slower pace. But that wasn't so in Havana; he'd have had to go to the countryside for that. Havana was just as busy as any comparable American city—maybe more so because it had an international flair. At some point, he'd decided it didn't matter; he loved Havana, and that was that.

He stopped briefly on the sidewalk, with people shouldering their way around him, and wiped his face with a handkerchief. He needed a break from the heat, someplace that had air-conditioning. He continued up the street and saw a sign hanging over the sidewalk: "Club de Los Bohemios. *Aire Acondicionado.*" Just a quick beer, a reprieve from the ghastly heat, was what he needed now. He scooted around two men sitting in small chairs with their knees up and a board resting between them, playing dominoes, and entered the club.

A small band in the back was playing "Siboney." The sensuous female lead singer was moving her body to the rhythm. Hunter liked the song, and he liked the singer even more. She was beautiful and reminded him of someone he'd known, at least from a distance. He saw that immediately. He sidled up to the bar and sat on a stool, glancing over his shoulder several times in her direction.

The air-conditioning felt good. Ignacio Navarro was still on his mind. So was Shaw Armstrong. He ordered a beer from the barman, glancing at the band again. He didn't want to stare, but he thought the girl had been looking at him.

The barman placed a bottle in front of him. Hunter reached into his pocket and then pushed some pesos toward the barman, enough for the beer and a tip. The barman nodded and slid the coins off the bar. Hunter didn't know him; he didn't know how the man would react to being raked over. Barmen knew and saw a lot, but they were known to be closed-mouthed, especially in Havana. People came and went and talked a lot in between. Most barmen knew other people's secrets, at least the barmen he knew. After he established a relationship with them, they were more willing to cough up information to him—for a price. They weren't paid well and had to supplement their incomes somehow. Other people's secrets were the commodity they sold in the marketplace of gossip and innuendo.

Hunter didn't have time to get to know this barman, so he decided to be up front with him and see what that got him. "Mind if I ask you a question?" he said in Spanish.

"*Sí*, senor. I am here to be of service. What can I help you with?"

"I'm part owner of the Paradise Inn, down by the Malecón. A couple from the States is staying with us for a week or so on vacation. They're looking for an American friend of theirs who lives here in Havana. Tall guy. Well dressed. His name is Shaw Armstrong. Looks like the American actor Tyrone Power. Ever heard of him?"

The barman looked down at the bar and then to his right as if he were thinking about it. Hunter noticed a seriousness in his demeanor that had not been there before. He swung his head toward Hunter again but didn't make eye contact.

"No, senor. I do not know the man."

He knew something.

"But you've heard the name before."

The barman looked around the club again. Hunter pulled out a twenty-dollar bill and laid it on the bar.

"I did not lie. I do not know the man," he said in a whisper. "But I have heard others say his name." He placed his fingertips on the bill and slid it back to Hunter. "The men—they were Americanos and not very pleasant people. You yourself are Americano, no? I am sorry, but they were not very nice, your countrymen. I would prefer they not come in here, but what can I do?"

"You think this Shaw Armstrong is with these men somehow? Like friends?" Hunter took a long gulp from his beer. He was much more comfortable now in the air-conditioning.

"I think that is the case. One time, just last week, they were talking about how this Shaw Armstrong liked to go to the Shanghai, and they were laughing about it. Sometimes they called him Shaw, and sometimes they said Armstrong, referring to the same man."

"The Shanghai, you say? A lot of people go to the Shanghai."

"But he goes there to collect money. Know what I mean? Maybe he watches the shows. I do not know. His friends seemed to think so. That's why they were laughing at him."

"I see. If this Armstrong ever comes in here, I'd appreciate it if you called me. You know what Tyrone Power looks like?"

"Sí, senor. My wife and I just saw *The Sun Also Rises* last month. It was from the book by Senor Hemingway. It was a private showing. We got tickets because my wife knows someone who knows someone who does some work for Senor Hemingway. It is not released yet, not even in America."

Hunter took his card out of his wallet, set it on top of the twenty, and pushed them both forward. "The couple I mention really want to see this guy while they're here."

"*Muchas gracias.* I will call you."

The band in the back of the bar finished their song and were about to take a break. Hunter looked over at them briefly and then back at the barman.

"By the way, would you mind asking the young lady over there, the lead singer, if I could buy her a drink?"

"I think that is possible, senor."

The barman went around the bar and made his way to the band. Hunter watched as he spoke to the woman, pointing back at him. The barman returned.

"She said she would join you in a few minutes. She first must do something."

Hunter reached over the bar. "*Gracias*. Ash Hunter, as the card says. I didn't get your name."

"Mateo," he said, shaking hands with Hunter. "Good to meet you."

Mateo seemed to be a reasonable man, and he didn't mind talking openly to strangers. Hunter could milk him for information in the future if the occasion arose. He'd have to come in there more often for friendly chats to establish a closer relationship. Mateo was definitely someone he could work with. He took a sip from his beer.

The singer with the band vaguely resembled the only woman he almost had married. She was about the right size, petite, with long black hair. But that had been his assessment from a distance with low lighting. He wondered how she'd fare up close.

Angie had broken his heart. Well, that wasn't exactly right. Her family had stepped between them. He didn't resent Angie; there was little she could have done. He had no doubt what kind of family she had been born into. He took another sip of beer.

"Hello! Am I interrupting your thoughts?"

Hunter swung around on his stool. For a second, he thought he was looking at Angie. "Not at all. You speak English."

"It's a second language for me. I have relatives in the States." She sat on the stool next to him.

"What are you drinking?"

She looked down the bar. "Mateo, would you bring me my usual?"

Mateo nodded, poured a brandy, and brought it to her.

"Salud!" Hunter and the singer said.

Up close, the woman could have been Angie's double. The hairstyle was a little different, and her jawline was less rigid, but

82

other than that, they could have been twin sisters. Why hadn't he come in there before?

"I'm Ash—"

"Yes, I know. You're Ash Hunter from the Paradise."

"You get around. Or maybe Mateo told you."

"I'm Maria Sanchez, and yes, I do get around. But your card, remember?"

She seemed a little distracted. There was a hard edge to her. She seemed more businesslike than relaxed, as one would have expected her to be when accepting a drink from a customer.

"You have a beautiful voice," Hunter said with a grin.

"Thank you. I had voice and singing instruction while growing up. You have a nice speaking voice yourself."

"I use it only for speaking. If I sang, I'm afraid it wouldn't be a very pretty thing to hear."

"Mr. Hunter," she said abruptly, "I will get to the point. I know what you do besides owning the Paradise Inn. I want to hire you."

Hunter was caught completely off guard. For a moment, he didn't know what to say. He stared at her. The woman's eyes, nose, and lips were Angie's. But instead of being warm and inviting, her eyes were cold—or maybe not cold but focused, as if she had just sat down to sign a contract for a business agreement. As she had implied, there was a point for her accepting a drink. Apparently, it wasn't social. It wasn't difficult for anyone to know he was part owner of the Paradise, but how did she know about his detective service? He could deny he had any such service, but it was obvious Maria Sanchez hadn't just made a wild guess. If she knew that much about him, what else did she know?

He angled his head slightly and narrowed his eyes at her, as if trying to read between the lines.

"As I said, Mr. Hunter, I get around."

"Apparently. Let's go sit down at one of those tables over there," he said, motioning with his head. "It'll be more private."

They sat down at a small, round table near a corner, away from other patrons. The place wasn't packed, but there was enough chatter that they could talk in a normal voice without fear of being overheard.

"Now, Miss Sanchez," Hunter said, "just what do you want to hire me for? You want to rent a room at the inn? It's high season, but I think I can manage one somehow."

Her face was stern and joyless. She picked up her brandy and sipped, looking at Hunter over the rim. She put the snifter down and said, "Let's not play games, Mr. Hunter. I don't want a room; I want to hire you as a private investigator."

He decided that a little denial wasn't a bad thing after all. He'd see where that took him—and her.

"What makes you think I'm in that line of work? I'm just an innkeeper, plain and simple."

"Mr. Hunter, I'm taking a considerable risk just in talking to you. I was going to come to you in a few days, but then you showed up here. It must be fate. How I know about you is not important. But it is important that you take me seriously. Will you do that, Mr. Hunter?"

He could see she was nervous. Her eyes darted around the club as she spoke. She appeared to be a woman in distress. He could finish the rest of his beer and leave, he thought. Maybe he should. He didn't like situations like this. She, a complete stranger, knew that he ran a below-the-radar detective agency, and that in itself wasn't good. Yet in some inexplicable way, he felt that Angie herself was sitting across the table from him and in some kind of trouble. Could he simply get up and walk away? Walk away from Angie?

"Why don't you tell me what's on your mind, and I'll see if I can help you?"

She looked around the club and then focused her eyes on Hunter again. "It's my husband. We've been married for five years now. Each year is worse than the last."

"There are some good marriage counselors here in Havana. I've never been married myself, so I'm afraid I couldn't give you much advice."

She looked at him as if he were being sarcastic. "It's beyond that point, Mr. Hunter."

"Please call me Ash, Miss Sanchez."

"Okay. Call me Maria then." She looked toward the entrance and then at the people sitting at the bar. Her eyes went from one to another, stopping briefly at each one, and then back to Hunter. In a voice just above a whisper, she said, "You see, my husband beats me. Everywhere on my body that can't be seen. In the beginning, he would always feel ashamed and say it would never happen again. And he would stop for a time. Then he would start again, especially when he was drinking a lot. Now it's every week. Once, I ended up in the hospital, but he told the doctor I had fallen down the stairs."

"Have you reported him? Filed a complaint?"

"It's not that simple. He knows a lot of important men in the city. They would support him without question. If I reported him, I would have to talk to the same men he knows."

"Maybe you should think about a divorce."

She went silent for a long moment. She took out a handkerchief and dabbed her eyes. If Hunter were to take her at face value, then this was serious, but what could he do?

"He's told me many times that if I divorce him, he will kill me. I believe him."

"What does your husband do that he knows these important people?"

"He's a captain on the police force. If I left him and hid somewhere, he would find me. He would have the entire police force out looking for me. If I filed for divorce, he would know. There is nothing I can do. I'm afraid he will beat me one day, and that will be it."

She was in a terrible, life-threatening situation. Hunter had known cases like hers there in Havana and back in Saint Paul, although he had never worked directly on them. More times than not, the women ended up in hospitals or dead. He wasn't about to walk away from Maria Sanchez, yet he had no idea how to help her. All the usual means she could use to protect herself seemed to be closed. She was in a prison cell without a key.

"Normally, I would tell you to go to the police, but obviously, you can't do that. When you decided to come to me, Maria, you must have had some idea how I could help."

She looked down at her drink. There was a little more brandy in it. She picked up the snifter, swirled the brandy, and then drank it. "I did," she said, looking up at him.

Hunter remained silent, waiting for her to continue. After a moment, she did.

"I want him dead."

Hunter was stunned. "Maria, I know you're in an awful situation, but you're talking about murder here. I do a lot of things here in Havana to make a living, but that's not one of them."

"Not you, but you must know someone who would be willing to do it."

Because he was a private detective, Maria must have assumed he knew a lot of criminals in the underworld, and she was right; he did.

"So you want me to be the go-between? That's still murder any way you look at it."

"Listen, Ash. I am asking you—begging you—to help me. Without your help, I will die very soon, and there is no one else I can go to who can prevent that. It will be either me or my husband."

He had walked in there only to get out of the heat. Now he had walked into a hellfire.

Hunter sat calmly, but his head was a roller coaster. He knew she was right. If what she said was true, eventually, she'd be lying on a slab in the morgue, and her husband would be savvy enough to get away with it scot-free. However, by helping her, he'd be guilty of arranging a murder. If things went sideways—there was always a chance they would, no matter how slim—and he got caught, that meant the death penalty in Cuba, and considering he'd be arranging the murder of a police official, he'd be led to the firing squad sooner rather than later. However, if he didn't help her, he could be signing Maria Sanchez's death warrant.

On the other hand, what if this woman wasn't telling the truth? What if she just wanted to get rid of her husband because she wanted to marry her lover? What if she wasn't the victim of her husband's beatings? Before he decided to walk down this rocky road, he'd have to have some proof, and there was only one way to get it.

"Maria, before I can give you an answer, I need to see some proof. We're talking about something very serious here. I'd be putting my neck on the line. I need to see the evidence." He paused for a moment and then said, "If we go through with this, it's going to cost you a lot of money."

"You want to see my body? I can show you all the evidence you need." Again, she looked around the bar, but Hunter guessed it wasn't because she was paranoid. "And I will pay anything it takes to rid myself of this beast."

To think, just a few hours before, he'd been cursing Hannigan for taking on risky jobs.

10

Looking for a Little Sin

The café at the Paradise Inn was beginning to thin out. Nearly every table had been full. Babs Hannigan was pleased. She walked to the back, where the view of the Malecón below was spectacular; stopped at a table; and smiled.

"I hope your meal was good tonight," she said to the couple sitting there.

"Marvelous. Just marvelous. Wasn't it, sugar plum?" Lizzy said.

Bradford smiled and wiped his mouth with a napkin.

"And what do you call what we just ate—I mean in Spanish?" she asked.

"You had one of our specialties. The *mojo*-marinated pork shoulder roast is called *pernil asado con mojo*, and the rice and beans are called *moros y christianos*. They're favorites here in Havana."

"Marvelous!" she said again. "It was just marvelous by any name."

"Instead of dessert, might I suggest a pineapple mojito?"

"Lovely, isn't it, Bradford?"

"Lovely," he managed to get out just under a grunt.

"Yes, we'll have the mojitos, please."

Babs went to the small bar toward the front of the café, fixed the mojitos, and returned with them.

"Oh, won't you join us?" Elizabeth Maddox asked Babs.

"I don't want to intrude."

"Oh, please, sit down. Please do. You definitely won't be intruding."

Babs sat down and motioned to Sammy to bring her usual drink. "How are you enjoying your stay in sunny Havana?"

"Oh, marvelous. Marvelous!"

Babs thought she either really liked using that word or had a limited vocabulary.

"We haven't done any of the tours yet. We'll keep that for last. Right now, we're just mingling with the natives." She leaned forward a bit and lowered her voice as if she were about to relay a secret message to a fellow spy. "They say that's the best way to get the most out of a vacation. You just muck in with the locals. At home, it would seem banal, but here everything seems so exotic."

"Marvelous," Babs said dryly, trying out the word to see how it fit. "*They* were right to tell you that. I guarantee you there's nothing in Havana that's banal."

Bradford Maddox reached into his inner jacket pocket and pulled out a torpedo—a Montecristo No. 2 cigar—and lit up, sending a cloud of smoke over the table. Sammy came over and set a gin and tonic in front of Babs.

Babs took a sip of her drink and set it down. "So you said you're from Tampa, Mrs. Maddox. What do you do there, if I can be a little nosy?"

"Oh, you're not being nosy in the least, and please call me Lizzy. All my friends do. Don't they, sugar plum?"

He blew another cloud of smoke over the table.

"In that case, Lizzy, you can call me Babs. All my friends call me that and even some of my enemies."

Bradford grinned and then winked at Babs, puffing on his cigar.

"Oh, I love your sense of humor, Babs. It's just—"

Here it comes, Babs thought.

"Marvelous!"

Bingo!

"To answer your question—" Lizzy suddenly stopped and turned toward her husband. "Oh, Bradford! Before I forget, remind me tomorrow to get some Coppertone, will you? I forgot to bring some with us." She turned back to Babs. "I burn so easily." She sipped her mojito and ran her tongue around her lips. "I'm a housewife, and Bradford here," she said, patting his shoulder, "does a little of this and a little of that."

"A little of this," Babs said, looking at Bradford, "and a little of that must be exhausting. You came to the right place. Havana can relieve all your stress." It was discreet, but Babs thought she saw Bradford eyeballing her. She was a good-looking woman and was used to men giving her a quick appraisal but not a husband whose wife was sitting next to him.

"And maybe create some more," Bradford said to Babs, glancing at his wife.

"If you're not careful," Babs said. "If you're worried about finding your friend—what was his name?"

"Shaw Armstrong," Lizzy said.

"If you're worried about finding Mr. Armstrong, Ash Hunter is the best man to locate him. If he can't do it, then Mr. Armstrong can't be found."

"Oh, I hope he can. We're so excited to see him again. He's a darling man and very good friend." She took a long sip of her mojito. Bradford had drunk most of his already. "Babs, if I can be personal just a tiny bit"—she held her hand out and squeezed her index finger and thumb together—"how did you come to Havana and start this inn?"

"Well, it was about ten years ago. Slane, Ash, and I were all working in a hotel in Saint Paul, Minnesota—that's where we're from. It's called the Saint Paul Hotel—very fancy and high class. Slane was the manager, I worked at the front desk, and Ash was one of the house detectives, although he had his own detective business on the side."

She went on to say they had saved their money with the hope of buying a small hotel somewhere in southern Florida because people were starting to flock there for vacations. They could run their own business and get away from the horrific Minnesota winters at the same time. Then they'd discovered an opportunity in Havana. They had done their research and discovered that because of the legal gambling, significant numbers of Americans were beginning to take vacations there. It was only ninety miles off the shores of Florida and was easily accessible by ship or plane, and more and more hotels were being built to accommodate them.

"So we bought the inn, eventually remodeled it, and haven't looked back. We love it here."

"And business is good?"

"The off-season can be a little dicey, but the high season makes up for it. We also have a charter service year-round that helps. You and your hubby here should book a cruise before you leave. The coast is stunning from only a little way out. You wouldn't regret it. The *Valiant Queen*—that's the name of our motor yacht. The beds are comfy, the cabin is cozy, we supply the food and drinks, and if you fish, we have all the equipment you'll need."

"Oh, that sounds like fun!" Lizzy said, clapping her hands and jumping up and down several times in her chair like a teenager anticipating her first kiss. "Doesn't it, Bradford?"

"A load of laughs," Bradford said, still working on the cigar. "Whoop-de-do." To emphasize the point, he stuck a finger in the air and twirled it.

Suddenly, Sammy appeared with his guitar and began strumming.

On dis island of love, people come, and dey go.
Two special lovers here from Tampa, who like the beautiful dove.
Dey look into each other's eyes, and dey surely glow.

91

Romance is what dey seek at the Paradise Inn,
for dis is *marvelous* Havana, the city of sin.
Da love is so strong, dis Bradford and Lizzy,
that it makes everyone around dem a tad bit dizzy!

Babs and Lizzy threw their heads back, cheered, and clapped their hands. Lizzy said that she loved calypso and that Sammy was clever. Sammy, beaming, bowed at the waist and said, "Thank you, thank you," and left. It was all part of the service at the Paradise Inn.

Babs glanced over at Bradford, who sat stern-faced with the torpedo in his mouth. She was beginning to feel uncomfortable with Mr. and Mrs. Maddox. Bradford clearly wasn't enjoying himself. Something was going on with this pair, and she didn't want to get in the middle of it. She slid the chair back and grabbed what was left of her drink.

"You two lovebirds enjoy the rest of the evening. A stroll down the Malecón at this time of night is lovely. It was a pleasure talking to you."

After Babs left, Lizzy spoke first. "Well, aren't you the life of the party," she said, running her fingers through her hair and shaking her head as if dispelling any remnants of displeasure that might have been ensnarled there.

Bradford puffed on his cigar again and then set it in the ashtray. "We didn't come all the way to Cuba for a party," he said, staring off into space.

"That doesn't mean we can't have a little fun while we're here."

"Fun?" he said, turning his head toward his wife. "Let's find that son of a bitch first. Then we can have all the fun we want."

"Bradford, darling," she said, sliding her chair closer to him and grabbing his arm, "you seem a little testy tonight. Are you testy, sugar plum?"

He looked into her eyes, his harsh countenance melting away. "You know I can never be testy with you, sweetheart. You're the love of my life. It's just that I wish this would all be finished so we could go back to Tampa. I feel this huge weight on our backs. Everything we do and everywhere we go, we're being weighed down. Don't you feel it?"

"It won't be long, Bradford. You heard Babs just a while ago. Ash Hunter is the best in the business. If he doesn't find Armstrong, that means he isn't in Havana, and we both know he's here. So when he finds Shaw Armstrong, we find Shaw Armstrong. And when we find him, all our problems will be solved. Just keep that in mind, darling." Her voice suddenly changed, becoming deep and seductive, nearly but not quite a whisper. "Then we can look for a little sin. After all, this is Havana, like the calypso man said. In the meantime, before we retire to our room and to our bed, what do you say we take a romantic stroll down the Malecón like the lady suggested? It could be marvelous!"

"Whoop-de-do," he said, again swirling his finger in the air, but this time, he meant it.

11

The Naughtiest Theater in the World

Havana was a complex city.

With its more than a million inhabitants, one could find many of the same things there as in other large cities, such as New York, London, and Paris—the rich and the poor, the pious and the sinful, the hardworking and the slothful, the glamorous and the depraved. One didn't have to look hard for crime and corruption in Havana. They were on the street corners, in the alleyways, and in every barrio.

American pleasure seekers came in droves by air and by sea for all of it.

The reasons they came were many and varied. They came for the liquor, the legal gambling, and the women. They came from Omaha, Cincinnati, and Dallas, seeking release from the tedium of their office and factory jobs in exchange for an exotic, tropical, mystical experience in a world so different from their own that they often were left exhausted from the excitement. They came in their bizarre mismatched Hawaiian shirts and Bermuda shorts, western boots and cowboy hats, linen suits and fedora panamas. But for all

94

the city's commodities they sought, one stood out in the mix: the debauchery.

Havana was one huge theater; its denizens and tourists were the players, acting out their never-ending parts by day and by night in the streets, restaurants, houses, hotels, classy nightclubs, and cheap dives. Inevitably, predictably, they all ended up at the queen of debauchery: the Shanghai.

A tattered, bulky building on Calle Zanja, between Manrique and Campanario, the Shanghai Theater originally had been a site for oriental drama. After Chinese opera had fallen by the wayside, the theater changed had hands and become a burlesque hall.

There, the impresario, Jose Orozco Garcia, served up—while the police turned their heads—an irresistible menu of live female flesh onstage and then spiced things up with debaucherous twosomes engaging in nookie in every inconceivable position on film. Guests found no tables, linen tablecloths, cutlery, water glasses, salt and pepper shakers, napkins, or waiters, save for Garcia himself. Instead, there were uncomfortable metal folding chairs—700 on the lower level and 350 in the balcony—occupied by men of wealth, men of poverty, and everyone in between, locals and tourists alike, who came there to fulfill their wildest and most sordid fantasies. The menu was unlimited and satisfying.

Ash Hunter opened the main door of the Shanghai and stepped inside. The woman in the ticket booth was reading a paperback. She looked up, and before Hunter had a chance to say anything, she spoke.

"The nine thirty show is full," she said in staccato Spanish. "You want a ticket for eleven thirty?"

"I'll pass on the ticket. I'm here to see Senor Garcia."

She looked at her watch. "He'd be in the dressing room with the girls. You still have to buy a ticket to enter. Even Senor Garcia buys a ticket whenever he comes in. So do I. So do the girls and the men."

Hunter paid for a ticket, asked where the dressing room was, and collected his change. He walked through the lobby, opened the doors to the auditorium, took several steps inside, and stopped.

It was still warm outside, but the temperature inside the hall must have been twenty degrees hotter. He could feel it radiating at the entrance. The ambient lights from the stage were bright enough for him to see most of the area around him. There were Chinese, Spanish, Americans, and Cubans, all men, and based on the languages he heard, there must have been at least a half dozen other nationalities. They were hooting and hollering and waving their arms in the air. The orchestra was playing a fast rhumba. The girls, all shapes and sizes, formed a chorus line and moved forward to the stage apron, at which time they reached behind themselves and collectively undid their snaps, letting their bras dangle while jiggling to the music.

Hunter had seen this act before and wasn't impressed, but it definitely pleased the crowd. He went to the left side of the hall and walked down an aisle toward a door next to the stage. Once inside, he pushed his way through a horde of girls, stopping to ask one of them where he could find the owner. She pointed toward the back of the room. Hunter spotted a short, paunchy man helping one of the girls zip up a costume. He was dressed in a dark pin-striped suit and vest, patent-leather shoes, and a black fedora. A long cigar stuck out of his mouth. Hunter shouldered his way toward the man.

"*Discúlpame, por favor,*" Hunter said. "Are you Senor Garcia?"

The man took his cigar out of his mouth, patted the girl he was helping on her behind, and said, "Sí, sí. I'm Jose Garcia. How did you get back here? You shouldn't be here."

"My name is Ash Hunter. I'm part owner of the Paradise Inn."

"Down by the Malecón?"

"Yes."

"Fine place. You want to rent some girls?"

"No, thanks anyway. I'm looking for an Americano. You may know him."

"Yes, well, I know many Americanos."

"His name is Shaw Armstrong."

"Armstrong? Ah yes. Tall man? Dresses well? Looks like a Hollywood movie star?"

"That's him."

"Never saw him. Don't know who he is."

Hunter cocked his head to the side.

"Don't be annoyed. That's just my humor. You've got to have a sense of humor in my business. What about him?"

"Do you know where I can find him?"

"No. He used to come here about once a week to collect—never mind. Haven't seen him lately."

"Why did he stop?"

"His woman caught him here. She came in looking for him. When she found him, she raised a fuss. Made quite a scene. Almost called the police on her. I don't like conflicts here; they can get out of hand fast. I heard her say things that shocked even me," he said, fingering his diamond stickpin. "Haven't seen the poor guy since."

Hunter was about to thank him, when Garcia spoke again.

"You might want to check out the casino at the Tropicana. He told me he gambles there a lot."

"*Muchas gracias*," Hunter said, and he started to leave.

"Hey, you might as well stay and see the show. After all, you bought a ticket for the raunchiest spectacle on earth!"

Hunter stood outside the Shanghai. He looked at his watch. It had been a long day, and he was exhausted. Tomorrow he'd have to get up early and go to the airport. He hadn't forgotten about Ignacio Navarro. He needed to check the flights out of Havana to make sure Navarro wasn't going to skip out. But right now, he had something important to do.

Maria Sanchez was waiting for him.

After he'd talked to her at the Club de Los Bohemios earlier that day, he'd rented a room at the Hotel Miami, a seedy little hole-in-the-wall in Chinatown. It was one of many small hotels in the city that catered to discreet rendezvous. They asked no questions, avoided eye contact when guests checked in, and required no identification. Still, he had to be careful. Maria's husband was a powerful man on the police force. Their eyes and ears were everywhere in the city. The hotel was only a few blocks north of the Shanghai.

He walked up the street. Behind him, a conjunto appeared from out of nowhere and followed him. Hunter enjoyed the music, but now was not the time. He stopped and turned around. He dug into his trousers, pulling out a handful of coins. He gave them to the guitar player. "*Gracias, gracias, pero no más, por favor.*" The man received the coins with gratitude, and they all nodded their thanks. Street commerce at its best. Hunter continued up the street.

He approached the hotel from across the street. He looked around for any suspicious activities and found none, except for a bum leaning against a building down the block. He knew the bum could be a police officer or, at the least, a police informant. Police often hung around those hotels to shake down the men and the prostitutes, who could cough up a little dough or spend a week behind bars—it was their choice. There wasn't anyone around the entrance, and few people were on the street, yet he was still taking a chance of being seen.

He crossed the street and went into the hotel. The lobby was tiny, and there wasn't a clerk behind the desk, so he climbed the steps to the second floor. He stopped at room 202 and knocked three times. "It's Ash Hunter," he whispered. The door pulled back, and he stepped inside.

"I thought you weren't coming," Maria said, closing and locking the door.

"Sorry. I got tied up on another case. Everything all right?"

"I don't think anyone saw me come in. I asked for the key at the desk. The man slid it over to me without looking at me."

"Good. He'll think you're just meeting someone here for a few hours."

The room was small, with a single lamp on the nightstand beside the bed. There was one window, but the shutters were closed. Maria stood by the end of the bed and took off her clothes. As she did, Hunter turned his back to her out of courtesy.

"You won't be able to see me with your back to me. I want you to see all the evidence. Every bit of it. I'm not embarrassed, so there's no reason you should be."

Hunter turned around and looked at her. "Please come over to the light so I can see better."

She moved to the other end of the bed by the nightstand and stood still with her arms hanging down and her head straight ahead; her face was rigid. He looked at her as if she were a corpse standing upright. Her ribs were bruised. There were welts between her breasts and on her stomach. The coloration varied, which indicated the marks had been made at different times. Hunter felt a sudden nausea well up in him. Her thighs were equally bruised, and he noticed what looked like strap marks.

"Did he use a belt on you?"

"Yes, when he wasn't using his fists."

"Turn around, please."

She did so, still holding herself still. He saw more bruises and welts on her back. They looked to be more recent. There were some older scars on the backs of her thighs. He looked down the middle of her back again; there were newer swellings and raw lesions. Maria was right; her husband was a beast—a monster.

"Okay, I've seen enough," Hunter said. "You can put your clothes back on."

Hunter was still fighting back nausea. He had never seen anything like this before, not on a woman. When he first had seen Maria up on the stage at the club, singing in her beautiful voice, he never would have guessed from looking at her what she had been going though. There were no visible marks on her body for the public to see. Clearly, she was a woman in danger. Hunter had no doubt that if she continued to live with her husband, one day he would kill her. Maybe not tomorrow or the next week but sometime soon.

Maria, now fully clothed, sat on the edge of the bed. "Will you help me?" she asked in a soft voice, looking down at her hands on her lap.

Hunter was fighting with a moral dilemma. If he did nothing, she would die; he was convinced of that. If he arranged to have her husband murdered, he would be implicated if caught. It would be a death sentence for him and for her. The way he felt at the moment, he would have had no problem killing the bastard himself. The only thing he knew for certain was that he'd have to do something now before it was too late.

He went down on one knee in front of her, reached under her chin, and raised it slightly. He looked into her eyes. *Angie?*

"Of course I will, Maria. Of course I will. But we should leave now."

She grabbed her purse from the bed and followed Hunter down the stairs to the lobby. The night clerk was sitting behind the counter, his head barely above the edge, but there was no indication that he heard them.

"Stay here," Hunter said to Maria in a low voice. "I'm going to flag down a taxi. I'll let you know when to come out."

With that, he opened the door and stepped down to the sidewalk. He looked at his watch. It was just after eleven o'clock at night, still early into Havana's nightlife. He looked up and down the street but didn't see a taxi. Hunter was a methodical man, not one prone to panic. However, there he was, in public, coming out of an ill-reputed hotel with the wife of a captain of the National Police. Still, he didn't resort to panic; however, he was somewhat concerned. *Have patience, my old friend. A taxi will be here soon, cruising the streets for customers.*

He'd told Maria he'd help, and he was a man of his word. However, he hadn't told her there'd be a condition. When he did tell her, if she rejected it, then there would be nothing else he could do. He would be adamant about that. He had but one plan up his sleeve; if she vetoed that, she would be on her own to solve her problem.

Just then, a taxi turned a corner onto the street he was on. He jumped into the street and waved to it with both hands. The driver dimmed his lights once to indicate he had seen Hunter. As the car approached, Hunter motioned to Maria to come out. She opened the door and was in the street in no time. The taxi stopped, and Hunter immediately opened the door. Maria swiftly, with one fluid motion, went from the sidewalk to the backseat of the taxi. Hunter hopped in after her and closed the door.

Just then, there was a reflection in the taxi of the lights of a car directly behind them. The car stopped a couple of yards from the bumper of the taxi. After a long moment, the lights went out, and so did the glare.

It was a police prowl car.

"Wait five seconds, and then just ease out," he said to the driver. "Don't rush away."

The other car's back door closest to the sidewalk opened, and a well-dressed young woman stepped out. Behind her was a man in the uniform of the National Police.

"¡Oh, *Dios mío!*" Maria said, greatly agitated. "That's my husband!"

"Drive slowly away, please—now!" Hunter said to the driver.

The driver did so.

"He was with his mistress. He doesn't know that I know he has one, but I have seen him with her before."

"Senor," the driver said, looking into the rearview mirror, "where would you like me to take you?"

"Just drive, and I'll tell you soon."

"The meter is still running, no?"

"Yes, yes, that's fine." He turned to Maria. "Maria, I said I'd help you, and I will. But you've got to make the break right now. You can't return home for any reason."

"But I need to collect my clothes. I have some important things to take with me."

"If you want me to help you, you can't go home. Your husband's with his mistress right now, but there's no guarantee he will be five minutes from now. He could change his plans and go home. If he does and he beats you again, it could be for the last time. I can get you out of this marriage, but you have to trust me. And you have to decide now."

She stared at him questioningly. She was about to say something but stopped before a word escaped. After a moment, she said, "Okay."

"You mean yes, you want to go through with it?"

"Yes, I want to go through with it."

"Once the plan is in place, there's no turning back. Do you understand that? Once it's in place, that's it."

"Yes, I understand."

"Say it again."

"Yes, I understand."

"Good," Hunter said. He turned to the driver and said, "Take us to the Paradise Inn, please."

"Ah, you have finally decided! That is good! The Paradise Inn— yes, I know the place. Down by the Malecón. That is where my relatives from Miami stay when they come to visit me. Very nice hotel! Okay, senor, I will take you and the lady to the Paradise Inn. Here we go." He made a sharp right turn and sped up. "Hang on to your hat, ha-ha! José is behind the wheel! José will get you there *muy rápido!*"

The taxi raced down the street and into the dark Havana night.

12

A Haze

Hunter had gotten up early that Thursday morning; brushed his teeth; combed his hair; thrown on his clothes; put on his hat, taking an extra second or two but no more to look in the mirror, making sure it sat with just the right tilt on his head; and grabbed a taxi to Rancho-Boyeros Airport. He had gotten up late in spite of the early hour and was in a rush, which had compelled to do the most unthinkable thing he could imagine: forgo his coffee. Granted, it had been a deliberate decision on his part, one for which he had taken full responsibility. Notwithstanding, if there'd been any blame to be had, it would have fallen squarely on the shoulders of Ignacio Navarro.

Navarro had lied to Hunter about where he had kept the jewels. Now Hunter had to consider what else he might have lied about. Navarro had claimed he was supposed to be traveling from Madrid to Buenos Aires with a short stay in Havana. Hunter wanted to verify that Navarro was indeed going to Argentina. He had to get to the airport fast; Navarro might even be boarding a plane now, for all Hunter knew, hence his spirited manner of getting dressed and his lack of stimulant to his central nervous system.

The ride to the airport forced Hunter to slow down. His thoughts changed direction; he began thinking about Maria Sanchez. He had given her a room at the Paradise the previous night without officially checking her in. He'd told her to stay there and not come out for any reason. Babs would look after her meals. At Hunter's behest, Maria would call her husband that morning and inform him she had been staying in town with a friend because she'd worked late last night. She had done so before; the police captain was used to it, so no suspicions would be aroused. She'd tell him she'd be home at the usual time that night after work. That gave Hunter the whole day to work out his plan.

When she didn't return home that night, her husband would become concerned. Sooner or later, he would set things into motion, suspicious that something wasn't right. When he couldn't find her, he would no doubt put out an alert to all or most of the police force to be on the lookout for her. Hunter would have to work fast.

He made a mental note to retrieve his .45 semiautomatic from the safe at the inn. It was registered, and he could legally carry it. Many business owners had guns, but he rarely took his own out of the safe. However, this time was different. He might need it. There was no imminent threat, but that could change.

At the airport, he checked the flights for Buenos Aires at Air Cubano. The woman he spoke to was in good humor and cooperative, but Navarro was not listed on any of the manifests. Hunter then went to the check-in desk of Pan American, the only other airline flying to Argentina. There were usually several flights each day to Buenos Aires. This had to be the one.

"*Buenos días, senorita,*" he said to the young lady behind the counter. "I have a problem that only you can fix." He jabbed a finger at her and gave her a million-dollar smile, and then he tipped his hat back on his head with the same finger. That gesture—tipping the hat back—was important. It suggested familiarity and relaxation. Only an honest person would do that—or a confidence man. Hunter hoped she'd see the former.

"How can I help you, senor?" she said. He could tell by her eyes, expression, and tilt of the head that she'd rather be on the beach, sunning herself. All that was missing was a yawn.

"Well, I found out that an old friend of mine is in town, but he'll soon be returning to Buenos Aires. Ah," he said, leaning back and throwing his arms out, "we go back a long way." Then he leaned forward as if he were going to let her in on a secret. "I can't tell you the times we had on Angel Justiniano Carranza Avenue. Oh, the nightclubs, the music, the wo—"

"How can I help you, senor?" she said again, this time with a heavy sigh.

"It's been *years*," he said, dragging out the word, undeterred, "since we've last seen each other, but I have it on good authority that he's somewhere in Havana. My problem is that I don't know where. I wonder if you could be so kind as to tell me whether he's scheduled to fly out of Havana soon. I would be forever in debt to you." Then he added, as if the idea had just jumped out at him, "Ah yes, I could even meet him here at the airport. His name is Ignacio Navarro." This time, he flashed her a two-million-dollar smile to make up for any ground he might have lost with her.

The young lady looked at Hunter skeptically for a long moment. Then she made a bizarre clicking sound with her tongue, reached to her left, grabbed a folder, and opened it. "Is he leaving today?" The words came out fast; she was becoming snippy.

"That I'm not sure about. Possibly. Maybe sometime this week."

She paged through the manifests for a moment and then slid a finger under a name. "Sí, I have an Ignacio Navarro here, but he is not going to Buenos Aires. He's scheduled to fly to Miami." She looked up at Hunter.

"Miami? Are you certain?" He dared to question her commitment to accuracy.

"He's on the manifest," she said with more snippiness.

"When is his flight?"

"Tomorrow morning at seven. It looks like he made the reservation yesterday."

"Are you allowed to tell me where he's staying?" He knew where Navarro was staying, but he wanted to verify that it was the same Ignacio Navarro. There could hardly have been two staying at the same hotel at the same time. "It would be very helpful. I could see him tonight." At that point, he decided to go into his routine again. *What the hell? It got me this far!* "What a time we'd have, reliving all those fabulous shenanigans we had in Buenos—"

"I'm not supposed to give out that information, senor," she said definitively, interrupting him again.

Hunter scratched his forehead; his hat slid back on his head even farther. Making himself even more obnoxious might do the trick. "Just think of the time we could have tonight, Juanita," he said, noticing her name tag and personalizing the dialogue, "if I knew where he was staying rather than meeting him here tomorrow morning. What? We'd only have minutes at the airport—mere minutes. We wouldn't be able to even scratch the surface."

The ticket agent stared daggers at Hunter; she appeared to be worn down to the bone. "The Hotel Sevilla-Biltmore," she blurted out. "He's staying at the Hotel Sevilla-Biltmore."

"*Muchas gracias, senorita,*" he said, pulling out his wallet and taking a few bills out. "Please have a nice meal for yourself and a companion on me. You see? You did solve my problem! And for that, you shall be amply rewarded." She had stuck out her neck for him, and he wanted her to remember him in case he ever needed some information in the future.

Coffee!

That was what he wanted now, so he went to a coffee stand, ordered an espresso, and found a small table to sit down at. Cubans and tourists with luggage hurried by him to their departure gates.

Navarro, he thought.

He had to admit to himself that Navarro was good. Why wouldn't he have been? He was a longtime gambler, after all. Deception was in his soul. He had fooled Gomez at the Tropicana and had nearly fooled Hunter himself with his sad story. Hunter could have kicked himself in the ass. It was clear to him now that Navarro had arranged for the jewels to be stolen by his two accomplices. He must have realized he couldn't stick around too long after Hunter interviewed him, so he'd reserved a seat on a flight out of the country. But why Miami?

With Navarro leaving, the Tropicana wouldn't have to pay for the supposed stolen jewels, but they were still out the money he'd lost to them. Navarro's debt needed to be paid. Hunter decided to confront him that night at his hotel if he had the time. Otherwise, he'd do it there at the airport tomorrow morning. He finished the espresso, got up, ordered an Americano, and returned to the table. He could feel the caffeine taking hold. It felt good. Caffeine withdrawal was insidious.

He was working on three cases—if Maria Sanchez could be considered a case—and needed to clear his head, if only for a short while. He generally felt refreshed and gained new insight into his cases whenever he did, but clearing his mind was dangerous. If he didn't have something immediately to think about apart from the cases, something deep and depressing would inevitably be on his doorstep. If he had a book to read, that usually did the trick, but he didn't.

It was useless for him to push things out of his mind without first deciding what to replace them with. The mind didn't stay a vacuum. Thoughts and images rushed in. If he didn't control what was coming in, he'd end up thinking about the war—painful memories, dark and depressing.

Baseball.

That was it. That should do it.

Now, who won the World Series last year? The Yankees beat the Dodgers four to three in seven, capturing their seventeenth championship. Don Larson pitched a perfect game in game five. The Dodgers scored nineteen runs in the first two games but only six in the remaining five games. One helluva series! He had picked up the broadcast on Mutual radio, listening to Vin Scully do the play-by-play.

Hunter's mental distraction was short-lived.

Soon, little by little, his mind began squeezing out the games, and in rushed Shaw Armstrong, Ignacio Navarro, and Maria Sanchez. At least it wasn't blood-soaked Italy.

He tipped his cup up, finished his coffee, muttered a few choice words at himself, left the airport, and got into a taxi.

He had a person to hunt down and a couple more to fix. He angled his head and looked out the rear window of the taxi at the sky. A haze was all he could see.

13

The Guan Yin Statue

Harry Smith opened the door and stepped into Wong's gift shop. The overhead bell ding-a-linged. He closed the door behind him, and sure enough, the damn bell ding-a-linged again, just as it had the day before. It hadn't bothered him then, but now it did. He felt like reaching up and ripping the damn thing out of the wall. The shop was peaceful and quiet, and the bell was an intrusion. The drapes behind the counter parted, and—*poof*—Mr. Wong suddenly appeared. There he was—a magician onstage.

"Mr. Smith," he said. "How nice to see you today."

"I'm early, but I was in the neighborhood, so I thought—"

"A bird that flies first will get to the forest earlier."

Smith angled his head.

Wong seemingly couldn't tell if he was confused, impatient, or offended. "Starting early helps achieve success, Mr. Smith," he said, clarifying the matter—if, in fact, it needed clarification.

"I understand the allusion, Mr. Wong. Speaking of success, how did it go with the statue?"

"Did *el papa* pray to God today?"

"I don't know. I haven't talked to him lately." Smith clearly meant the comment to be sarcastic. His patience was fragile.

"Neither have I," Wong said, missing the irony, "but I can assure you he did." He reached under the counter and brought out two identical white statues. "Can you tell which one is the original?"

Smith leaned down, and his eyes ran around the details of both figurines, flickering from one to the other. Then he turned the statues around, looking intently at both.

"Please pick them up, and feel the weight of each," Wong said confidently.

Smith did so. "They seem the same," he said. "Exactly the same."

"That is because they are the same—the Guan Yin and its perfect duplicate."

"Which one is the original? I can't tell."

"The one on your right is what you brought to me. The one on the left is what I created." Wong picked up a red ribbon and tied it around the base of one of the statues. "So you can tell the original," he said.

"You definitely earned your bonus, Mr. Wong. Wrap them up, will you?"

"Of course, Mr. Smith."

As Wong wrapped them up, Smith took out his wallet and laid three twenties in US dollars on the countertop: twenty-five for the statue and the rest as a bonus.

"It's been a pleasure doing business with you," Smith said, smiling, as he put the statues in a leather bag with a shoulder trap.

"One smile undoes one thousand worries," Wong said.

"A single smile removes all your troubles."

"That is a very good translation of the original."

Smith then leaned toward Mr. Wong, mere inches away, face-to-face, and even though there wasn't another soul in the shop who could eavesdrop, he whispered, "Remember, mum's the word." As if the meaning weren't clear, he added, "Translated, that means don't tell anyone."

Once outside, Smith stuck his hand up to hail a taxi.

110

A passing *manisero* in a tattered baseball cap stopped beside him. *"¿Miseria, senor?"*

Smith didn't feel like eating peanuts that day. As a matter of fact, he didn't particularly like peanuts any day, but he reached into his pocket for some change and gave it to the man. "See that old woman over there, sitting on the steps?" he said in English to the peanut vendor, pointing across the street. The manisero followed his finger and looked across the street, clearly not understanding English. "Go give her the peanuts. She'll like them." Then he motioned with his hands toward the woman for the man to go with the peanuts.

The meaning clicked, and the manisero affirmed the transaction with several nods. *"Sí, sí, sí."*

A taxi pulled up, and Smith got into the backseat.

"Take me to the bus depot," he said to the driver. Most taxi drivers understood some English because of the American tourists.

Smith couldn't have been any happier. The duplicate statue was perfect; it couldn't have been any better. The original was his ticket out of Havana—his and Margot's ticket out of Havana. This was all going to be a big surprise to Margot. He was still concerned about how she'd handle the news.

I've got it! He snapped his fingers. *That's it!* She always had wanted to go to Paris. He'd bring up Paris. That would be the clincher. She wouldn't be angry about that. If she accused him of keeping secrets, he could say he'd wanted to surprise her, and it wouldn't be a lie. That was what he'd do—bring up Paris.

The taxi pulled up to the bus depot.

"Wait for me," he told the driver. "I'll be about five minutes."

He walked into the building and went directly to the lockers in the rear. Kneeling down, he selected a locker at the bottom and put the original statue inside. He closed the door, put some coins into the slot, and pulled out the key.

Back in the taxi, he told the driver to take him to the Hotel Capri in Vedado.

It was about a half-hour drive to the hotel in heavy traffic, and Smith nearly fell asleep on the way. He opened his eyes when he felt the taxi come to a stop at the entrance. He paid the driver, giving him a little extra for waiting at the bus station, and went inside. In the huge, elegant lobby, he saw a man dusting off a large poster resting on a three-legged wooden frame near the reception desk.

"Hey, George," Smith said. "How are they hanging?"

The man turned around and grinned. "They're hanging just fine, Shaw," George said, winking at him, "just like they did thirty years ago. Probably better than yours are right now."

George Raft was an aging Hollywood movie star who was branching off in other businesses now that his career had tanked. He once had been a matinee idol adored by women across the globe to the point of adulation. He'd started off as a dancer and a good one at that. When a mobster friend he'd grown up with in Hell's Kitchen had told him he should be in the movies, he'd decided to move to Hollywood. The decision to go had been a relatively easy one, as the husband of a woman he'd been seeing had threatened to shoot him on sight. He had hopped a train at Grand Central twenty minutes after talking to his friend.

In no time, he'd landed supporting roles with the best of them: Spencer Tracy, Jimmy Cagney, and Loretta Young. Then the starring roles had started coming to him, and he'd been off and running. The photo on the poster he was dusting off showed him as the handsome, suave, and sophisticated actor he had been nearly two decades earlier. In the picture, he had dark brown hair with a dandy part in the middle. Now he was gray, with a receding hairline and a hint of a paunch. He was part owner of the Capri and served as official host of the hotel as well as the casino.

"How do you like the poster?" Raft asked. The picture of Raft's mug was actually a publicity photo taken about twenty years earlier. The text above the photo read, "George Raft invites you to the breathtaking Casino de Capri." Below, in smaller letters, were the words "No cover charge. No minimum anytime."

"It's okay, George," Shaw Armstrong said. "More than okay. You were a handsome devil back then." He corrected himself. "Still are!" He stared at the photo for a moment. "That must have been taken about the time when *Casablanca* came out. You know, I still think you should have taken the part of Rick Blaine. Playing opposite Ingrid Bergman—well, you know what I mean. Instead, you let that hack Bogart get the part, and see what that got him."

"It got him a lot of money and fame. The part of Blaine was too namby-pamby for me. Remember, I usually played a killer."

"Yeah, Killer Raft—that's what I like! Is the boss in?"

"He's in his office."

"Mood?"

"He's a butterfly today—he's all over the place. Driving me crazy."

The Capri had just opened its doors the week before. Armstrong knew his boss would be preoccupied. That could play in Armstrong's favor.

He walked down a long hallway, stopped at the boss's door, rapped once, and then walked in. "Hey, boss," he said.

The boss was alone in his office. He had his back to the door, sliding a book in place on the bookshelf. He turned around. "Shaw. You got it?"

"Did el papa pray to God today?"

"How in the hell would I know? You got it?"

Armstrong walked over to the large desk in the back of the office, set his leather bag down on the floor, took out the package, unwrapped it, set the statue on the desk, and threw his hands up. "In all its glory."

The boss remained by the bookshelf and stared at the statue. "Goddamn it, it's finally here. Do you know how long I've been waiting for this?"

The boss was Santo Trafficante Jr., one of the most powerful Mafia dons in the United States, who controlled organized crime in most of Florida and in Cuba. He also had legitimate business interests in several casinos and hotels in Cuba, as well in several restaurants and bars in his hometown of Tampa. He had taken over the Trafficante crime family business three years earlier when his father, Santo Sr., died of natural causes. Junior was a short, thin man of forty-three who wore expensive but conservative suits and black-framed glasses. One could easily have mistaken him for an accountant or a podiatrist.

One would have expected his office to be lavish, but it wasn't. There were a couch, two armchairs, and a half dozen wooden chairs against the wall. The decor was clinical and businesslike, with no colorful, elaborate paintings on the walls or artwork scattered around—nothing to distract the boss from conducting business. That was the way it was, and that was the way he liked it.

Trafficante walked over to his desk and picked up the statue. "Do you have any idea what I'm holding in my hand, Shaw?"

More than I can tell you, Armstrong thought. "Yeah, boss, I know."

"It's the Guan Yin, the goddess of mercy," Trafficante said, as if he hadn't heard Armstrong. "She's venerated by Mahayana Buddhists because she shows compassion to the world. And now she belongs to me. It's worth a fortune."

Of course, Armstrong knew all this already because Trafficante had talked about it enough over the last year. Armstrong also knew why it was worth a fortune. It wasn't because of the intricate details of the statue itself or its history, although both played a part in its value; it was because of what was inside. Though not at all religious, he said a silent prayer that Trafficante wouldn't break it open now. If he did, Armstrong's plan would be shot to hell, and eventually, he would be too. In a few days, it would be fine. But not right now.

"What are you going to do with it, boss?"

"It's going in the safe for the time being. I'll take it out every so often and look at it. When the time is right, I'll crack the son of a bitch open like an egg, and you'll see just how magnificent it is."

Relieved he wasn't going to do it now, Armstrong said, "That's a good idea, boss—let the suspense build up." Then a magnificent idea popped into his head. "Maybe you should wait for Josephine, when she flies in from Tampa next week. She'll get a real kick out of seeing you split the bastard open with a hammer." Josephine was Trafficante's wife, who lived part of each year at their home in Tampa.

"Hey, I think you're right. I hadn't thought about that, but you're right. Josephine would love to see me crack it open. Maybe I'll let her do it herself. Whaddaya think?"

"I think she'd love it, boss—doing it herself."

"It's settled then. I'll wait for Josephine."

Trafficante set the statue down on the desk, opened the lid of the humidor, and took out a cigar. He clipped one end of it and lit the other with a match, sending a cloud of smoke between him and Armstrong. "Maybe that Corsican in Saigon isn't such an asshole after all," he said. "Maybe I had him all wrong."

"Everything went like clockwork. The freighter was where it was supposed to be, and they had the statue, just like the man said they would."

"Still, I don't trust the son of a bitch until I break it open and see for myself. Whaddaya think, Shaw?" He picked up the Guan Yin again and held it with both hands, looking at it. "Maybe I should crack it open right now." He raised his head and looked at Armstrong. "Hmm?"

Jesus almighty Christ, Armstrong thought. A lump formed in his throat; he couldn't talk, yet he had to say something.

"Santo," he said. He rarely called the boss by his first name, and whenever he did, they were usually three sheets to the wind. "Think about Josephine and how much pleasure she'll have taking a hammer to it. She'll be here soon enough. What's a week?"

Trafficante set the statue down, walked around the desk, and sat down. He puffed on his cigar, blowing more smoke into the air. He was quiet for a minute, thinking. "A week," he finally said. "If that

Corsican bastard cheated me, I suppose a week isn't going to make much of a difference. And if he didn't, to see the look on Josephine's face when she smashes the Guan Yin into pieces and sees what's inside will be worth the wait."

"It will be, boss," Armstrong said, with the stress of the moment suddenly gone. "It will be. It'll be positively priceless!"

14

Lady Luck

The sign outside advertised two drinks for the price of one.

Ash Hunter sat at the bar of the Bajo las Estrellas in the Tropicana, on the same stool he'd sat on four days earlier on New Year's Eve. He'd been drinking a mojito and smoking his pipe that night. He was doing the same thing now. As Lady Luck had had it, Alfonzo Gomez had wanted to see him in his office before the bomb went off. The end of the bar had been blown to high heaven, but it had been repaired so well that someone who didn't know there had been an explosion would have been none the wiser. But the news had made all the papers, so everyone knew what had happened. Maybe the two-for-one special was to draw people in and announce that business was as usual.

He wondered what had happened to the girl in the red dress. She had been gorgeous. She probably still was, notwithstanding half her arm was missing. The chilling fact was that she was a terrorist. She'd tried to murder as many people as she could and cause chaos. What was a revolution without a little murder and chaos thrown into the mix? She couldn't have been much more than eighteen or nineteen. A good-looking broad like that was an easy mark to be manipulated. Inexperienced youth were often seduced by grandiose rhetoric, slogans, and images of the ideologically insane; by the time they discovered that the love wasn't real—that they were simply an expendable means to an end—it was too late. They had become murderers and terrorists.

Yet Hunter couldn't help feeling sorry for her. She'd spend many years in prison. Quite a few people had shrapnel wounds from flying glass and wood, but no one had died. Lady Luck had intervened again, and that was good, or the girl in the red dress would have been the star attraction at a firing squad. When she got out of prison a much older woman, a pariah, what would she do? Where would she go?

Hunter was late for the afternoon entertainment and too early for the evening show. That was fine with him. He was there on business. He picked up his drink and made his way to the casino with a trail of pipe smoke wafting behind him. Alfonso Gomez was leaning against a wall in the back, talking to a few of his employees. When he saw Hunter, he walked over to him.

"*Buenas tardes*, Ash," he said, talking his cigar out of his mouth. "Any news?" He was referring to the Navarro case and the missing jewels.

"I'm working a lead. I want to let it play out before I say anything. But I should have something for you in a few days."

"I hope so. Senor Fox is very upset, to say the least."

"Like I said, I'll have something in a few days. I came for another reason, though. Do you know a gambler by the name of Shaw Armstrong?"

"Armstrong? Of course. Everyone knows him here."

"What can you tell me about him?"

"He works for Santo Trafficante at the Capri. Does legwork for him. Quite close to him, apparently. At least that's what I hear. Is he in trouble?"

"If he works for Trafficante, he probably is in some kind of trouble. But that's not my concern. A couple from Tampa hired me to find him. All I need is an address. They're old friends of his and want to see him while they're in town."

"He gambles here and loses a lot. Santo won't let him gamble at any of his casinos, so he comes here. He's also a heavy drinker when he's gambling. Many times, we've had to call a taxi for him, so we keep his address." He took out a little black book from his suit pocket and flipped it open. "He lives in Old Havana. Let's see; I have his address here. Here it is: 39 Tejadillo, just off Monserrate. Apartment three."

"I know where it's at," Hunter said, jotting the address down and puffing away at his pipe. "Walking distance from the Paradise. Okay, thanks, Alfonso. That's all I need. I'll be in touch soon."

Outside, Hunter wondered why a nice couple like the Maddoxes had a good friend who worked for the mob. It was none of his business, so he stopped wondering about it and grabbed a taxi for the thirty-minute ride to the Paradise.

"Listen to me now, Maria," Hunter said, "because from now on, things are going to move fast."

"I'm listening," Maria said.

They were sitting on the edge of the bed in Maria's room at the Paradise. Hunter could see she was tense. She had every right to be. Her husband likely was making phone calls at that moment, and soon he'd have the police force out searching for her across Havana. They would start at Club de Los Bohemios, where she worked, and when they couldn't find her there, they would contact her friends and family. Captain Ricardo Sanchez would be relentless in his search for his wife. When he found her, she would get the beating of her life—maybe the last one she'd ever receive. Maria knew this and was frightened. But if Lady Luck was on her side, that wouldn't happen.

Hunter had a plan that he knew would work. However, he was less certain how Maria would receive it. No doubt she would see it as extreme, but her life was in danger, which called for extreme measures. She was running out of time and had few options.

"But first, I need to ask you a question," Hunter said.

"Of course."

"Are you willing to do what it takes to be rid of your husband for good?"

"Yes, of course. That's why I'm here."

"What if I said you'd have to leave Cuba for good and start a new life somewhere else?"

"Why would I leave Cuba?" She looked confused, as if she'd never considered that. "You said you would help me and take care of things."

"I never said I would hire someone to kill your husband. That's murder, and I won't be a part of it." That was technically true, but for a brief moment the day before, he had considered contacting a local hit man.

"But that's the only way I can have my freedom. My husband must be dead."

"You're wrong, Maria. There's another way, but you've got to be willing to leave Cuba for good."

She stood up and threw her hands in the air. "No, no, no!" she shouted. "Ricardo must die, or I will find no peace. He knows too many people. He'll search for me wherever I go and take me back."

"You're not thinking this through, Maria. Just listen to my plan, and then you can decide. I can't force you to do something you don't want to do. But right now, you're in a box and can't see outside of it. Having him killed will only bring you new problems. You have another option, a better solution."

Hunter was still sitting on the edge of her bed. She threw herself onto the floor in front of him, on her knees. She put her hands together as if in prayer. For a moment, she looked like a wild beast about to be devoured by a greater wild beast.

"No, no, no!" she shrieked, choking on her words, with tears running down her face. "He will find me and kill me. Please, Ash! Please have him stopped for good. I will pay whatever you want. Pay anything. Money—I have it. But he must be stopped, or he will kill me."

She put her forehead to the floor, covering her face with her hands, with her hair splayed out in all directions, sobbing. Hunter's heart broke for her. He knelt beside her and held her, caressing her head. She cried hard tears. Hunter could feel her body trembling. She was scared out of her mind and desperate.

If she wouldn't listen to his plan, if she wouldn't at least consider another option, he was concerned she might do something foolish, and then she would be trading one problem for another. The fact was that he couldn't force her to do anything. She had come to him for help. His only hope was for her to listen to him and acquiesce. But first, he had to wait. He needed her to cry herself out completely. She had to empty herself of all the built-up tension to the point of exhaustion. Only then could he lay out his plan in a calm and rational way.

So he waited while she continued to shake and cry.

He waited and waited.

A half hour went by. She was still in the same position, but she was quiet now. She hadn't moved an inch; her breathing returned to normal.

"Maria?" he whispered.

She didn't answer.

"Maria?" he said again, slightly louder this time.

"Hm?"

"Let me help you up." He stood up and helped Maria to her feet. He led her to the rocking chair not far from the bed. "Here. Sit down, and relax."

Once she was settled, he sat down on the floor directly in front of her. Her long black hair was a tangled mess, and she looked as if she had just woken up after a long sleep. Her face was pink but dry.

He looked into her eyes without saying anything for a long moment and then calmly said, "I won't hire anyone to kill him, and I won't do it myself. If you listen to what I'm going to tell you, you'll be free from him for good. You'll never have to see him again, and he'll never find you. Do you understand that, Maria?"

She nodded.

"Will you hear me out?"

She nodded again.

"Okay then, here's my plan." He decided he was going to tell her every detail of it. She had a big decision to make that would affect the rest of her life, and she needed to know everything. "Let me tell you everything first. If you have any questions, wait until I finish to ask them. Okay? Good. When we're finished here, I'm going to take you to a man I know. He'll take a photograph of you. He'll use it to make you a new passport. He'll also make other documents that will verify your new identity. You'll have a driver's license, a national health card, and a social insurance card, all with valid numbers on them, as well as a birth certificate. All the documents will be legitimate. Are you following me so far?"

"Yes, I understand," she said resignedly.

"This man is an expert at what he does. He's the best I've seen anywhere. I don't know how much he'll charge, but it'll be a lot. Will you have the money to pay him? He'll want it in cash before he starts."

"I've kept money hidden from my husband. I keep it with me at all times. It's in my bag over there," she said, pointing at it. "It's in US dollars."

"Good. I'm guessing he'll charge as much as ten thousand dollars. He'll want it in American currency, so you're covered there. Do you have that much?"

"That is not a problem. I have much more than that. A great deal more."

"Good. Tomorrow night, I'll take you to the airport, and you'll board a flight to London, using your new passport. You'll be safe and free. Your husband will never think to look there. If he thinks you left the country, he'll assume you went to Spain, Argentina, or maybe Colombia or other countries where Spanish is the language. He might even think you went to the States since you have relatives there."

"I think you're right. He would never consider England."

"Your new name is Luciana Ruiz. You were born in London of Spanish immigrants. It will say so on your birth certificate. All the necessary supporting documents will be registered within a week of your arrival in London. This man I'm taking you to see will give you all the information you'll need to establish your new background. He's done this many times before. It's foolproof. You'll need to memorize it all. This man helps people like you who are in trouble and have no way out. He makes little for himself. Most of the money goes to the people in England who process the documents. You can now see why he charges so much for his services."

"Yes, I understand."

"You'll have to forget you were ever Maria Sanchez. If you're walking down a street in London and someone calls out the name Maria, you will spontaneously want to acknowledge it. But under no circumstance are you to turn around to see who called out that name. You'll want to, but you can't. Can you do that?"

"That won't be difficult."

"It'll be more difficult than you think. Don't think for a second it'll be easy."

"Okay."

"You are Luciana Ruiz now, not Maria Sanchez. Luciana Ruiz. Say it."

"Luciana Ruiz."

"Keep saying it in your head until you believe it." He paused for a moment and then said, "Good. Is this all acceptable to you?"

"Yes, it is acceptable to me."

"Say it again."

"Yes, it is acceptable to me."

Lady Luck, be with us for a few more days, Hunter thought. "Then let's go see this man."

15

The Bait

"What is it?" Margot asked as she poured some lemonade into two large glasses.

Shaw Armstrong sat in an armchair in his apartment and looked across the room at her. Margot Reed was beautiful, with dark brown hair, a petite body, a thin nose, and luscious lips. He wanted to marry her. He had never actually asked her, and whenever the subject of marriage came up in a general way during conversations, she was coy about it, never expressing an opinion or commenting one way or the other. If anything, she seemed indifferent to it, or at least that was how he saw it. He'd have to be strategic, laying the groundwork, gently hinting at it first. Margot never liked for anyone to shove something in her face, especially if she had to make a decision about it. Now that he had the bait, he would make his case and then reel her in little by little.

"It's our future, Margot."

She turned around, walked across the living room, and handed him a glass. "I'm afraid you'll have to narrow that down a bit," she said, sitting down on the davenport across from him. She crossed one leg over the other. "It looks like a plaster Chinese statue to me, the kind you'd find in those knickknack shops in Chinatown." She took a sip of her lemonade.

The statue stood on a coffee table between them. Armstrong marveled at the possibilities it harbored that would affect the rest of their lives. It seemed to radiate before his eyes.

"Yeah, baby, you're right. It's a plaster Chinese statue but a very special one. It's called Guan Yin. If I were to take a hammer to it and crack it open, you'd find it's made of solid gold. It's worth at least a half million dollars. With the right buyer, I could get a million for it."

Her response came immediately, as he'd expected it would. "You're joking with me, right? A gag? Very clever, Shaw."

"It's no gag, Margot," he said. "It's the real deal."

She stared at him for a long moment and then said, "My God, you're not joking, are you, Shaw?" Suddenly, her eyes widened, and her jaw hung down. "Where did you get this? Where did it come from?"

Armstrong had decided earlier that he would tell her the truth. He loved her and didn't want any secrets between them. Secrets, he knew, ruined many relationships, and he felt a pang of guilt because he hadn't told her from the beginning what he'd been planning. But he trusted she'd do the right thing, and if she felt the slightest sense of disloyalty, it would be short-lived.

"Trafficante bought it from his Corsican dope dealer in Saigon. Where the Corsican got it is anyone's guess. I had it picked up from a freighter off the coast." He went on to tell her that he had had a double made there in Havana and had taken the copy to his boss. "I kept the original in a locker at the bus station and just picked it up before I came here."

"Then it belongs to Santo." She uncrossed her legs and leaned forward. "He'll kill you when he finds out! Maybe he knows already."

"No, he's waiting for his wife to fly in from Tampa next week before he breaks the shell. When he does, the first thing he'll think is that he was scammed by the Corsican. By the time he finds out the truth, it'll be too late. We'll be gone."

She flinched. "Gone? Gone where? Like you and me gone?"

"Like you and me, baby. Gone with the wind."

"I know Santo better than you do. He'll hunt us down until he finds us."

Now's the time to spring it on her, he thought. "You always wanted to go to Paris. It's a big city. Besides, he won't have a clue where to look for us. You could live like a queen in Paris, Margot. The value of the Guan Yin is not only in the gold but also in its history. If I find the right buyer, we're looking at a cool million—more if I find a couple of buyers. They'll bid against each other. The price will go up."

"Paris!" She used the French pronunciation. "We're going to live there? But how will you find a buyer? You can't just advertise it in the newspapers."

Shaw grinned. One of the things he loved about Margot was her innocence, her naivete. "I'll handle that, Margot. I won't have a problem finding people who want this. I just have to find the right ones who'll want it for the gold as well as for its historical significance. That's the key, but I can do it. I'd be looking for rich collectors of Chinese art. They're all over the world. Rich collectors—that's the key. They won't be hard to find."

Margot got up and began to pace the room. She was frowning and looked worried. Shaw followed her with his eyes.

"I thought you'd be happy about this," he said.

She managed a half smile. "I am, darling. I am. But I'm worried about Santo. He can be brutal. Does he know you're seeing me?"

"It doesn't make any difference if he does. In a day or two, we'll be out of Cuba."

She went over to him, and they held each other tightly.

"As long as we have the statue," she whispered, "and we're here in Havana, we won't be safe."

"Tomorrow we'll book a flight to Paris. We'll spend the day doing the town. The next day, we'll be gone. How does that sound, baby?"

"It sounds like I'm going to be nervous for the next forty-eight hours."

"Just stick with me, kid, and everything will be just fine."

There was a long moment of silence. Now was the time for Armstrong to pop the question, but Margot spoke first.

"Shaw, darling?"

"What, baby?"

"Maybe we could get married in Paris. Would you like that?"

Shaw was wildly excited, but in a calm voice, he said, "I'd like that just fine, baby."

Slane and Babs Hannigan were going over the books and counting the day's receipts; Slane was sorting through the receipts, and Babs was totaling them on an adding machine, punching in the numbers and then pulling back on the mechanical arm the way one did on a slot machine. Slane liked this time of the day. He liked the typewriter-like clicking sound when she tapped the keys and the metallic clacking noise as she pulled back the arm. He was always amazed how Babs could pick up each receipt with one hand and use the other hand to type in the numbers and pull the arm down without ever looking at the adding machine. However his day had gone, this time always made him believe that all was good in the universe.

It was quiet at the Paradise; it was the end of the day. Most of the guests were back in their rooms, exhausted after a full day of exploring the ins and outs of how to maneuver about in Havana. As in all tourist cities, they learned by trial and error. Some had had late-night suppers and then gone to bed. A few of the more adventurous ones had gone out to the nightclubs to drink, take in the shows, and maybe gamble a bit and would stumble in at around three or four o'clock in the morning. Hannigan hoped that some loudmouthed drunk wouldn't wake up the other guests.

"We did all right today," Babs said in the neutral voice of an accountant. "We're up twenty-three percent over last year at this time." During the high season, Babs always compared each day's take with what they had done on that day the previous year.

"A few more days like this, and we can buy more bar soap for the guests and fix the plumbing in 108!" Hannigan said jokingly. "Maybe we could actually pay Sammy his salary."

"Yeah, and in 112 too!" Babs said, extending the joke.

"What's wrong with 112?" Hannigan asked, not catching on at first.

"Nothing that a little cash won't fix."

"Listen, Babs, you're not cooking the books and lying to me to make me feel good, are you?"

"Would I do that to you?"

"Only if you thought you could get away with it," he said, grinning at her. "How about we call it quits and go out on the veranda to unwind a little before turning in?"

"Thought you'd never ask."

"Go on out back. I'll fix some drinks and meet you out there."

Babs made her way to the veranda, sat down on an Adirondack, flipped off her sandals, and made a sound somewhere between an aah and an ooh. A few minutes later, Hannigan appeared with two gin and tonics. He sat down beside Babs and gave her one of the drinks.

She held her glass in the air and said, "Here's to today's take! May there be many more days like this."

"Hear! Hear!" Hannigan said, raising his glass. "That's something to drink to."

Clink!

"Ah, that tastes delicious," Babs said.

Slane reached for the cigar humidor on a small table between their chairs and pulled out a panetela for himself and a cigarillo for Babs.

"No, give me a panetela too," she said.

"I've never seen you with a panetela before."

"That's because I've never had one before."

"Go for it, girl," he said, handing one to her. "Just don't smoke it in public. People will think you're a dyke."

"With all due respect, my adorable husband, I will smoke a panetela whenever and wherever I please. I don't give two hoots what people think."

"Like I said, go for it, girl!"

They both lit up, sending clouds of smoke around them. They sat in silence for a few minutes, drinking their gin and tonics and enjoying their panetelas and each other's company. A pleasant breeze was coming off the bay. They heard only distant, faraway night sounds. It was quiet and peaceful.

"This is the life, eh, Babs? The life of Riley!"

"I could stay like this for the rest of my life. A fine cigar, good booze, money in the till, a quiet night, a half-refined companion to share it with—what more could a body want?"

"Whaddaya mean *half-refined*?" he asked, twisting in his Adirondack to see Babs better. "When we go out, don't I polish my shoes? Don't I use Vitalis in my hair? Don't I wear a tie? Didn't I buy a pair of Florsheim shoes yesterday? A body couldn't ask for more than that!"

Babs grinned.

She loves getting me stirred up, Hannigan thought. But he loved every minute of it.

They went silent again.

Babs is right, Hannigan said to himself. *We've made a good life for ourselves in Cuba.*

Then a thought occurred to him.

"If we'd stayed in Minnesota, Babs, what would we be doing right now?"

"We'd be plowing through two feet of snow, trying to get home in the middle of a blizzard."

"Ah yes, I remember those days. The snow blowing sideways. Our noses and lips freezing in the subzero temperatures. Falling on the ice, cracking our heads open. Those were the days—blessed times that are now all but faded memories of things past, dim recollections of tribulations overcome and never to be resuscitated."

"Gee, Hannigan, you sound so poetic tonight. I never thought you had it in you." She paused for a moment and then added, "You stir me, Hannigan. Stir me deeply."

"It's the sweet, warm breezes of Havana that bring out the poet in me." He turned in her direction. "I'm a refined man, don't you know?"

"No regrets?" she asked, and the amorous mood was suddenly gone in a flash.

"Regrets? About what? Leaving Saint Paul?"

"You did spend twenty-five years there."

"Minus my time in Italy during the war. But that was in a different life. We've all reinvented ourselves since—you, me, and Ash. We're all different people, Babs. Our environment makes us that way. We adapt, and then, over time, we change. You know what they say about trees, don't you?"

"No. What do they say about trees, dear?" she asked, blowing out smoke.

"Trees either bend in the wind, or they break. No, I don't have any regrets about leaving or about anything else in life. When you regret something, you wish you would have done something differently, because you made a mistake. But mistakes are good— they give you an opportunity to learn from them and grow. If you stop learning, you become static, just like the tree that refuses to bend. You end up breaking."

"So you're saying that you're not perfect and that you've made mistakes."

"I'm saying I've learned from my mistakes. You can't get anything worth having in life without falling down along the way. Getting back up is what counts."

"You're a philosopher too, Hannigan. You never told me that when we got married."

"You never asked. Besides, if I'd told you everything about myself all at once, you'd have been bored with me by now and traded me in for a new model."

"I like the model I have right now."

"It's getting a little run down. There's a dent or two in the fenders, and the tires have a little wear on them."

"That's okay. Those flaws give you character."

Hannigan grinned. "I love you too, Babs."

"Even after all these years?"

"Because of all those years."

"You're getting syrupy-sweet on me. Are you trying to woo me, Hannigan?"

"If you like."

"Oh, I like. Shall we take our leave?" She started to get up from her chair.

"Let's finish our cigars first, and then I'll woo you all you want."

"Is that a promise?"

"Promises shmomises. It's a statement of fact."

"Whoopee! The lady is going to be wooed tonight!"

They were silent again. The view from the veranda was gorgeous anytime of the day but especially at night.

"Do you remember when that drunk wandered into the Saint Paul Hotel, Hannigan?" Babs asked. "I'd been on the front desk for only a few weeks, and you had your eyes on me even then."

"Love at first sight, it was."

"The drunk tried to climb over the counter to get to me."

"How could I forget that?"

"You grabbed him by the back of his collar and by the seat of his pants, pulled him off the counter, ran him across the lobby—his shoes barely touching the floor—and threw him out the front door. He landed in the street in a heap."

"Yeah, and I didn't find out until the next day that he was the new mayor who had taken office just a month before."

"That was when the mayor's office threatened to bring charges against you."

"And I threatened to release photos of the episode that I didn't have to the *Pioneer Press*. Never heard back from them."

They sipped their drinks and puffed away on their cigars. They heard someone come out onto the veranda.

"Sammy," Hannigan said. "Just the man I wanted to see. Play us a tune, will you?"

"Of course, Mr. Slane. That's why I brought my guitar. What shall I play? Something soft and romantic or something playful and witty?"

"Can you combine the two?" Babs asked.

"I can try my best. My best is all I have."

He strummed on his guitar for a minute or so and then began singing:

> Dere was once a couple from Minnesota; dey came
> to seek deir fortune and to seek deir fame.
> Dey bought a boat; dey bought a run-down hotel.
> Da man, he was handsome, da lady a gorgeous bombshell!
> Dey worked very hard and made many renovations.
> Den dey hired a very skillful man by the name of Sammy
> to cook and clean and look after da public relations.
> When all was said and done, the Paradise Inn
> climbed beyond their expectations!

"Very witty, Sammy," Babs said, "but that wasn't romantic. But I do appreciate the bombshell rhyme."

"Thank you, Miss Babs, and you're quite right that it wasn't very romantic. It's been a long day, and I do have my limitations."

"We all do, Sammy," Hannigan said. "What say we all turn in for the night?"

"Good night," Sammy said, yawning out the words. "Mr. Ash is on the desk tonight, but I have to relieve him early because he must go somewhere. See you in the morning."

After Sammy left, Babs grabbed Hannigan by the arm and gave him a steamy smile. "I hope you haven't reached *your* limitations quite yet," she said.

"Not by a long shot, kiddo. Not by a long shot."

16

A Little Pain, Nothing Serious

The coffee tasted good. It always did, especially the first cup.

Ash Hunter was on his third espresso. He was sitting at a small, round table near the Pan American boarding area at Rancho-Boyeros Airport, tucked away behind a pillar. From there, he had a clear view of the waiting area in front of the gate. It was beginning to fill up with passengers, but as of yet, there was no Ignacio Navarro. He looked at his watch: 6:15 a.m. The plane would be boarding soon.

What would he say to Navarro when he arrived? Hunter had no authority to detain him. If Navarro had the jewels in his possession, that was no crime, because he owned them. Big deal. There was still the matter of the gambling debt he owed the Tropicana, but that was between the Tropicana and Navarro. Gomez had made it clear to Hunter that he did not want to involve the police. Perhaps the only thing Hunter could say to Navarro was that the Tropicana knew about the scam and would involve the local police in Miami. There was ongoing cooperation between the Americans and the Cubans regarding criminal activities.

Whether the Tropicana would actually pursue that avenue was another question, as was whether skipping out on one's debts even rose to the level of being criminal. Perhaps it was simply a matter for the civil courts.

Hunter lacked an edge with Navarro, and Navarro would be savvy enough to know that. So the question remained: What would Hunter say to Navarro when he arrived? He didn't know. Perhaps something clever would extemporaneously pop into his head. He was good at that. But if it did, it certainly wouldn't get the jewels back and probably would not encourage Navarro to pay his debt. Hunter was left in a quandary.

An announcement over the loudspeaker called for passengers to board flight 064 to Miami, Florida. One by one, they began queuing up, moving out the door, and crossing the tarmac toward the plane. Still, there was no Ignacio Navarro. The boarding area quickly emptied. Hunter ordered another coffee and then sat down at his table again. He'd wait for the time it took him to finish the coffee.

Fifteen minutes later, with all the passengers on board the outbound Pan Am, another announcement came over the loudspeaker: "Senor Navarro, please report to the Pan Am desk. Senor Ignacio Navarro, report immediately to the Pan Am desk."

If Navarro came at that point, Hunter wouldn't even get the chance to talk to him.

Ten minutes later, the loading stairs, on wheels, were rolled away from the aircraft; the door was closed; and the plane began to taxi to the runway.

Navarro never showed up.

Hannigan was feeling particularly happy that morning. He always did after having wooed Babs the night before.

He reached behind him at the front desk and put a record on the phonograph. A little Pérez Prado mambo music was just the thing needed to set the mood for his American guests before they ate breakfast and set off on their adventures in tropical Havana. When the music came on, he lowered the volume so it could be heard just in the background.

He turned around as an older man with gray hair opened the door and walked into the Paradise. Hannigan didn't peg him for an American—maybe Cuban or Spanish. He had a mustache, and Latinos were big on them. His clothes looked expensive, but he himself appeared a little weatherworn. Maybe he'd been drinking all night and had a hangover. He wasn't carrying any luggage, which was always a bad sign for business.

"*Buenos días, senor.* How may I help you? Do you need a room?"

"No, no room. I'm here to see Senor Ash Hunter."

"Ash isn't here, but he's on his way."

"I see then. Can I wait for him?"

"You can wait over there in our café," Hannigan said, pointing. "We serve a hearty breakfast, if hearty is what you're after, and all the coffee you can drink. You pay once; refills are free."

"That will be good. I'll wait there."

"Babs," Hannigan said to his wife, who'd just appeared at the front desk, "could you show this gentleman to a seat in the café?"

Babs led the way to a table near the entrance. The man eased himself unsteadily onto a chair.

"Can I get you some coffee?" she said, frowning, leaning down a bit. "You don't look well. Are you all right?"

"I'm fine," the man said. "Some coffee would be good. Yes, and some water as well, if you don't mind."

Babs brought him both and then went back to Hannigan.

"That gentleman doesn't look well, Hannigan. We should keep an eye on him."

Hannigan glanced over at the man and noticed that his arms were folded on the table with his head resting on them. "I'd better go over and see if he's okay," Hannigan said, and he walked over to the man. "Senor, are you okay? You don't look well."

The man raised his head and sat up straight in his chair. He ran a hand across his face and then, with both hands, smoothed his hair back. "I'm fine, thank you. I have a little pain in my stomach. It's nothing serious. I think it must have been some bad food I ate last night."

"Do you want me to call a doctor? Maybe you should rest in a bed. I don't have any rooms open, but we have one in the back room behind the front desk. I could take you there. You could rest and wait for Hunter there."

"No, no. That won't be necessary. I'll be fine. I'll just wait for Senor Hunter here. I'll be fine. *Muchas gracias.*"

"Okay, it's your stomach. But if you change your mind, just give me a shout. I'll be at the front desk."

A half hour later, Ash Hunter arrived at the Paradise.

"It's about time you got here," Hannigan said. "There's a sick guy waiting for you in the café. Over there. Says he wants to talk to you."

By that time, the café was filling up with guests.

"Jesus, what in the hell did you feed the guy, Slane?"

"Very funny. He walked in looking like death warmed over. His face looks green like an avocado. You'd better see what he wants before he croaks."

"We can't have that, now. It'll be bad for business. The guests might start boycotting us."

Hunter walked into the café and over to the table. The man had his head down again.

"I'm Ash Hunter. You wanted to see me?"

The man lifted his head and sat upright again.

Hunter immediately recognized him. "Ignacio! What's wrong? You don't look well."

Navarro was breathing heavily now, and he was grimacing in agony. "Ash, I think I've been poisoned." His stomach pains suddenly became excruciating, and he toppled to the floor.

Hunter grabbed him before he fell too far and eased him down. Some of the guests eating breakfast nearby put their knives and forks down and stood up. Nothing like a good look-see during a crisis. Something to write home about.

"Slane!" Hunter shouted. "Call an ambulance. Tell them it's an emergency. Tell them to get here pronto." Hunter was on his knees, cradling Navarro by the shoulders, with Navarro's head resting on Hunter's chest. "Help is on the way. Just try to relax. Take some deep breaths." It wasn't the right time to ask Navarro any questions, but he did nevertheless. "Ignacio, I've got to ask you something. Did you scam the Tropicana?"

Navarro was breathing heavily, grimacing in pain.

Hunter immediately regretted asking him anything. "Never mind. Just lie still. Don't say anything. The doctor will be here soon."

Navarro managed to open his eyes, looking up at Hunter. "No, I swear. What I told you was the truth." He grimaced for a moment and then continued. "I got sick after eating breakfast at the hotel this morning. Room service. I felt fine until I ate. I passed out briefly. I'm sure I was poisoned. I took a taxi here to find you." He closed his eyes again in pain. After a moment, he opened them again and whispered, "The jewels. The jewels."

"What about the jewels?"

"Delgado. Find him in Havana. Find Santiago Delgado. The jewels. Delgado."

And then he passed out.

The ambulance arrived shortly after, and Navarro was taken out on a stretcher. Hunter followed along and told the doctor the man's name and that Navarro had said his breakfast had been poisoned. The doctor looked confusedly at Hunter. So did Hannigan and Babs.

"Not by us," Hunter said. "He told me he was poisoned at breakfast in his hotel room this morning. The Hotel Sevilla-Biltmore."

As the ambulance sped away, Mr. and Mrs. Maddox appeared and sat down for breakfast.

"What's all the excitement about?" Lizzy asked Hunter, who had followed them into the café.

"There's always excitement here during the tourist season," Hunter said, sitting down.

"That involves an ambulance?" Bradford asked sarcastically.

"Especially ambulances," Hunter said. "People drink too much, and they get sick. What can I say? Happens everywhere."

Sammy brought coffee to the table for all three.

"And to the best of us, eh?" Bradford added.

"So let me guess," Lizzy said. "You found Shaw Armstrong." Her voice was tinged with optimism.

"I didn't find him, but I did find out where he lives. That's what you wanted, right?"

Their faces lit up.

"Oh, that's wonderful," Lizzy said, clapping her hands fast and jumping in her seat. "Just marvelous!"

Hunter wondered whether they knew their friend was involved with the mob. Based on what they'd told him, they hadn't seen him in years. People could change during that time, and some did. He thought for a moment about telling them but decided against it. It wasn't any of his business. It wasn't a crime in Cuba to have a friend who was a gangster. If that had been the case, the authorities would have had to arrest el presidente, his cabinet, and half the politicians.

Hunter took out his notebook, paged through it, tore out a page, and laid it on the table. "Any taxi driver would know where it's at. Actually, the address isn't far from here."

"You were right then," Lizzy said.

"About what?"

"Being a good detective. This is a big town. It couldn't have been easy."

"I know a lot of people. It helps. So what are you going to do with the rest of your time here in our big town besides visiting your friend?"

"We're just going to take in the sights. Right, Bradford?" she said, glancing at her husband. "We're going to the Tropicana tonight as part of our package deal. It'll be refreshing to gamble legally in the open for a change. We're told not to miss the stage show."

"You were told right. The shows are not to be missed." Hunter finished his coffee and got up. "I hope you have a great reunion with your friend."

"It's bound to be a doozy. Right, Bradford?"

"Yeah, a real doozy," he said, grinning from ear to ear.

Hunter left them with a gracious smile and a mock hand salute and walked back to the front desk. Initially, he had liked the Maddoxes, but now he had a bad taste in his mouth. He had been willing to give them the benefit of the doubt, but after his little chitchat with them, he had to reconsider. It was just a gut feeling. Lizzy seemed as phony as a three-dollar bill, and Bradford was a wise guy if ever he had seen one. Neither quality made them particularly bad people. But something did, he thought.

"So when are the lovely couple checking out?" he asked Hannigan.

"You mean the Maddoxes? They're booked for the week."

"Make sure you add two hundred bucks to their bill for services rendered. Don't let them leave without paying that."

"You think they're flimflam artists? Ash, you ought to be more trusting."

"I ought to be a lot of things. Just make sure they pay up."

"I take it you found the man they were looking for."

"All they wanted was an address, and I got one for them." He glanced sideways into the café. The Maddoxes were eating their breakfast and laughing up a storm. "By the way, how's Maria doing?"

"Babs took her breakfast and chatted with her while she ate. She seemed in good spirits."

"She's staying put in her room?"

"Hasn't left the accommodations since you muscled her in, then out, and then in again."

"Nobody's been by looking for her?"

"Nary a soul, my friend. Babs and I have that covered just in case. Sammy too. All is copacetic."

"Good. I don't like that her husband's a well-connected cop. It makes things more difficult. But I can't do anything about that. I'm taking her to the airport tonight for her flight out of the country. That's going to be the tricky part, getting her from here to there. Any suggestions?"

"I think you've got your bases covered. As long as she wears the wig you got her, the one she wore in the passport photo, she'll be okay. Babs is going to redo her face before she leaves."

"And the clothes?"

"Babs took care of that too. Maria will be in some warm clothes when she gets to London. It'll be cold there at this time of year."

"Thanks, Slane. I owe you and Babs."

"Don't be a silly ninny. We're all in the same boat here. The girl's in trouble, and what are we if we don't lend a helping hand?"

Hunter leaned over to glance at the Maddoxes again, but they were just walking past him.

"Adios! Ciao! Au revoir! Ta-ta!" Lizzy said gaily. "We're off to see the sights!"

"Have a fun time with your friend, folks," Hannigan said joyously.

Hunter twisted a smile at them and stared as they went through the door.

"Trust," Hannigan said to Hunter. "You gotta have a little faith in humanity."

"Hmph" was all Hunter said.

The Long-Overdue Reunion

"Okay, babe, it's this way," Shaw Armstrong said. "While you were getting your beauty sleep this morning, I was at a travel agency, booking a late flight to Miami."

"Miami?" Margot said, speaking louder than she should have.

"Hush, baby. Keep your voice down."

"But I thought we were going to Paris."

"We are, but we've got to play this intelligently. We'll go to Miami. I can borrow a car there from a friend, so it can't be traced. We'll drive up the coast to New York. We'll catch a flight to London, and then we'll hire a car to take us to Dover. Once there, we'll cross over to Calais on a ferry, hire another car, and voilà—we're in Paris." He smiled, looking pleased with himself. "So how's your French?"

"It's only high school French but not bad," she said. She looked confused. "Why don't we fly directly to Paris?"

"Come on, baby; think about it. Once Trafficante puts two and two together, the first thing he's gonna do is have his boys go to the airport and check the manifests. He's got contacts there, so it's going to be easy for him to find out where we went. They'll see that we flew to Miami. Next thing Santo's gonna do is make a few phone calls. The red flags will go up, and his boys there will be searching

143

every square inch of the city for us. Maybe they'll even go to Tampa too. If they do track us to New York—there's no frickin' way they can, but let's say they do—they'll see that we went to London. Santo will make a few more calls, and the hunt will start all over, only it's gonna end there too. There's absolutely no way he'd find us in France."

They had spent most of the day eating, drinking, and gambling. Exhausted, they were now sitting at a table in Sloppy Joe's, each enjoying, appropriately, a Chartreuse.

"You were a little busy beaver this morning," Margot said.

"I've got all our bases covered, baby. Once we're in Paris, we can start our new life. No one's going to bother us there, because no one's going to even know we're there. I wish I could see the expression on that little wop's face when he breaks open that statue and finds a rubble of plaster. It's almost worth—"

He was interrupted by an older man standing over them. The man was bulky, but not fat; well-dressed in a khaki shirt and pants, but somewhat scruffy, with a baseball cap on the back of his head and a frizzy gray beard on his face. He appeared to be drunk. He leaned into Margot and placed an arm around her shoulders.

"Margot, my little hot tomato, where've you been? I haven't seen you in months." The words slurred out of his mouth.

Armstrong watched from his chair, fuming. The intruder was American. Suddenly, Armstrong stood up.

"Back off, old man. You're drunk. You've got the wrong woman." He pushed him lightly on the chest with his fingertips as an encouragement; the old man went backward a few steps before catching his balance. Those sitting near them stood and formed a half circle around them, perhaps anticipating a little action. "Do yourself a favor, and go back to your table and leave us in peace. I'm asking you politely. We don't want any trouble."

Armstrong didn't want to hurt the old man, despite his being disrespectful to Margot. The man appeared to be twice Armstrong's age—maybe in his late fifties or early sixties—but in good shape. Armstrong just wanted him to leave.

"Why, you son of a bitch, push me, will you?" the old man said, slurring his words. "I've chopped down bigger trees than you in my time."

The man got into a classic boxing stance with his fists held up nicely in front of him and started moving around Armstrong, pumping his fists back and forth slowly like pistons before springing into action. He had his chin neatly tucked into his shoulder, as professional fighters did, instead of hanging out in the breeze and waiting to be clobbered, as drunks did. Clearly, the old guy had some experience, drunk as he was.

Armstrong followed suit; soon the two men were circling each other. Those around them pushed tables and chairs out of the way. Several glasses fell to the floor and smashed. Margot, shocked, stood up and backed away. There was some moaning and groaning that the fight wasn't fair, as their age difference was too great. Neither the old man nor Armstrong seemed to hear, or if they did, they didn't seem to care. Then, suddenly, without telegraphing his punches, the old man threw a combination left jab and right cross that nicked the end of Armstrong's nose. The old goat had more steam in him than Armstrong had thought.

Armstrong countered with a left hook that landed flush on the side of the man's right jaw. Those who witnessed the action would later say he pulled his punch out of respect for the man's age. They could have been right. Nevertheless, the punch was hard enough to put the old man on the floor, unconscious. No one was certain whether it was the punch itself or the amount of alcohol the man had consumed that did the trick. The patrons would debate that for the next week. Notwithstanding, the man was out cold, spread-eagle on the floor.

Armstrong looked at Margot and said, "Let's get out of here."

Before they could do anything, a young man wearing a panama fedora and a white linen suit and vest hurried to Armstrong and said,

"I'm a reporter from the *Miami Herald International*. Do you know who you just knocked out?"

"Yeah, a drunken old man who was disrespectful to a lady and started a fight. You can print that."

"That was Ernest Hemingway!"

"I don't care what his name is. He started it, and I ended it."

"Can I quote you on that?"

Armstrong took Margot's hand and led them through the crowd that had formed and went outside. "The old geezer knew your name," he said. "Do you know the guy?"

"I might have met him around town, but I don't remember."

"Anyway, sorry that happened. It's getting late. We should go to my apartment and pack."

"Listen," she said, fixing the knot in his tie, "I'll meet you there. I've got to pick up a few things I don't want to leave behind."

Armstrong hailed a taxi for Margot and then got one for himself.

A taxi pulled up to 39 Calle Tejadillo. The back doors flew open, and Bradford and Elizabeth Maddox got out. Bradford paid the driver, while Lizzy adjusted her dress and patted the wrinkles out. When she'd finished, she leaned over and looked at her reflection in the rear window, turning her head this way and that, fluffing up her hair. The surrounding lighting could have been better. Her arms were a bit pink from being in the sun earlier, because Bradford had forgotten to tell her to buy some Coppertone. Together, hand in hand, the lovely couple made their way to the apartment building.

"What's the number of the apartment, sweetheart?" Bradford asked. He hadn't called her that in months.

"Number three, sugar plum."

"It pains me to mention this, sweetheart, but did you remember to bring it?"

Lizzy looked up at him and grinned. She appreciated his little gestures of affection. "Of course I have it, dear. It's in my purse."

"Do you think Shaw will be surprised to see us? After all, it's been quite some time now."

"I think he'll be as giddy as a schoolgirl. I can't wait to see his face."

Like a gentleman, Bradford held the door for Lizzy and followed her into the building, up a few steps, and down a long, dimly lit hallway. They looked at the numbers on the doors as they passed them. They stopped at number three.

"Are you ready, Bradford?"

"I've been ready for five years now." He spoke somewhat gruffly but then flashed her a smile.

Lizzy was surprised at his tone at first, but she guessed the smile was to patch things over in case she took it the wrong way. She appreciated that too.

She knocked on the door, and they waited. After ten seconds had gone by, she knocked again. They heard a muffled voice say, "Use your key, babe." Lizzy and Bradford looked at each other and grinned. He was in. She knocked again.

The door swung inward, and a voice said, "Sorry. I was just packing and—"

"Going somewhere, Shaw?" Lizzy asked pleasantly.

Armstrong froze in place, his eyes wide and his jaw hanging down, unable to finish the sentence.

"It's impolite not to ask us in," Lizzy said with an edge to her voice.

Armstrong backed up, and the Maddoxes walked in, closing the door behind them.

"What brings you to Havana?" Armstrong asked watchfully, his eyes darting from Lizzy to Bradford and back again.

"What brings anyone to Havana during the tourist season?" Bradford said. "The sun, the beaches, plenty of rum, and gambling. Oh, and let's not forget the shows. We thought we'd see for ourselves how the other half lives. How Shaw Armstrong lives—on our money. We have a vested interest in that. Know what I mean?"

Lizzy's eyes flicked to Armstrong's hand sliding into his jacket. She quickly opened her purse; took out a double-action, snub-nosed six-shot revolver with a two-inch barrel; and pointed it at him. "Don't try it, Shaw. It's loaded, and you're not fast enough."

Armstrong let his arm fall to his side. "How'd you find me?"

"A little bird told us," Lizzy said.

"Listen," Armstrong said, his palms out toward her, "I was going to send you a telegram and tell you the whole thing is off. I'm moving off the island. It's ended. You paid enough."

"We paid too much, Shaw. Has anyone ever told you that you're a greedy man?"

"I can explain. It's not the way you think."

"And just what do I think?"

"You've got it all wrong. I was just—"

"Where's the gun, Shaw?" Bradford asked, jumping in.

"It's under the mattress in the bedroom."

Bradford retrieved it and returned while Lizzy kept her gun steadily on Armstrong.

"I have to say one thing for you, Shaw," Lizzy said. "You were clever to steal from my house the gun that I used to kill Travis Reed and then run a ballistics test on it. Did you decide right away to blackmail us, or was that an afterthought?"

"You've got it all wrong. I can explain."

"On second thought, I don't think it's necessary to hear your explanation." With that, Lizzy fired three quick shots into Shaw Armstrong's chest. He slumped to the floor with his back leaning on the couch behind him.

"Let's go," Bradford said. "Someone is bound to have heard the shots."

They left the building and walked east on Tejadillo until they found a taxi. Once inside the car, Bradford asked Lizzy, "Did you notice that lovely Chinese statue on the coffee table?"

"Oh, I did indeed!"

"I'll buy one for you before we fly back to Tampa."

"How thoughtful of you, sugar plum. It was beautiful. I have to say one thing for Shaw: he's got marvelous taste."

Margot Reed's taxi pulled up to Armstrong's apartment house. She had collected a few of her belongings at Casa Marina, a bordello in Vedado, near the sprawling seaside Malecón. She'd left most of her things there because she didn't want to tell Doña Marina she was leaving. She worked there as a prostitute, albeit for only a few months, because she needed money, and the money was good. Armstrong had protested vehemently at first, saying he would give her what she needed, but she wouldn't give in. She was proud of her independence.

She paid the driver and got out of the taxi. As she made her way to the door with her small bag, she thought about the dangers of what she and Armstrong were in. Turning against Trafficante was a foolish thing to do, but she had faith in Armstrong's judgment. Margot knew Trafficante better than most. But if Armstrong thought they could get away with it, she had to have faith that they could.

She knocked twice on the door and then said, "Shaw, it's me." When he didn't answer, she dug into her purse for her key and stuck it in the lock. She turned it but realized the door wasn't locked. That was unusual; Armstrong always made sure it was locked.

She opened the door and saw Shaw immediately. He was half lying against the couch, and the front of his shirt was soaked with blood. She quickly covered her mouth with her hand and made a horrible sound.

After closing the door, she ran to him, knelt beside him, and held his head. She buried her face in his hair and moaned, making a low, guttural sound, unable to believe her lover was dead. He had been alive just a few hours before, telling her how they would get to Paris. They had been excited, spending their last day in Havana. They had their tickets. They were to fly out that night.

Then a dreadful thought occurred to her.

Trafficante found out.

She got up and began pacing the room. She had to think of something quickly. Armstrong's buddies who also worked for Trafficante knew he was seeing her. If they knew, then Trafficante probably did too. He might have them come after her.

Her eyes caught sight of the white statue on the coffee table. If Trafficante's men had killed Armstrong, why hadn't they taken the statue with them? It didn't make sense. Maybe they'd opened the door and shot him without coming in. Maybe they hadn't seen the statue. Maybe they'd realized their mistake by then and were on their way back. She picked up the statue, put it in her bag, and zipped it up. Trafficante's men would be coming back—for the statue and for her.

She ran out of the apartment, out of the building, and into the street and disappeared into the dark, sultry Havana night, crying her eyes out.

Ash Hunter reached over and placed his hand on Maria's.

They were sitting at the gate, waiting for the announcement to board the Pan American for London. Maria was wearing a blonde wig; Babs had earlier made up her face and given her a pair of stylish nonprescription glasses to wear. She had warmer clothes on now, along with a winter coat she kept draped over her arm and a snap-brim on her head. For all intents and purposes, others would see her as a tourist returning to London from a holiday. She was no longer Maria Sanchez; she was now Luciana Ruiz.

"It's going to be all right, Luciana." Hunter insisted on using the name so she'd get used to it, even though he felt awkward doing so. "You're over the worst of it. In about ten minutes, you'll board the flight to London and leave your old life behind. Your husband will never know where you are."

"I don't know how to thank you, Ash. You and Babs. You've been so kind."

"There's no need to thank us. You were in trouble, and we helped you out. That's what human beings do. Someday you may have to help someone else. That'll be thanks enough." He thought that sounded sappy, mawkish, and maybe even somewhat insincere, but he couldn't think of anything else to say.

"If I were bold enough, I would ask you to come with me."

Hunter looked into her eyes. He was looking at Maria, but he saw Angie. He wasn't surprised she'd said that. From the beginning, he'd felt a connection to her. Based on what she'd just said, she felt a connection too. But was the connection real? He really didn't know her. How could he have? A few days ago, he hadn't known she even existed. Perhaps it was nothing more than animal lust. That would be fine for a few months or a year, perhaps longer, but it wouldn't sustain a relationship if that was all their connection had to hang on to. Maybe his feelings for her were really leftover feelings for Angie that he'd harbored all these years. Only time would tell—but they were out of time.

"In another life, Luciana, if things were different, I might very well get on the plane with you. But I have a life here in Havana, and yours will be in London. You'll settle in, find work, and meet someone who'll treat you the way you deserve. You'll make a good life for yourself."

The loudspeaker blared, "Pan American flight 014 to London, England, is now boarding. All passengers on this flight, please go now to the boarding gate."

The passengers around them picked up their carry-on baggage and filed through the door to the plane. Hunter and Maria waited until the last one was through before getting up. Hunter accompanied her to the tarmac and to the stairs leading up to the aircraft.

"So long, Luciana," he said. He placed his hand gently on the side of her face. "Here's to a wonderful future."

She leaned up and kissed him hard on the lips. When she pulled away, he was slightly embarrassed and glanced over to the waiting room. The glance suddenly became a stare; he saw three uniformed police officers walking around and scrutinizing the passengers for the other flights. They were checking passports. Maria noticed a raw expression on Hunter's face, squinted toward the waiting room to see what he was looking at, and saw the officers as well.

"Hurry, Luciana. Get up the stairs and into the plane. Go. Hurry."

Maria hurried up the stairs. Hunter waited where he was, thinking of what he could do to stall the officers if they came outside. The door to the plane closed, and the ground crew wheeled the stairs out of the way. One of them told Hunter to return to the building because the plane was getting ready to taxi to the runway.

He walked back toward the building and was almost there, when two of the officers came through the doors. Hunter looked back at the plane. It was slowly moving toward the runway. Would they attempt to stop it?

"Gentlemen," he said to the officers, "it's a fine evening tonight. Fine indeed. So fine that I'm going to buy you guys a beer. How does that sound, fellas?"

The police officers looked at each other and then at Hunter. One of them said, "Dis another officer inside. Heem too?"

"Yes, *heem* too! I'm feeling so happy tonight that I might even buy the whole damn National Police force a beer! Let's go, gentlemen. Let's go partake!"

And that was precisely what they did.

In the meantime, Pan American flight 014 gained speed, gently lifted off the runway, and dipped to the right after reaching the proper altitude, ramming its way into a heap of low-level cumulus clouds, until the flashing navigation lights on the aircraft faded and soon could no longer be seen.

Inside, Hunter raised a bottle of beer in a toast. "Here's to the Cuban National Police! May they continue to protect and always remain vigilant!"

18

Trouble in Dodge City

"For a second, I thought about going with her, and then the thought was gone."

"What stopped you?" Hannigan asked, sipping his coffee.

Hunter glanced at him, picking up his cup. "It's too complicated. I'm not sure whether I fully know."

Hannigan seemed impatient with Hunter and irritated. "Hell's bells, I'll tell you why you didn't go with her, and it's pretty simple. Listen up now. You'll learn something. You live here in Havana, see? Babs and me—we're your partners in a business that's doing well. Deep down, you didn't want to throw all that away and split with a gal you've known for all of a few days. It took you a second to come to your senses. You're not a reckless man, but sometimes …" He sipped his coffee. "There. I've uncomplicated the matter for you."

Hunter grinned. "You have a way with words, but you're probably right."

"I know I'm right."

"But I still have this nagging feeling I didn't give it a chance. If we had had more time—"

"Time? Time for what? For you two to dig your graves? For Christ's sake, Ash, Maria is a married woman—married to a police captain at that. What were you going to do with more time?"

Hunter stared down at his coffee as if he were being berated by his father. "I suppose get to know each other better. We both felt a spark between us."

Hannigan grimaced and then looked at him with disgust. "If I didn't know better, I'd think you were ready for a straitjacket. Jesus, Mary, and Joseph, the good Lord gave you—"

"The good Lord?"

"Yes, the good Lord gave you the sense to work things out like that. Thank God you took a second to figure that out. And remember, there's a spark just before dynamite goes off and blows everything to smithereens."

Hunter put his hands together as if in prayer. "Thank you, Lord."

"You can make all the fun you want about that, but you *should* thank the Lord that you came to your senses. Show a little humility, man."

They were suddenly quiet for a minute. Of course, Hannigan was right.

"On top of all that, you'd have had to settle in England, of all places." Hannigan wasn't finished yet. He was on a roll. He took a deep breath and continued. "We stepped up to the plate during the First World War to save their asses, and how did they show their appreciation?"

"Do tell me," Hunter said, enjoying the moment and egging him on. He was always entertained by listening to Hannigan get his knickers in a twist.

"I'll tell you how: by having us step up again for a second go-around twenty years later. I'm getting sick of all these European family feuds. And what did they do after we saved their necks a second time? I'll tell you that too!" He jabbed a finger at Hunter. "They turned socialist on us; that's what they did. They give away free this and free that with tax money, and if someone doesn't want to work and make a living for himself, well, no problem there, buddy; he just goes on the dole or collects social benefits. No, sir," Hannigan said, slapping the table, "you did the right thing. No upstanding American would want to live in a welfare state."

The door of the Paradise opened, and the newsboy stepped in. Hunter was glad for the interruption. Although his tirades were entertaining, he knew Hannigan was capable of going on for the entire morning—and perhaps for a good chunk of the afternoon.

"Hey, Chico!" Hannigan said. "You're early this morning. How about a shot of strong coffee on the house?"

"Gracias, Senor Slane, but I am very busy today. Here is your paper," he said, taking a newspaper out of his sack, folding it once, and handing it to him. "You must excuse me; I must leave now. Have a good morning, senor, and you too, Senor Ash." He opened the door, stopped, and turned around. "There's trouble in Dodge City this morning, but Matt Dillon is on the way to save us!" He giggled and was gone in a flash.

"Thanks for the warning, Chico," Hannigan said as the door swung shut. "The kid watches *Gunsmoke* on TV through the window at the El Encanto department store every day. He can't hear the show, so he makes up the dialogue." He thought for a moment. "Now, that little rascal is gonna make something of himself. I'll bet a dollar to a doughnut he'll end up owning the *Post* one day."

Hunter smiled wearily and drank some more coffee. His thoughts were still on Maria, who was probably in London by then, he thought.

Hannigan picked up on his mood and said, "Cheer up, Ash. She'll be fine. She's a strong woman." He poked him in the ribs for good measure. Then he unfolded the *Havana Post*, Cuba's English-language newspaper; spread it out on the table; and drank some more coffee. After a moment, he said, "Well, I'll be a monkey's uncle. I know this guy."

"What?" Hunter asked. "Who do you know?"

"This guy," Hannigan said, pointing a finger at a picture on the first page. "That's the guy who hired the Valiant Queen. I picked up that package for him. But they got the name wrong. This is Harry Smith, but they say his name is Shaw Armstrong."

That caught Hunter's attention. "Let me see."

Hannigan swung the paper around to him. Hunter looked at the picture and then read the short article underneath it.

"It says he was murdered in his apartment yesterday. Three shots in the chest with a small-caliber handgun." He looked over to Hannigan. "Shaw Armstrong was the person the Maddoxes hired me to find. Remember? I gave them his address yesterday morning." He thought for a moment. "And he was found dead the same day." He looked at the picture again and then pushed the paper back to Hannigan. "Does this guy look like a famous movie star to you?" He watched Hannigan as he looked at the picture.

"Babs always said he was a knockout, but yeah, maybe like Tyrone Power, but his hair is a little different."

"Precisely. That was who the Maddoxes said he looked like: Tyrone Power. That's what they told me."

"You think they knocked off this guy?" Hannigan asked, incredulous. "The Maddoxes?"

"All I'm saying is I gave them his address, and the same day, he was murdered. But you said this is Harry Smith. I wonder if this has anything to do with the package you picked up for him."

Hannigan and Hunter looked over toward the entrance at the same time to see the Maddoxes entering the café.

"Good morning, Slane, Ash," Lizzy said cheerfully. "Isn't it lovely outside?"

The couple sat down three or four tables away. Sammy poured them coffee and took their order. Hunter picked up the paper and went over to them. He sat down without waiting to be asked.

"Marvelous! You're going to have breakfast with us," Lizzy said.

"No, I ate already," Hunter said. "I was going to ask you whether you saw your friend yet. Shaw Armstrong."

"No, not yet. We were going to go to his apartment yesterday, but the day got away from us, so we decided to wait until today. We're planning on going there this afternoon to invite him to lunch. Maybe if he's available, we could have dinner here tonight. I could introduce him to you. He's a lovely man."

Hunter eyed them carefully. Lizzy had the same smile plastered on her face as she normally did. Bradford looked bored, as usual. They looked like typical American tourists to him. Could they have been capable of murder? Given the right circumstances and the right motivation, anyone was capable of murder. Should he tell the police what he knew?

"I'm afraid you won't be having lunch with him today." He spread the paper out between them and watched their reactions. "Or dinner."

Lizzy was first to react. She looked up at Hunter with shock. "My God, he's been murdered!" She looked down at the paper again. Bradford didn't react aside from narrowing his eyes, as if concentrating on reading the article.

"Then that's Shaw Armstrong's picture?" Hunter asked.

"It most certainly is," Lizzy said. She sat back in her chair and took some deep breaths. "I can't believe this. Who would want to murder poor Shaw?"

"That's what I was going to ask you," Hunter said. "Did he have any enemies in Florida who might want him dead? The police would want to know. The article says they don't have any leads."

Lizzy looked at Bradford, who said, "Everybody knows someone who doesn't like them. But no, we're not aware of anyone who would want him dead." He paused for a moment and then said, "As Lizzy said, he was a lovely guy."

There was something about his tone that Hunter didn't like.

Lizzy swung her head around to Hunter. "He was such a nice man. He got along with everyone."

How far was Hunter going to take this with them? He decided to push them a little to see what happened. "When I was asking around town about him, trying to find where he lived, someone I greatly trust said that Armstrong worked for a man named Santo Trafficante. He's a mobster. Has a home in Tampa."

"Listen, bub," Bradford said, "if you're saying that—"

"I'm not saying anything, Mr. Maddox. Your friend was murdered. I just thought this was something that might interest you. Maybe Armstrong wasn't the person you knew."

Lizzy put her hand up to her husband to shush him. "We've always known Shaw as an upright citizen who worked as an insurance investigator. As we told you, we haven't seen or heard from him in many years. We have no idea what he did here in Havana to make a living. But you have to understand, it would be very difficult for us to believe he changed so dramatically. I would say it would be against his nature to be a criminal. Perhaps the person you trust so much was misinformed. We are shocked and saddened by this."

Hunter quickly glanced at her husband, who sat mute, staring at him. "Anyway, I'm sorry to be the one to break the news to you."

"Do you know if the funeral is going to be here or in Tampa?" Lizzy asked, patting her eyes with a handkerchief.

"I don't know. I just saw the news in the paper myself. You could check with the police. They might have some idea." He got up to leave as Sammy came with their food. "I'll leave you to your breakfast."

"Thank you, Ash," Lizzy said. "You've been very kind and helpful."

Bradford continued to stare daggers at him.

Hunter went to the front desk, where Hannigan was, just out of earshot of the Maddoxes.

"Well, how'd they take it?" Hannigan asked in nearly a whisper.

"I've got this pain right here," he said, putting his fingertips to his forehead. "This happens whenever I'm talking to someone who's bullshitting me. They know something. I just don't know what."

"You think they had something to do with it?"

"I don't know, but it's a police matter now. I can't go to the police, because they'll ask too many questions, but maybe I can send them an anonymous note telling them to look at the lovely couple." He stopped for a moment and then continued. "On second thought, maybe I won't. They're staying here. We don't want the cops coming to the Paradise and questioning our guests. I guess I'm out of it now, but the Maddoxes know something they're not telling. I'm certain about that."

Hunter went behind the desk and picked up the phone. "I need to find out how Ignacio is doing," he said to Hannigan while dialing zero. When the operator answered, he said, "Connect me with the Havana Centro Hospital, will ya? Thanks." He waited a minute and then said, "Hello. My name is Ash Hunter. I'm a friend of a patient who was taken there yesterday. His name is Ignacio Navarro. I'm calling to find out how he's doing. Yes, I'll wait." He cupped the receiver and whispered to Hannigan, "Bradford Maddox is a real asshole. I wouldn't be surprised if he—yes, this is Hunter. Yes, yes." He listened for a minute or so and then said, "Yes, I understand. Yes, yes, you should do that. I understand. Thank you very much." He hung up.

Hunter looked at Hannigan. "He died about five hours ago. The hospital's going to contact the police because they found poison in his system."

"Jeez, you're losing clients left and right."

"Navarro wasn't exactly a client, and neither was Armstrong, but I see what you mean."

"Whaddaya going to do about the jewels now?"

"Before Navarro passed out, he said the name Santiago Delgado. He said that this Delgado knows about the jewels or stole them—I don't know. He was vague."

"Maybe Delgado was one of the two guys who nicked them."

"Or the guy who poisoned him."

"You're not going to get the bonus Navarro promised you, but if you find the jewels, maybe Alfonso will up the ante. After all, the

Tropicana will own them for the debt. They'd be rolling in dough over this. That'll be good for the Paradise!"

"I think Navarro was mostly truthful with me, but he was holding something back. Maybe that got him killed. I've changed my opinion about him. He was a good man. He deserved better. I'm going after Delgado. If I find out he killed Navarro, I'll—"

"Hold on there, Ash. Calm down a minute. This sounds like a vendetta to me. Revenge doesn't suit you."

"It's not revenge; it's justice."

"God Almighty, after all these years, after all we went through in Italy, you still believe there's a difference between revenge and justice. It looks like we're gonna have to have another sit-down so I can talk some sense into you and straighten you out—again."

19

A Major Headache and Then Another One

Santo Trafficante rose at the usual time of six o'clock that Saturday morning. He showered, shaved, brushed his teeth, combed his hair back, and cleaned his glasses, as he did every day. That day, he selected a gray silk suit with a dark blue tie—his favorite combination because it was understated. At seven o'clock on the dot, his breakfast came: sliced banana, mango, papaya, and mammee. After that, he downed two cups of espresso so sweet it could have been served separately as a dessert. In a few years, he supposed, he'd cut down on his sugar intake—diabetes ran in his family—but he enjoyed it too much to give it much concern yet.

He sat behind his desk in his office at the Hotel Capri with his legs stretched out and his feet, one ankle over the other, resting on the desk. His Testoni loafers sat below him on the floor. He reached for his cigar humidor and selected a belicoso with which to start the day. He snipped the tapered end and then put the flame of his lighter to the other end, turning the cigar until it was evenly charred. He then put it in his mouth and took a few puffs, sending smoke above him.

This was his peaceful time of the day, a time to think and plan. It would be the only time of the day when he could do this. The rest of the day, until he climbed into bed, would be too hectic. He had a large organization to run there and in Florida and a dozen or more phone calls to make, but right now he had to focus on the Capri, because it had just opened its doors recently, and he needed to concentrate on seeing that it was operating smoothly and steadily. It was like a newborn baby who needed constant care. So far so good. That was what he'd expected, as he had paid off enough government officials to see that it was. His father, Santo Sr., would have been proud of him.

He puffed on his cigar and looked over the tip of his socks at the Guan Yin. Earlier, he had taken the statue from his safe to admire it. He had waited more than a year for it. Now it was sitting on his desk in all its glory. The details were magnificent. It was a good thing Shaw Armstrong had suggested he wait for Josephine to fly in from Tampa to do the honors of breaking it open. Trafficante had another week to admire its beauty. He reminded himself to have Shaw take some pictures of it before they cracked it open.

Just then, the door burst open, and two men, out of breath and panting, rushed in. No one came into Trafficante's office without first knocking and then waiting for an answer, except Shaw Armstrong. But it wasn't Armstrong; it was two underlings, Jacopo and Stefono. Jacopo had a newspaper in his hand.

"Boss," he said, trying to catch his breath, "did you see this morning's paper?" They went around the desk, and Jacopo dropped it onto Trafficante's lap, opened to the front page. "Someone pumped some lead into Shaw. He's dead."

Trafficante picked up the paper with both hands, with his cigar in his mouth. First, he saw Armstrong's picture; then he read the article below it. Jacopo and Stefono stood over him, waiting for a response.

When Trafficante finished reading it, he laid the paper on his lap again and smoothed it out. "Did you check with the police?"

"Yeah, with our contact there—Luis," Stefono said. "He said they found Shaw's luggage packed with his things and two tickets to Miami for last night."

Trafficante continued to puff on his cigar and watched the smoke rise. *Two tickets to Miami*, he thought. *Two, not one. So he was skipping out with someone. A lady friend?* "Jacopo, get me a hammer."

Neither Trafficante nor Stefono said anything for the minute Jacopo was gone.

"Here it is, boss," Jacopo said when he returned.

Trafficante grabbed the handle of the hammer and stood up. He swung the hammer up and then down, directly hitting the top of the Guan Yin statue with more force than he intended, reducing the statue to a pile of shattered plaster and leaving a nice dent in the desk.

"Goddamn it!" he shouted. Jacopo and Stefono backed away from the desk, having never seen their boss this angry.

Trafficante was generally a methodical man who kept his cool under fire. Sometimes he would erupt like a volcano, but those times were few and far between. He took a deep breath and then let it out. There were two possible explanations for the statue. His immediate thought was that the Corsican in Saigon had scammed him. Trafficante had no doubt the bastard was capable of that. If that were the case, it would take Trafficante weeks to deal with him. His second thought was more immediate: Armstrong had scammed him.

It made sense now. Armstrong had persuaded him to delay cracking open the statue until Josephine arrived next week. That would have given him time to skip out of the country with the real statue. He could have bought a similar-looking one or maybe even had a duplicate made. But who was the second ticket to Miami for? And more importantly, who had killed Armstrong?

"Do you know of anyone Shaw was seeing?" he asked the two men. "Some broad?"

"Yeah, he was doing a line with a prostitute who works out of a bordello in Vedado," said Stefono.

"Casa Marina," added Jacopo.

"You have a name?"

Jacopo looked at Stefono, shrugged, and said, "Margot something."

Trafficante's eyes widened, his blood pressure dropped, and his face paled. "Reed? Margot Reed?"

"Yeah, boss, I think that sounds 'bout right. Margot Reed."

Trafficante went to the window in his socks and looked out at the garden. *Margot Reed.* He couldn't believe it. He'd had no idea she was even in Havana. *A prostitute? Christ Almighty!* A light breeze made the palm fronds dance. Two colorful butterflies were fluttering back and forth near the window in some courtship ritual. *Shaw Armstrong.*

Trafficante suddenly turned around to the two men, who jumped a little when he did. "Find Margot Reed. Bring her back to me. No rough business. Go!"

After Jacopo and Stefono left, Trafficante sat down behind his desk again. His cigar had gone out, so he relit it. Was he disappointed in Armstrong or in himself? He wasn't sure. He'd put a lot of trust in Armstrong—and the son of a bitch wasn't even Italian—because he had proven himself over the years. Trafficante had thought the man was loyal to him. Obviously, he'd been wrong.

Santo Sr. had told him time and again that he shouldn't trust anyone. Sooner or later, everyone would betray him. The exceptions were just that: exceptions. If his son was going to one day take over the operations, he had to learn that one fact. Santo Jr. had told his father what he wanted to hear, never fully grasping what he'd been told. When his father had died and he'd taken control, he had done what he felt benefitted the Trafficante family. He had to rely on the men underneath him in the organization. In order to do that, he had to have a certain amount of trust in them; otherwise, how could he run the operation? He never had understood his father's warnings. Now he did.

As if this Armstrong business wasn't bad enough, now he also had to deal with another big problem, this time with an Italian.

The world was going to hell in a handbasket.

He pressed the button on the intercom for his secretary. "Lucy, send Carbone in here."

He put his cigar in the ashtray and pressed his thumbs to his temples. He felt the onset of a headache coming. He hadn't had one for a while now. When they did come, they could lay him out for two days. He reminded himself to have Lucy make an appointment with his doctor in Tampa. He didn't trust doctors in Cuba.

There was a knock on the door.

"Come in," Trafficante said. The door opened, and Carbone peeked his head in. "Come here, Joey. Sit down."

Trafficante was short in stature and thin, but Joseph Carbone was shorter and thinner, with a beak for a nose. He made up for any shortcomings by having a sharp, analytical mind—the best there was. That was the reason Santo Sr. had hired him a few decades ago as an accountant—*the* accountant—for the Trafficante crime family organization. After Santo Jr. had taken over the operations of the family, he'd kept Carbone on, based on his past loyalties to his father and because of his impeccable performance. He knew the tax laws in Cuba as well as he knew them in the United States, and he knew exactly how to manipulate them to the benefit of the family. He also knew how to launder money. He had been an invaluable asset.

"Mr. Trafficante, if you don't mind me saying so, you look unwell," Carbone said in the soft voice of an accountant who had just made an assessment after having calculated the evidence.

"Actually, I feel like shit, Joey." He picked up his cigar again and relit it. "And do you know why I feel like shit?"

"No, Mr. Trafficante, I do not."

"Then let me tell you. You don't mind if I tell you, eh?"

"I don't mind, Mr. Trafficante."

"Good. Because if you did mind, I'd still have to tell you. Know what I mean?"

"I do, Mr. Trafficante."

"Good." He paused briefly, puffing on his cigar, collecting his thoughts. "I went over the books for the construction of the Capri. Now, I admit it took me quite some time to do it, because, well, I don't have your skills and knowledge. But I went over them nonetheless, not once but twice, and you know what I found? I found a shortfall of three hundred thousand dollars. That's a three with seven zeros behind it, if you include the zero cents, which I admit I like to do. Then I got to thinking that because I don't have your skills and knowledge, I must have made some kind of error in the calculations. Now, Joey, please tell me I miscalculated."

Carbone sat silently for a moment. His face looked as if he were mentally computing. He swung one leg over the other and placed his hands on his lap with his fingers intertwined. "If I may say so, Mr. Trafficante, I think—"

"You may say so, Joey, because I have to tell you that this is a big concern of mine. Three hundred grand is a lot of money by anyone's standards."

"Yes, sir, it is." Carbone paused to swallow some phlegm. "I've kept track of the construction costs with a fine-toothed comb, including the payoffs to the building inspectors. Everything balanced on an ongoing basis. This discrepancy must have been the result of how I presented the figures rather than something you did wrong. If you'd like, I could walk you through the books."

"Yeah, Joey, I'd like that very much. I'm going to be tied up for the rest of the day. Be here tomorrow morning at nine sharp. The files are sitting over there," he said, pointing. "So all I need is you, and I'll want to see every penny accounted for. Like I said, I don't have your skills and talent."

"Every penny is accounted for, Mr. Trafficante. I assure you. I'll go over every little detail with you."

Trafficante reached under the desk and slid his feet into his Testoni loafers. Then he stared at Carbone with steel eyes. "I know you will, Joey. I know you will."

Joseph Carbone left the office, and for a brief moment, he no longer had control over his central nervous system. Roadblocks were set up along the highway of communication between his brain and his body, preventing his thoughts from freely passing through. His brain ceased to interpret his external environment; his senses malfunctioned.

Then he snapped out of it.

He went to his office to collect a few things and then took a taxi to Havana Centro and had the driver let him out in no particular place. He started walking with nowhere specific in mind. How could he have let himself get into such a mess? It wasn't just a mess; it was a catastrophe of monumental proportions. He'd thought he had covered his tracks. He had meticulously worked on the books, covering himself with each transaction during the entire construction of the hotel. He hadn't stolen the money in one lump sum; that would have been too obvious. Instead, he'd done it little by little while adjusting the entries. It had been a foolproof scheme. The books were straight, at least to the untrained eye.

He hadn't counted on Trafficante himself examining the books. His father never had. Why had Trafficante all of a sudden decided to look at them? He never had in the past. He took after the old man in that way.

But that was all water under the bridge now. There was nothing he could do. Trafficante had the books in his office, out of reach of Carbone's hands and sharply tipped pencils. In fact, if the books had been on another planet, he might have had a better chance of getting to them.

He had to see his boss at nine o'clock sharp tomorrow morning. Sometime before noon, Carbone would be a dead man.

A conjunto appeared out of nowhere, as they often did, and began following Carbone. He turned back and shooed them away with his hands, trying to discourage them from following any farther. He knew they could be persistent. He crossed the Prado and then walked another block and crossed Monserrate into Old Havana. They decided not to follow him. There he saw La Floridita bar. He needed a drink.

At the bar, he ordered a daiquiri. Then he changed his mind and ordered a straight double whiskey. The bar wasn't crowded at that time of day. That was good. There'd be few distractions. He had to come up with a plan, and he had to do it now. He couldn't meet with Trafficante tomorrow or any other time. He'd never walk out of his office alive. He'd be carried out.

Carbone had always been a smart man. From grade school through high school, he had been the teacher's pet and received top grades, but he always had earned them. He'd been an honor student at the University of the State of Florida and graduated top in his class. A year after receiving a master's degree, he had gone to work for Santo Trafficante Sr., a friend of the family.

He made a more-than-decent living. He never had married, so his expenses were not great. He could have lived a highfalutin lifestyle but chose not to. He always dressed in modest suits, usually purchased in low-end department stores. He'd tried dressing flashily once, but it just wasn't him. Even Santo Sr. had commented. "Kid," he'd said, "your clothes—you need to do something with them."

With his minimal expenses and restrained lifestyle, most of his money went into a savings account and low-risk investments. If he'd retired right then at the age of forty-eight, he'd have had more than enough money to last him the next twenty or thirty years—longer if the markets were good and he lived long enough. So why had this crazy fuck decided to steal $300,000 from the most powerful Mafia boss in the state of Florida and Cuba and probably one of the top three or four in all of the United States?

He didn't know with certainty, but if he'd had to guess, he would have said it was just a whim, just to see if he could do it.

He did know with certainty that he had to get the hell out of Cuba before Trafficante knew he was gone. Florida was only ninety miles away. He could rent a car in Key West and be in Tampa seven hours later. There he would close his bank account and liquidate his investments, and then he would disappear. But to where? Maybe Alaska wouldn't be such a bad choice.

But was it far enough?

Carbone walked to the end of the bar, where the management had a telephone for public use. He grabbed the directory under the phone and paged through the *p*'s. There it was. He dialed the operator and gave her the number. After three rings, someone answered.

"Paradise Inn! Slane Hannigan here. How can I help you?"

"I'm interested in hiring your boat for tonight. Is it available?"

"That depends. Where're you heading?"

"Key West."

"There's going to be a storm passing through tonight, so it's nix on that. If it's clear tomorrow, probably in the afternoon, we can set off at that time. You all right with that?"

Carbone thought for a moment. It would be the same with the other boat owners too. *Damn the storm.* "It looks like I have no choice. Please reserve the boat for me then. The name is John Smith."

"Okay, Mr. Smith, she's all yours. But like I said, it all depends on the weather. Three o'clock good for you?"

"That's fine," he said, and he hung up. He caught the bartender's attention. "Another double whiskey, please."

Trafficante would be looking for him at nine o'clock sharp. When he didn't show up, the boss would know for sure he'd cooked the books and stolen the money. He'd send the Bobbsey Twins, Jacopo and Stefono, out looking for him. Carbone would need six hours to hide out somewhere. Once he was on the boat to Key West, he'd be home free. The bartender set the whiskey in front of him. He gulped it down in one go.

Goddamn that storm, he thought.

20

A Stormy Night

Casa Marina stood like a castle on the corner of Twenty-Fifth Street and the seaside Malecón in the chic Vedado district of Havana. Its owner, Doña Marina, a Spaniard, had established herself after the war as the Queen of the Madams in her palatial two-story residence. The bordello was renowned for its white-coated servants and luxurious decor, complete with plush draperies and period furniture in the tradition of the old French *maison de joie*. It was cosmopolitan by anyone's yardstick. The menu included French, Chinese, Cuban, and American girls for her clientele who could afford them. Those who couldn't might have other services provided. As an added benefit, she had two trained nurses on duty twenty-four hours a day in a spotlessly clean clinic to guard the health of the famous and the wealthy as well as her employees.

Doña Marina ran a tight ship and didn't put up with any nonsense, so her reaction came as no surprise to Margot when she shared her little problem with her. They were sitting together on a bench in a corner of Doña Marina's office.

"Let me see if I understand you," Doña Marina said. "You said that Santo Trafficante might be after you. Right? And you want my help."

"Yes."

The clouds rumbled outside, and thunder shook the universe. Rain poured down loudly on the clay roofing tiles, so the women had to raise their voices slightly to be heard.

"What in the world could you have done so bad that Santo Trafficante might be after you?"

"I can't say."

"You can't say." Doña Marina ran her hands down her dress to smooth it out, even though it didn't need to be smoothed. "But you want me to help you. Am I correct to think that?"

"Yes, you are correct. I've come to ask you for help."

"I assume you know who Santo Trafficante is, and I also assume you know that he could snap his fingers and put me out of business if he so desired." She thought for a moment, made her calculations, and then said, "You might be in trouble with him, and you want my help, but you won't tell me what this is all about. Is that correct?" Sitting with her back straight, she once again ran her palms down her thighs, attempting to smooth out her already-smooth silk dress.

"It's serious, and I don't want to involve you, Doña Marina."

"If what you're saying is true, you do understand that you cannot work here any longer. Santo and I are on a first-name basis. We are friends, although we're not that close. But that won't prevent him from shutting down my house if he believes I have conspired against him in some way."

"That's why I don't want to tell you my problem."

"That's kind of you," she said sarcastically. She straightened her back even more. "Here's what I will do for you. Take your belongings, and leave. If Santo's men come looking for you, I will tell them you quit, gave no reason, and just left. I will do that and nothing more."

"Thank you, Doña Marina. Thank you very much."

"You can thank me by never coming back and by never mentioning this conversation to anyone."

Outside, overhead, there was a flash of lightning, followed by a sharp, loud crack of thunder that made both Margot Reed and the Spanish madam flinch.

"Batten down the hatches, folks!" Hannigan yelled. "This is going to be a humdinger!"

"Hannigan!" Babs shouted, squinting out the window. "Look! Our beautiful neon sign outside fell down. It's lying in the mud."

"That's not the only thing that's going to be in the mud before this storm is finished. Did you get the extra supply of candles out?"

"I put them in the office." Babs continued to peer out the window. "Our gorgeous sign lying facedown in the mud. Where's the justice in this crazy world?"

"Forget the sign, Babs. We've got to check on our guests and get them some candles. They've got to have some light to see. We got enough matches?"

"Loads of them. Where'd Sammy go?"

"I sent him out to the Valiant Queen to secure her. This feels like a typhoon."

"I think you mean a hurricane, dear. You're in the wrong part of the world."

"Hurricane, sugarcane. What we have is one hell of an old-fashioned tropical storm."

"Look, Hannigan! I think I see someone coming. There!" she said, pointing out the window.

Hannigan peered over her shoulder. It was pitch dark, and the rain was lashing down with tremendous force. "I think you're right. I can't make 'im out, but whoever it is, he's carrying a suitcase."

"I think he's too small to be a him. I think he's a she."

Hannigan went to the door and opened it. A lone figure was trudging slowly toward the Paradise with shoulders sloping, toting a piece of luggage. "Here! Over here!" he yelled, waving a hand. "Come on!"

When the figure got close enough, Hannigan ran out the door, grabbed the suitcase, grabbed the person's arm, and made for the door. By the time they got inside, they were both drenched.

"Oh, you poor dear," Babs said. He, in fact, was a she. "You're soaking wet. You've got to get out of those clothes."

"Thank you," the woman said. "I was wondering if you had a room for tonight."

"We'll fix you up with something, sis," Hannigan said. "Don't you worry your little head about that. Babs, take her to 2B. That's vacant now. Get her into some dry clothes before we have a sick girl on our hands." He himself was dripping wet.

"Do you have a safe here?" the woman asked. "I need to put something in it." Rain dripped from her clothes and puddled on the floor by her shoes.

"That's fine, sis. When we're finished, Babs here will take you to your room. She'll bring you a couple of candles so you can change properly. Whaddaya want to put in the safe?"

"My name is Margot Reed." She bent over, unzipped her suitcase, and pulled out a package. "If you could put this in your safe, I'd greatly appreciate it." She handed it to Hannigan.

He looked at it and felt its weight. It was wrapped in the same kind of paper Armstrong's package had been wrapped in. He looked back at her skeptically and said, "Sure, sis, we'll put it in the safe for you. What is it, if I'm not being too nosy?"

"Just something special is all. I don't want to lose it."

An hour later, Babs and Hannigan sat in the office with a candle between them. The rain outside fell heavily on the roof, making it difficult to speak. Most of the guests were tucked away in their rooms, waiting out the storm. Babs and Hannigan had provided them with candles and matches and cautioned them to keep an eye on their candles. They didn't want the Paradise to go up in flames.

"How's the girl?" Hannigan asked.

"She's fine now, the poor thing. I helped her change her clothes and gave her some hot coffee and a chicken sandwich to eat. I wonder why she was outside in this kind of weather. She's not a tourist; she says she lives here in Havana."

"I don't like it, not one bit. Didja see the package she gave me?"

"I couldn't see it very well."

"Well, I did. It looked like the same one Harry Smith—I mean Shaw Armstrong—had us pick up. It weighed about the same too. Now Armstrong's as dead as a doornail. No, I don't like it one bit."

"You don't think that girl had anything to do with his death, do you?"

"I don't think nothing, Babs. I just don't like it. I have half a notion to go ask her about it right now."

"Let's wait until the storm is over. Let her rest up. She was exhausted when I left."

"Fine. I'll let her rest. But after that, I'm going to get to the bottom of this. We don't need the Paradise involved in any shenanigans."

"Since when is a murder a shenanigan?"

"When it involves us!"

"Do you really think that little girl is capable of pumping three rounds into a man's chest?"

"How many times have I told you, Babs? Anyone is capable of doing that if the price is right. A little girl can even the score when she's holding a loaded revolver in her hand."

21

I Feel It in My Bones

At sunrise the next day, the sky was a canvas painted a light blue, and there wasn't even a hint of a breeze. The air hung over Havana, creating a furnace below. Hannigan, Babs, and Sammy were standing over the neon sign with their hands on their hips, trying to come to some kind of consensus as to the best way to get it back on the roof.

"I think if we tie the ends with rope," Hannigan said, "Sammy and I could get on the roof and hoist it up. We'll have to replace a couple of tubes. I'm surprised they weren't all busted up."

Sammy bent his knees, squatting in place with his heels touching his rear end. "The braces seem to be okay, Mr. Slane. We'll just have to pound them into the roof once we get it back up."

"Babs, while we do that, would you mind having a look at the Valiant Queen? I hope she came through it okay. She's booked for a run to Key West this afternoon. With the storm and all, I forgot to tell you."

"I'll go over her with a fine-toothed comb. If there's no damage, I don't see why we can't go. We should spend the night there. Get some rest."

They all looked behind them when they heard someone walking their way.

"Well, look at what the dog dragged in," Hannigan said. "We thought you were washed out to sea. We were just going to have a memorial service for you."

"I knew I couldn't make it back in time," Ash Hunter said, "so I stayed at the Hotel Nacional overnight. They have their own generator. We should think about getting one."

"Yeah, classy," Hannigan said. "I hope they fed you."

"Steak and lobster with *moros y cristianos* and champagne last night and eggs Benedict this morning—with more champagne, of course."

"King- or queen-size bed?" Babs asked jokingly.

"King, of course, with silk sheets. I was cozy."

"Creature comforts," Hannigan mumbled.

"Actually, I stayed with a friend in Chinatown. Had to sleep in a hammock. Fed me beans and rice, though, and all the warm beer I could drink." Hunter surveyed the area. Besides the Paradise Inn's sign falling down, there was mostly debris from falling tree limbs and blowing trash. Their flower garden was a mess. "What a way to start the week."

"You've got that wrong," Hannigan said, taking off his hat and running his fingers through his hair. "Today's Sunday. The Bible says that God worked his rear end off for six days and rested on the last day. That happened to be a Sunday. Monday starts the week, and Sunday ends it."

"And what in holy heaven would you know about the Bible?" Hunter asked.

"I read a lot. You should try it sometime. It's good for the soul."

Hunter shook his head. After a moment, he asked, "How did our guests manage the storm?"

"They're fine," Babs said. "No one set fire to their room. Oh, and we got a late-night check-in, if you can believe it. A pretty young lady toting a treasure through the wind and rain. Wanted to use our safe."

They told him about the curious package and how it resembled the one Hannigan had gotten for Armstrong off the freighter.

"We should open it," Hunter said. "We can't afford to be stowing any contraband."

"Nix on that," Hannigan said. "That would be unethical. The Bible says so." He paused briefly, looking at Babs and Hunter. "Okay, you twisted my arm. When should we do it?"

"I need some coffee before we do anything," Hunter said. "Sammy?"

"Coffee coming up," Sammy said, making his way inside.

Once the coffee finished brewing, they all went into the café and sat around a table. Sammy brought in a baguette. They all pulled off hunks of it and ate. Hunter appeared to be somewhat dejected.

Hannigan eyed him. Thinking he might be concerned with the sign, he said, "We'll have the sign up in an hour; no need to worry about it."

Hunter looked up from his coffee. "It's not that. I was just thinking how I could get more clients." He swung his head to Babs. "Babs, why don't more men cheat on their wives? It's good for business."

"You're asking me?" Babs said, laughing. "You should be asking Hannigan. Better yet, you should take a survey. You'd have an answer in an hour."

"Why should he ask me?" Hannigan said to his wife. "I've never come close to cheating on you."

"Well, that's the point, isn't it?" Babs said. "You could tell the gentleman here why you don't cheat on me, and he'd have his answer. But I still think a survey's a good idea."

"Maybe, Mr. Ash," Sammy said, "you should go to the fancy hotels where all the rich American tourists stay and hand out your card to all the ladies you see."

"Good idea, Sammy, but remember, I'm not licensed here, and I prefer not to be deported. My cards could get into the wrong hands."

"That is a very good point, Mr. Ash."

"Sammy, how 'bout a little song to inspire us to get that sign back up?"

"That too is a very good point, Mr. Slane. One must have a certain motivation for a particular task." He reached behind him for his guitar, strummed a few chords to warm up, and then began singing:

Havana, oh, Havana!
We all come to you from lands afar.
We work, we toil, we sweat under de beautiful sun.
You give us de fruits of our labor, but in truth, it's all bizarre,
because den da hurricane comes. Wind
and rain—dey are not much fun.
Our poor neon sign is sitting in da mud,
so again, we must toil, and we must sweat.
To get the sign up high, we must spill our blood.
Den we drink coffee, we laugh, and we eat da baguette!
Havana, oh, Havana!

They all laughed, shouted, and hooted.

"That was great, Sammy," Hannigan said. "Now, drink up. That sign isn't going back on the roof by itself."

"But, Mr. Slane," Sammy said, "I am not finished. I have one more verse to sing."

"Sing away, Sammy."

On de night of the storm, in de wind and de rain,
comes a mysterious woman looking very sad.
Her face tells us she is in much pain.
Den we realize dat she could be quite mad.
She carries a suitcase with a treasure inside.
"Can I use your safe?" she asks Mr. Slane.
He looks at her upside down and inside out like she is insane,

but he does not rant, and he does not rave;
instead, he says, "I will certainly abide!"

They laughed some more, but Babs said, "That was good, Sammy, but your rhymes were a little misplaced."

"I know, Miss Babs. It must have been the storm."

Suddenly, the bell over the entrance rang, and a man appeared, carrying a briefcase. He was short and thin and dressed in a lightweight brown suit. Hannigan walked over to the front desk and greeted him.

"Welcome to the Paradise Inn," he said. "If you don't already have a reservation, I'm afraid we can't help you with a room. We're all booked at the moment."

"Actually, I've hired your boat to take me to Key West today. My name is Smith. John Smith."

"There seem to be a lot of Smiths in Havana these days. You're early, Mr. Smith. The boat's not ready because of the storm. We should be ready to hoist anchor this afternoon sometime. If you come back around—"

"No, that's fine. I'll just wait, if that's okay with you."

"It's fine with me, but it's going to be a long wait. We have to go over the Valiant Queen and make sure she's seaworthy. You could wait in the dining room. We'll fix you up some grub if you'd like."

"I'd like that just fine," Smith said. "And some coffee too."

Hannigan led the way into the café.

After Ash Hunter helped Hannigan and Sammy secure the sign on the roof, he showered, shaved, and put on some fresh clothes. He'd decided to make one more attempt to find the Perón jewels. If he actually found them—and that was a big *if*—it would mean a hell of a lot more working capital for the Paradise. They might even be able to pay off the mortgage.

If he himself had stolen the jewels, he would have been out of Cuba in a flash. But in the event the thieves were still in town, they might want to find a fence to take care of the jewels; that way, they wouldn't have to worry about being searched when leaving Cuba and arriving wherever they were heading. The jewels would have to be broken down into individual diamonds; otherwise, they would be too recognizable. Hunter knew a Cuban in the city who was both a jeweler and a fence.

He took a taxi across town to the Hotel Comodoro. Designed in the late moderne architectural style, it was located by the sea on Seventy-Second Avenue in the exclusive Miramar district. The taxi pulled up under the kidney-shaped entrance canopy. Hunter paid the driver, got out, and walked into the hotel. The lobby was full of small shops that catered to the rich and famous. To the left of him was Hollywood Jewelers. He walked past an old woman selling flowers, nodded, and entered the shop.

It was small but elegant, with a long aisle down the middle and showcases on either side. In the back, facing the aisle and behind the counter, stood a tall man of about forty-five. He was impeccably dressed in a light tan suit and burgundy tie. He had black hair combed back and a thick mustache. His name was Valentino Valenzuela. He was a successful businessman whose sole claim to fame was that he had never been arrested or incarcerated—at least not since he was fifteen years old—which bestowed upon him a certain amount of bragging rights.

"Ashton Hunter!" Valenzuela said with his arms stretched out in front of him and his fingers splayed wide, as if he had just introduced the guest speaker at a dinner party. "How are you, my friend? You're looking fantastic!"

"I'm fine, Val. How are you doing?" *Oops*, he thought as he approached him. He shouldn't have asked him that.

"Me? I'm always in motion. Life is like riding a bicycle. To keep your balance, you must keep moving. There are peaks and valleys." He demonstrated the concept with his hands, throwing them above his head and then below his waist. "The secret is that you don't let the peaks get too high or the valleys too low. Life is beautiful, and when you love life, my friend, you have the key to eternal youth. In the morning, when I get up, I burst with joy. Every morning is like that for me. I have my wife, I have my children, and I have my humble shop. I ask you: What more can a man want? A man who dares to waste one hour of time has not discovered the value of life."

Hunter stood with his arms crossed, grinning. He knew Valenzuela well enough not to interrupt him once he got going. When he was certain his friend had finished, he waited a moment longer before saying anything. It was better to be safe than sorry.

"Good for you, Val," Hunter said, looking at his watch. "I don't have much time, but I was wondering if I could talk to you in private in the back room." If he didn't want to spend an entire morning or afternoon listening to Valenzuela, he had to introduce time constraints from the onset; otherwise, it would be hopeless.

"Of course you can talk to me in private." Valenzuela opened the curtain behind him, which led to the office, and said, "Alicia, would you watch the shop for me for a minute?"

A stout woman who looked as if she could be his *abuela* came out immediately and sat on a chair behind the counter. She was silent and eyed Hunter suspiciously. Valenzuela and Hunter entered the back room.

"First, a drink!" Valenzuela said, producing a bottle of Hennessy. "Nothing but the best!" He poured some into two glasses. "To our friendship over many years!" They clinked glasses.

Getting down to business before Valenzuela went off in another direction, Hunter said, "I have a problem I want you to help me with if you can."

"Name it, and I will help!"

Hunter told him the entire story involving the Tropicana, Ignacio Navarro, and the stolen Perón jewels. To his surprise, he wasn't interrupted once. After he finished, Valenzuela poured more cognac into their glasses.

"First of all," Valenzuela said, "no one has come into the shop wanting to sell the jewels. Second, now that the man who owned them has been murdered, it would make the jewels too hot for me to handle. I would never do that. Too risky. So how can I help you, Ash?"

"Does the name Santiago Delgado mean anything to you?"

"No, I have not heard that name."

"He's somehow involved in the theft and maybe the murder. I really need to find this man. You have contacts all around town. I'm asking you, as a favor to me, to make use of them." Hunter knew he'd have to sweeten the pie a bit. "If I end up finding the jewels, I could make a lot of money. A lot! I'll cut you in fifteen percent."

"Make it twenty percent, my friend, and I will be your diligent servant forever. You know what they say about—"

"Twenty percent it is," Hunter said, cutting him off at the pass. He had been willing to go as high as twenty-two percent if necessary. "Delgado might be Cuban. Or he could be an Argentinian or a Spaniard—I don't know. But put the word out—not too conspicuously, though. I don't want Delgado to know he's being sought."

"You might be surprised by this revelation, but I was not born yesterday, my friend. Now, on the chance this man walks into my humble shop and offers to sell them to me, what would you like me to do?"

"That's a good question." Hunter thought about it for a moment. "He's going to want a lot of money for them; that goes without saying. Tell him you're very interested in buying them, but you'll need twenty-four hours to collect the cash he wants. Tell him you have a buyer in mind, and you'll need to contact him first. That should work without scaring him off. You do that a lot anyway, right?"

"For certain items, yes, that's not at all unusual."

"Try to get as much information about him as possible. He's not going to want to say much, but try anyway. I don't know if it's going to be possible, but try to find out where he's staying. When he leaves, call me at the Paradise. Leave a message if I'm not in."

"My friend, the sun shines bright in the Western Hemisphere! I feel it in my bones that this confederacy of ours is going to produce wonders like the papaya tree produces fruit. Or better yet, like your ship sinks, and you swim to shore, thinking you're in Papua New Guinea and will be eaten alive by the residents, only to find you've landed in Tahiti, where the natives welcome you with pleasure and wealth. My bones, Ashton—"

Hunter didn't have the heart to interrupt him again, so he pointed to his watch, waved goodbye, and left.

"It's in my bones!"

22

A Nice Send-Off

Santo Trafficante rubbed his left arm. Every so often, pain shot up to his shoulder and down to his wrist. It wasn't bad, just something he'd have to live with—an annoyance more than anything. Three years earlier, he, Josephine, and their two girls had just finished dinner at his father-in-law's house in the Ybor section of Tampa and gotten into his Mercury with two of his bodyguards, when another car had passed by and blasted them with buckshot. He'd been the only one injured. It had been only a slight wound, but it had given him a problem ever since. A little nerve damage, the doctor had told him. Santo Sr. had been in ill health, and Santo Jr. had taken over the family operations. A rival Mafia faction had decided to take advantage of the transition to expand their own territory. Two months after the incident, Junior had put them out of business.

There was a knock on his office door.

He was expecting Jacopo and Stefono. The men entered the office, looking a little weather-beaten. They had been up all night during the storm. Their suits had been wet but were pretty much dry by now. They hung wrinkled on the men, with spots of dirt on them.

"Sit down," Trafficante said. "You guys look like shit." He reached behind him for a bottle of whiskey and poured two glasses.

"Here. You could use a stiff drink." After a moment, he said, "What about the girl?"

"We went to Casa Marina. Talked to Doña Marina. She sends her regards," Stefono said, and Trafficante nodded. "She said the girl was gone; she doesn't know where. She packed her bags yesterday and left. She could be anywhere. Sorry, boss."

Damn it, he thought. He had to find her before she decided to take off. "How about Carbone? You been keeping an eye out for him?"

"Yeah." Stefono was doing the talking. Jacopo looked as if he were about to doze off. "The bad news is, we followed him around yesterday but lost him during the storm. It was raining sideways. We couldn't see our hands in front of our faces."

"I hope there's good news."

"Right, boss, there is. We were scouting out the Malecón this morning and spotted him. We followed him to the Paradise Inn. We called Jake to take over so we could report back. Carbone's still there. Do you want us to pick him up?"

The Paradise Inn, Trafficante thought. *Slane Hannigan.* Trafficante didn't know the man personally, but he knew that Hannigan had a boat for hire. Trafficante himself had told Carbone to tell Armstrong to hire Hannigan's boat to pick up the statue. Apparently, Carbone was going to do a little business with Hannigan for himself.

"No, don't pick him up. He's probably going to hire the boat at the Paradise to take him to Key West. Go back there, and keep an eye on him. When the time is right, I want you boys to give him a nice send-off. Understand?"

"Sure, boss, we understand. Give him a nice little send-off he won't forget."

Trafficante raised his head and sniffed. "You guys smell like a wet sheepdog. Take a shower first. Change your clothes. Put on a little Old Spice. I want you guys looking spiffy, but do it quickly!"

"The Valiant Queen is gassed up and ready to go, Mr. Smith," Hannigan said. "Do you have any luggage besides your briefcase?"

"No, that's it. Just the briefcase," he said, finishing his sixth cup of coffee in the café.

"Good enough then." Hannigan looked over his shoulder at Sammy. "We'll either be back late tonight, or we might decide to stay the night and come back tomorrow. If we're staying, I'll give you a call. Hold down the fort until we get back."

"I understand, Mr. Slane. The fort will be tied down securely until you get back."

"Let's shove off then, Mr. Smith. The harbor is a fifteen-minute walk from here. We'll get you to Key West in no time."

Babs was waiting for them outside, and the three of them made their way to the Valiant Queen. Babs and Hannigan walked ahead on the cement path just above the shoreline with Mr. Smith following behind. Blue skies and little wind—it couldn't have been a better day for a trip on the motor yacht.

"The weather is going to be perfect all the way there," Hannigan said over his shoulder by way of making conversation, "so we should make good time, Mr. Smith. Are you from the Key West area?"

"I'm from Tampa, but I've been living here in Havana for a while."

"I see. Tampa's a good city. Good indeed! I've always said that, haven't I, Babs? Tampa's a good city to raise a family, if you're so inclined. You're going for a little visit?"

Babs looked at her husband with a sour expression that said, "Stop it!"

"Yes, a little visit."

"A little visit. Gotta get away once in a while, yes indeed. You don't want to get stale staying in one place. I used to say that all the time too."

Babs's look intensified.

"Look, Mr. Hannigan. I would like to pay you now for the trip—get it done with."

"Naw, that won't be necessary, Mr. Smith. We'll take care of things on the other end. There's no rush. We just want you to relax and have a nice trip. We threw in some grub, if you get hungry along the way. Some beer too. That's standard. You don't have to pay extra."

"I appreciate all the amenities, but I insist, Mr. Hannigan," Smith said, slightly out of breath. "I'd like to pay you now, before we leave."

"Are we walking too fast for you?" Looking at Babs, Hannigan said, "Let's slow down a bit."

As they were talking, a dark blue Buick approached them on the road parallel to the cement path. The driver was going fast and then slowed down when the car got to them. Hannigan looked over his shoulder. There were two men in the car. He couldn't see them well, but maybe they were trying to get his attention. He was still looking at them as the man in the passenger seat stuck his arm out the window. *A gun!* Hannigan grabbed Babs by the waist, threw her down onto the grass beside the path, and landed on top of her.

Seconds later, he heard six shots being fired and the car speeding away.

"Are you all right, Babs?" he said, out of breath.

"I'm fine. Jesus, that was gunfire. Where's Mr. Smith?"

Hannigan got up and helped Babs to her feet. They looked behind them. Smith was lying on the sidewalk on his back, riddled with bullets.

"My God," Babs said. Her hand went to her mouth in shock. "They murdered him. Murdered him in cold blood."

"Yeah, they certainly did that. But who's *they*?" Hannigan picked up the briefcase and gave it to Babs. "Take this back to the Paradise. Put it in the office, and then call the police. Tell them where we are. I'll stay until they get here. Don't mention the briefcase."

"But, Hannigan—"

"No buts, Babs. Just do it. I've got to think this through."

"But—"

"Babs, please. Just go now. Let me think."

Trafficante sat behind his desk, talking on the phone to his wife, Josephine, who was in Tampa.

"Yes, darling, I can't wait to see you and the girls. I miss you too."

Someone knocked on the door.

He covered the receiver with his hand and said, "Come in."

Jacopo and Stefono entered and sat down on the chairs in front of Trafficante's desk.

"Yes, dear. Kiss the girls for me. See you soon. I love you too." He hung up the receiver and looked at the two men.

"It's done, boss," Jacopo said.

"What? The send-off?"

"We gave him a good one. He was walking to the harbor, just like you thought. Never knew what happened."

"Witnesses?"

"There were two people with him—a man and a woman. Probably the owners of the boat. They ducked out of the way when Stefono started firing. Fell in the grass. It happened so fast that they didn't have time to see nothing. We're okay on that."

Hannigan and his wife, Trafficante thought. "They're okay, right?"

"They're fine. Like I said, they fell in the grass, where it slopes toward the harbor. I think the guy saw the gun but nothing after that. We hid our faces."

Trafficante thought for a moment and then said, "Good job then. Here's what I want you to do next: bring the guy to me but not his wife. His name is Slane Hannigan. He owns the boat and the Paradise. That's the guy who picked up the statue. I want to see what he knows about it."

"Should we have a little talk with him first, boss?" Stefono asked.

"No, just bring him here. Be gentle with him. No rough stuff. I need him here on friendly terms. Tell him I'll pay him for his time. Be gracious about it. I know you can be gracious when you want to be."

"Okay, no rough business, boss. We'll be gracious. We can do that. Right, Jacopo?"

"Right."

Trafficante rubbed his arm again as his mind went three years back in time.

23

Danger on Two Fronts

"Now, this is the way to start the week off!" Hannigan turned around to Babs and Sammy with his arms folded across his chest. "Ash thinks Sunday is the first day of the week. But it's not; Monday is. How d'ya like them?" He turned toward the conjunto in the rear of the café. Four men were playing a lovely, spirited country song. "Great, eh?"

"Yeah, great," Babs said dryly, "but how can we afford them?"

"I hired them for the week on a test run. After a week, we'll see how things go."

Babs persisted. "But how can we afford them?"

"I told them they could keep all the tips they could get."

"Yes, dear husband, but how—"

"I haven't gotten that far yet. Maybe we could cut down on the bar soap."

Sammy jumped in. "If they don't work out, maybe I could play a little calypso for our guests on a regular schedule. You could keep the tips."

"No, Sammy," Hannigan said. "We need you to help run the place."

All three of them turned toward the entrance when they heard the bell over the door ring. Two men entered, wearing suits and hats. Hannigan didn't like the way they looked.

"Good morning, gentlemen," he said. "Our rooms are all booked until Wednesday, if that's what you're looking for."

"We ain't lookin' for a room," the tall one said. "We're lookin' for Slane Hannigan."

Hannigan eyed them suspiciously. They didn't look like tourists or businessmen. They were well dressed but looked seedy. They were tough guys—guys who made a living out of violence. There was no doubt about that. There was an unmistakable aura about them. He'd seen enough of their kind in his time and always kept his distance. What in the hell were they doing in the Paradise, looking for him?

"I'm Hannigan. What can I do for you boys?"

"Our boss wants to see you. He wants a little word with you."

Babs and Sammy looked at each other at the same time. Hannigan was hesitant to ask who their boss was but did anyway.

"Santo Trafficante," the shorter man said. "He said you should come with us."

This wasn't how the week was supposed to start. Then, suddenly, his mind flashed back to yesterday, to the man who had hired him to take him to Key West, John Smith. *Six bullets in his body. Blood everywhere. Trafficante.* He knew him by reputation. Monday was going to be a bad day.

"We had a little excitement yesterday by the harbor. You wouldn't happen to know anything about that, now, would you?"

Babs was standing behind Hannigan. She put a hand on his shoulder and whispered, "No, Slane. Stop." That might have been the first time she'd called him by his first name since their wedding day. Sammy looked worried.

"Not a chance," the tall one said. "Don't know what you're talkin' about."

"Hey, there's nothing to worry about," the shorter one said. "We'll have you back here in a couple of hours. Mr. Trafficante said we should tell you he'll pay you for your time. He knows you're a busy man."

"Suppose I gave you a no for an answer. You gentlemen wouldn't just leave peacefully, would you?" He knew he was pressing his luck. Babs, behind him, was in the first stage of going into a tizzy.

The two men folded their arms across their chests in unison and leaned their heads to the side. Their smiles were crooked. Their moves seemed choreographed and practiced.

"Okay, boys, I hope you weren't just cracking wise about paying me for my time. Time is money in my business."

"Same with ours. When Mr. Trafficante says something, he means it," the taller one said.

Hannigan looked between the men out the window beside the entrance and saw their car sitting in the parking area: a dark Buick. It looked like the one used in the shooting the day before. He had given the police as little information as possible yesterday without straining his credibility. One never knew who the good guys and the crooks were. Sometimes they were the same.

"Let me get my briefcase in the back room, and then we can tallyho."

In the background, the conjunto continued playing their sonorous tune.

The shorter man looked at the other. "We should come here more often, Stefono. They have good taste in music."

Santo Trafficante poured two fingers of whiskey into each glass and gave one to Hannigan.

"*Buon anno!*" he said. "*Alla tua salute!*" They clinked glasses. "I want to apologize for taking you away from your place of business on such short notice. As a businessman myself, I realize the importance of your time."

They were on the couch in Trafficante's office, sitting like old friends.

"Your boys were persuasive. Polite but persuasive."

"I'm glad they were polite. We have a reputation to uphold."

"Wasn't that George Raft, the movie star, I passed in the lobby?"

"George is part owner of the Capri. He does some publicity here—draws customers into the hotel and casino. I'll introduce you to him on your way out if you'd like. He's a real gentleman—quite different from on the big screen. But first, I know you must be a busy man, so I'll get down to business." He took a sip of his whiskey and puffed on his cigar for a moment or two. "Last week, I told a friend of mine to hire your boat. You picked up a package from a Liberian freighter. Now that package has disappeared. It happens to belong to me. What I was wondering is this: You wouldn't happen to know anything about that, would you?"

"You're talking about Shaw Armstrong, right?"

"That's the man."

"Said his name was Harry Smith. I read that he was shot in his apartment."

"Shaw was funny that way. He liked to use different names. But yes, he's no longer with us."

"I kept the package in my safe overnight. He picked it up the next day. I didn't see it or him after that." Hannigan sipped his whiskey and then added, "Shaw Armstrong must have been a popular guy, eh?"

"Why would you say that?"

"An American couple checked into the Paradise a few days ago on vacation. Said they were looking for him—that they were old friends."

"Oh?" Trafficante said, caught off guard. "What're their names, if you don't mind me asking?"

"Don't mind at all. Bradford and Elizabeth Maddox. She goes by Lizzy. They were going to see Armstrong on the day after he was killed."

Trafficante was stunned but hid it. "Are they still at your hotel?"

"It's an inn, but yes, they're still there."

Trafficante thought for a long moment, and then he asked Hannigan if he knew a Margot Reed.

Hannigan hesitated briefly and then said, "Never heard of her. Should I know her?"

Trafficante ignored the question. He took another sip of whiskey and ran his tongue across his lips. Then he knocked some cigar ash into the ashtray. "You have a good reputation here in Havana, Slane. I'm going to be up front with you. That package you gave Armstrong is a valuable Chinese statue. It would mean a lot to me to get it back. I'd like you to keep an eye out for it. It's white plaster with detailed designs about so big"—he used his hands to show its height and width—"and it's quite heavy. If you find it or know where we can find it, it's worth five—no, ten—grand for you."

"Ten grand, you say? That's a lot of dough to find a statue."

"Like I said, it means a lot to me. Now it means a lot to you."

"I'll see what I can do, Santo."

"You do that, Slane," Trafficante said, getting up from the couch. "Thank you for coming. I appreciate it. Again, I apologize for any inconvenience. My men will drive you back to your hotel. Sorry—I mean your inn."

Hannigan rose from the couch and said, "By the way, we had a little excitement yesterday on the way to my motor yacht. Someone dropped this briefcase in all the hubbub. I brought it here just in case it belongs to you."

Trafficante took the briefcase and went over to his desk. He opened it and found it stuffed with money—his money—in nice little packets. *Carbone. The bastard*, he thought. He peeled off five one-hundred-dollar bills and then turned to Hannigan. "Like I said, you have a good reputation. You're an honest man. Here's a little something for your trouble." He gave him the bills. "Oh yes, and remember about the statue."

"I'll do my best, Santo," Hannigan said.

Later that night, Hannigan was telling Babs and Hunter about his encounter with the mob boss.

"He was polite. He was a gentleman of the first order. He called me Slane. That's more than I can say for you."

"He's a gangster, Hannigan," Babs said. "Plain and simple. And a killer."

"Babs is right," Hunter said. "You shouldn't have taken the money. There are strings attached. There always are."

"Listen. His two business associates came and got me and—"

"You mean his two thugs," Babs said, interrupting him. "I saw them, remember? I was right there. They didn't ask; they told."

Ignoring the interruption, he continued. "I was back in two hours, like he said. He paid me for my time. Five hundred smackers! You can't beat that, no sirree. And he apologized several times on top of that! Santo isn't such a bad guy."

"Listen to him, Ash," Babs said. "He's calling him Santo!"

"We're on a first-name basis, him and me."

"Yeah, I wonder if he'd call you Slane," Babs said, "just before he plugs you full of holes."

"You're cynical, my dear wife. How'd you get that way?"

"You should listen to your dear wife, Slane," Hunter said. "Your friendship with a mobster can't have a happy ending."

"You always take her side. You two are always ganging up on me."

Just then, the phone rang.

"Paradise Inn," Hannigan said into the receiver, "where your friends stay and all your kin."

Babs rolled her eyes at him.

"Yep, he's right here. I'll put him on," Hannigan said before handing the receiver to Hunter.

"Ash Hunter. Yes, hello, Val. Yes, good." Hunter listened for a minute and then said, "Let me get a pen out." He jotted down something on a notepad and then said, "Thanks, Val. I owe you." He paused for a moment to listen and then said, "No, not twenty-five percent. We settled on twenty, and that was if I find the jewels. Yes, yes. Okay." He hung up.

Babs looked at Hunter. "You have a lead on the jewels?"

"Got to go. I'll fill you in later."

He went into the back room, opened the safe, and took out the .45 semiautomatic. He dropped the magazine, checked to make certain it was full, and then slammed it back in. He closed the safe and spun the dial.

"Don't wait on supper for me," he said to Hannigan and Babs.

With that, he was out the door.

Babs looked at Hannigan. "The cowboy took his gun."

"Yeah," Hannigan said reflectively. "I hope he's not going to the OK Corral. You know what happened to those boys, eh?"

Hunter stood behind a huge tree on San Isidro, looking across the street at a ground-floor apartment. It was at the corner of Avenida de Belgica, near the Old City Wall. The fence, Valentino Valenzuela, had come through for him. He had located an Argentinian with the name of Santiago Delgado. Hunter knew this might be his last opportunity to find the jewels and bring some justice to Navarro. Hannigan had been wrong; Hunter wasn't looking for revenge, at least he didn't think so. Justice was what he sought. But there was a slippery slope.

He'd been standing there for nearly an hour, watching the windows for a sign that someone was there. The lights were on, but so far, he couldn't see anyone inside. He was prepared to stay there as long as it took. How many Argentinians with that name were there in Havana? He didn't know, but there couldn't have been many.

Maybe there was just one.

Suddenly, the lights went out, and someone came through the door—a man about Hunter's size. The area wasn't well lit, so he could only see the man's silhouette. The man walked up San Isidro and turned right onto Picota. Hunter followed him from the other side of the street. The man continued on Picota for half a block and then went into a shop.

Hunter waited across the street, hiding in the shadows. A few minutes later, the man came out of the shop and continued down Picota. At the end of the street, he turned right again, onto Belgica, and continued straight until he got to San Isidro again. He had made a circuit. Hunter watched him enter his apartment. He crossed the street and hid behind the tree again. The light came on in the apartment.

Valenzuela's unexpected phone call had come so suddenly that Hunter hadn't had time to do much planning. How would he handle the situation? If Delgado had killed Navarro, then he was dangerous and would be capable of killing Hunter as well. Hunter was glad he had remembered to bring the .45.

He waited for a half hour, and nothing changed. The lights were still on, and once every so often, he could see the man inside. He decided to wait until Delgado went to bed and had been sleeping for a time before he did anything. Hunter had the element of surprise, and he had his gun. He would have the advantage.

Finally, after another hour, the lights went out. Delgado did not leave the apartment, so he must have gone to bed, Hunter figured. It was somewhat early to do so, but maybe the man was simply tired. It was going to be a long night, but to maintain the upper hand, Hunter needed to enter the apartment after Delgado was in a deep sleep. He was getting tired himself, so he sat down on the curb.

He waited for two hours and then got up, stretched, and made his move. He crossed the street and went to the door. He tried the knob, but it didn't budge. He took from his wallet the small tools he always carried with him and used them to unseat the lock. He fiddled with it for about thirty seconds, turned the knob, and then carefully eased the door open. The hinges squeaked, so he slowly pushed the door inch by inch to reduce the noise.

Once he was fully inside the apartment, he decided to leave the door open, fearing the noise would wake Delgado. It was pitch dark. He'd have to move slowly and carefully and grope in the blindness so he wouldn't bump into anything.

But that was all water under the bridge in a moment, because the light suddenly went on.

"I knew you'd be showing up," someone said in Spanish.

Hunter spun around and faced a man pointing a gun at him. He took a deep breath. The first thing that crossed his mind was that the fence, Valenzuela, had double-crossed him. It was unlikely, but he didn't have another explanation. Delgado had been waiting for him.

"Oh yeah? Did Valenzuela tell you I'd be here?"

"I don't know a Valenzuela." He switched to English. "You're American, no?"

"I'm American, yes."

"I see," he said. "CIA?"

That caught Hunter off guard. "What makes you think that?"

The phone on the table beside Delgado suddenly rang, and he jerked his head in that direction for just a second. That was all the time Hunter needed. Hunter leaped forward and rushed him like a football tackle, and both of them fell to the floor, with Hunter on top. Hunter struggled with him and got his gun, but Delgado threw him off and ran out the door.

Hunter, breathing heavily, got up with the gun and ran after him.

The Ball of Twine Unravels

"I tell you, the guy isn't as bad as he's made out to be," Hannigan said to Babs and Sammy. "Didn't I tell you that before? I did. I remember it."

"So says the man who's on a first-name basis with a killer," Babs said, smirking.

"Mr. Slane," Sammy said, "if I may take some liberty and freely speak—"

"Sammy, I've never muzzled you in the past, and I ain't about to start now. Speak freely. Take all the liberty you want. You're family."

"I think Mr. Trafficante is a criminal of the first order. He has a reputation for being a ruthless, dangerous man. He is not someone you want as a friend."

"You're right; I know." Hannigan gulped down some of his gin and tonic. "I didn't tell you this," he said, looking at Babs and then at Sammy, "but the guy who got knocked off, John Smith—well, that wasn't his name. His real name was Joseph Carbone. The police told me when they interviewed me." Hannigan had lied and told the police he was the only witness to the murder. He hadn't wanted Babs involved.

"John Smith wasn't his real name? Well, will wonders never cease?" Babs said, rolling her eyes.

"And he worked for—"

"Let me make a wild guess," Babs said. "He worked for your buddy, the one you're on a first-name basis with. What was his name, now? Oh yes, it's good old Santo, the one who was so polite and gracious to you. They must have had a falling out. Stealing money from your boss, if he happens to be a Mafia don, will do it every time."

"Anyway," Hannigan said, "he treated me with respect, even before I gave him the briefcase full of his cash."

They paused for a moment with their drinks, and then Babs said, "It's getting late. We should go to bed, but I'm worried about Ash. He left with the gun. I don't like it."

"Neither do I," Hannigan said. "Sammy, why don't you hit the sack? Babs and I will stay up. If we're up all night, you could take care of things in the morning."

"Okay," Sammy said. "I forgot to tell you that the Maddoxes checked out today, so there's a room free. It's clean; I did it myself. Good night to all."

After Sammy left, Babs said, "I had a bad feeling about the Maddoxes. They gave me the creeps. I'm glad they're gone."

"What about the girl who checked in Saturday night? How's she doing?"

"She hasn't left her room since she got here. Orders room service for her meals."

Hannigan thought for a moment about his conversation with Trafficante. "You know, Santo asked me about her by name. Wanted to know if I knew a Margot Reed. I said I didn't."

"You think she's mixed up with this mess somehow? She looked desperate when she came in."

"What I'm wondering is if she was involved with Shaw Armstrong in some way. That package looked just like the one I picked up for him—the one Armstrong had, the one Santo's looking for, the one that's missing and worth ten grand if I find it."

"Maybe we should—"

"Maybe we should go have a look-see, eh?"

They got up and went to the safe in the back room of the office. Hannigan knelt, spun the dial, and opened the safe. There was the package, nicely wrapped in brown paper and tied with twine. He took it out and set it on a desk. Babs used scissors to cut the twine, and Hannigan unwrapped it.

"Looks like a Chinese statue to me," Hannigan said. "White plaster and detailed designs, just like Santo said."

"What are we going to do?" Babs asked.

"It looks like Armstrong stole it, and somehow, the girl ended up with it."

"We can't go to Trafficante with it. He'll want to know how we got it. The girl will be in danger."

"Not only that, but he might figure we had something to do with the theft. He could have his thugs come around again and burn the Paradise down—or worse."

"We need to talk this through before we do anything. Those two men of Trafficante's scared the hell out of me. Remember what they did to John Smith?"

"Yeah, I'm remembering, Babs. I'm remembering right now."

Ash Hunter rushed out of the apartment and ran up San Isidro with Delgado's gun in his hand and his own in his belt, at the small of his back. No one else was on the street. It was dark, but he could still see Delgado running up the street. The man fell, and Hunter sprinted to catch up. He reached Delgado as he was getting up. Panting, Hunter grabbed him by the back of his shirt and stuck the barrel of the gun to his neck.

"We're going to walk back to your apartment now, nice and easy, and finish the conversation we were having," Hunter said in a low voice. "I won't have a problem using this gun if you take off again. I'll be damned if I'm gonna run after you a second time."

"Why don't you just shoot me now and save all the melodrama?"

"I like a little melodrama once in a while, Delgado. It spices up my life."

Delgado didn't resist. They walked the short distance to his apartment. Once they got there, Hunter closed the door and locked it.

"Sit down there," Hunter said, indicating a wooden chair.

Delgado did.

Hunter maintained a safe distance from him with the gun still in his right hand. "Now, tell me all about Ignacio Navarro."

Delgado looked up at Hunter and smirked. "Who?"

Hannigan and Babs stood outside Margot Reed's room. They could see light under the door.

"She's still up," Babs whispered.

"Let me do the talking, okay?"

"Fine, but ask her about the Maddoxes. I still think they're involved in something. Maybe she knows what."

Hannigan rapped on the door lightly with his knuckles. "Miss Reed? It's Hannigan, the manager."

"Yes?" Her voice was faint.

"I'm just checking to make sure you're all right."

"I'm fine, thank you."

"Could you open the door? I'd like to talk to you for just a moment. It'll take just a second or two."

The door swung inward, and Margot stepped back to allow them in. Babs closed the door behind them.

"We're glad you're fine, Miss Reed," Hannigan said. "You didn't look at all well when you checked in."

"Thank you for asking. I wasn't—you know, the storm and all. But I'm good now."

"Well, we're happy about that." He paused for a moment, trying to decide how to broach the subject. "Uh, would you mind if we asked you something?"

Margot looked a little nervous and asked, "About what?"

"Mind if we sit down a bit? It's been a long day. Sorry we're here so late."

Hannigan and Babs sat on the only two chairs in the room; Margot sat on the edge of the bed.

"That's okay. I slept most of the day and was up reading when you knocked."

"Well, we were wondering. I mean, you see, we had a couple of guests here—Americans. They're gone now. We thought you might know them: the Maddoxes."

Margot shot up from the bed, and Hannigan and Babs drew back, thinking she was going to attack them.

"Maddox! You mean Elizabeth and Bradford?"

"That's right," Hannigan said. "You know them?"

She paced the small room once and then stopped and swung her head around. "Did they ask about me?"

"No, they didn't."

She sat down on the bed again with her head down and her hands folded on her lap. Tears welled up in her eyes.

"Do you want to talk about it?" Babs asked.

They waited for her to respond, and when she didn't, Hannigan spoke.

"I have something to confess. The package you had me put in the safe—we opened it. We thought you might be in some kind of trouble. We know about the Chinese statue."

At that, Margot moaned and started crying, covering her face with her hands.

Babs went over and sat down next to her, putting an arm around her shoulders and pulling her close until her head rested on Babs's shoulder. Margot didn't resist.

Hannigan and Babs remained silent for the next few minutes. Gradually, Margot's crying became sobs, and after a minute more, the sobbing ceased too.

"Why don't you tell us about it, Margot?" Hannigan said, speaking more tenderly than intended. "It could help a girl unburden herself. Besides, we might be able to help."

Margot slowly pulled herself away from Babs, glanced over at Hannigan, and then turned to Babs. "It's a long story and dreadful. I'm not sure anyone can help. And I don't want to involve either of you." For a moment, it looked as if the floodgates were going to open up again.

"I think we're involved already," Hannigan said. "Just let it out, and you'll feel better."

Margot sighed deeply. She stared at her hands on her lap and sighed a second time. Then she looked up at Hannigan. "Elizabeth Maddox is my mother, and Bradford is my stepfather. I had no idea they were in Havana, but now it makes sense. My mother killed my father for his insurance money and then married Bradford Maddox. I was seeing my boyfriend at the time. They didn't know him at all then, because I never introduced him, but he was the insurance investigator who had the case. Shaw and I talked about it and—"

"Shaw?" Hannigan said.

"Shaw Armstrong, my boyfriend. Anyway, he and I talked about it. He was convinced my mother had killed my father. He broke into my mother's house one night while she was gone and found a gun that had recently been fired. He took it and had it tested, and the gun was a match to the bullets that had killed my father. After that, we decided to blackmail my mother to punish her. Shaw demanded she give him money every three months. At that time, he was also working for a gangster in Tampa."

"Santo Trafficante?" Hannigan asked.

206

"Yes. You know him?"

"Go on."

"Shaw decided to work for him full-time in Havana, and I went with him. So he had my mother send the money to a post office box. When Shaw was murdered, I thought Santo had had his men do it because he'd stolen the real statue from him. Shaw had a duplicate made and gave it to Santo. Now, because you said my mother and Bradford were here, I think maybe they're the ones who killed Shaw. My mother is quite capable of that."

"Do the Maddoxes know you're here?"

"No. I've had no contact with them since I found out my mother killed my father. They have no idea I even know Shaw—I mean knew him."

"Listen, Margot," Hannigan said, "I don't want you getting all emotional on me again, but I don't think you're safe. That statue belongs to Trafficante, and he wants it back. His men are out looking for it, and they'll do anything to get it back, if you catch my drift."

"You're saying you think Santo would harm me? I thought so too at first, but after thinking about it, I realize that's not possible. He was our neighbor back in Tampa. I grew up next door to him. I babysat his two daughters when they were young, and I watched his little dog, Chuckles. He treated me like his own daughter. He wouldn't be capable of harming me."

Hannigan and Babs looked at each other in amazement.

Although Hannigan thought Trafficante wasn't such a bad guy, he knew down deep how mobsters worked. They'd kill their closest friends if the matter involved money.

"Just the same," he said, "it wouldn't be a bad idea to take some precautions. We could help you with that, but you'd have to cooperate. Whaddaya think?"

"Well, if you think it's necessary."

"I do. I want you to stay put while we come up with something. Okay?"

"Okay."

207

Hannigan and Babs left Margot in good spirits, went out to the lounge, and sat in the Adirondack chairs.

"I don't care what the girl says," Hannigan said. "She's dead meat if Trafficante finds out she has the statue."

"I thought he was Santo to you. I thought he was your new best friend."

"This isn't the time for cracking wise, Babs. The girl's life is at stake. We gotta come up with something."

"Yeah, something that isn't going to dig a grave for you and me."

"Well, there's that too!"

"What do you have in mind?"

"Trafficante's boys are probably staking out the airport and cruise ships. They know Armstrong was seeing the girl; otherwise, why would Trafficante have asked me about her?" He hit the palm of his hand to his forehead. "Dammit, I shouldn't have lied to him. Now we have to cover my tracks. We've got the girl, and we've got the statue. We're involved right up to our necks."

"I know, and we're sinking in quicksand and need someone to throw us a rope."

"And I think I have just the rope."

"Is it a strong one, Hannigan? We need a strong one."

"I think it'll be strong enough. Here's what we'll do. Feel free to kibitz if you want to."

"When have you known me not to kibitz if I wanted to?"

"We have the girl. She came here at night, during the storm. She hasn't been out of her room since. So no one knows she's here but us."

"Go on. So far so good."

"We need to change her appearance—like you did with Maria Sanchez. You're good at that."

"Cut her hair, dye it another color, and get her different clothes. I'm following you."

"A little change, and you have a new person. She can't stay holed up in her room all the time; she'll go batty. We'll put her to work. Give her a uniform and let her clean the rooms."

"You're forgetting one little detail, Hannigan."

"What's that?"

"Margot doesn't believe she's in any danger. Maybe she won't go for it."

"I'll make her believe. She knows Trafficante only as her kind next-door neighbor who treated her like his daughter. He had me fooled too until you talked sense into me. I'll talk sense into her too."

"Did he treat you like his daughter?"

"Don't jerk my chain, Babs. Not now. Do you think it'll work? Just give me a yes or no."

"When have you known me to give you a one-word answer, darling?" she said, drawing out the last word.

"Yes or no?"

"Yes, but she's the one you've got to convince, not me."

"I'll do just that!"

"What about the statue? What are we going to do with that?"

"I'm going to bury the damn thing in the back. If I'd listened to you about Harry Smith in the first place, we wouldn't be in this mess now."

Babs didn't say anything right away. Instead, she took some time to reflect. Finally, she looked her husband in the eye. "No comment," she said.

25

The Interrogation of Santiago Delgado

"Ignacio Navarro," Hunter said, repeating the name slowly and deliberately.

It had been a long day. He was tired and wanted nothing more than to return to the Paradise, have a stiff drink, and turn in for the night. That would have to wait. He raised his arm and pointed the gun at Delgado. "I'd just as soon pull the trigger than say the name again."

"You're CIA, so you tell me who he is," Santiago Delgado said.

Hunter could see hatred in the man's eyes. Why would Delgado think Hunter was with the CIA? It didn't make sense.

"I don't know who you think I am, but I'm really a decent guy. And because I am, I'll make this easy for you. I'll just take you to the police and let them interrogate you. They always have something in their bag of tricks to make people talk. Pliers, scalpels—those sorts of things."

Delgado wasn't easily intimidated. He seemed self-assured, if not arrogant. "What am I supposed to have done? I broke no laws."

"I'm sure it says somewhere in the Cuban statutes that stealing and murder are serious crimes. You're going away for a very long time." He paused for a moment and then added, "But then again, maybe they'll give you a break and put you in front of a firing squad."

Delgado looked both surprised and confused. His foundation seemed to be crumbling but only slightly. "I don't understand. You think I stole something from this Navarro and then killed him? What proof do you have that I did those things? Even in Cuba, you need evidence for a conviction, or am I mistaken about that?"

"The last thing out of Navarro's mouth before he died was the name Santiago Delgado. Three witnesses, including myself, will testify in court that we heard him say your name."

Delgado stared at Hunter, but the hatred in his eyes dissipated, replaced by resignation. "Who are you, if not CIA? What's your connection to Ignacio Navarro?"

Hunter debated whether to answer him. He didn't want Delgado to get the upper hand and turn the interrogation on its head. But fatigue was getting the best of him. He decided to tell him the truth and see where that led. He didn't have much more energy for anything else.

"Someone hired me to find the jewels you stole from him. Why did you poison him? Let me guess: because he knew it was you." Hunter wondered why Navarro hadn't told him about Delgado from the beginning during their interview.

Delgado lowered his head and stared at the floor like a guilty man with a noose being placed around his neck. Hunter had his man. He would take Delgado to the authorities and let them deal with him. Before he did that, however, he'd have to think of a story to tell them about why he was involved in this situation in the first place. He couldn't tell them he was a private investigator hired by the Tropicana to find the stolen jewels. They'd ask him to show them his license. One step at a time, though. He'd try one last thing

211

with Delgado; he wanted the jewels first, and then he'd take them to Gomez at the Tropicana, out of reach of the hands of the police.

"If you give me the jewels, I'll release you." That was a lie, of course, but Hunter had to use everything in his own bag of tricks. "I'll forget about taking you to the police."

Delgado remained silent, staring at the floor. Hunter decided to give him a few minutes to think about it.

One minute went by. Then two and then three.

"Okay, get up. Let's go," Hunter said.

"Ignacio was my brother-in-law and a dear friend. He was family."

The statement came so suddenly and unexpectedly that Hunter was stunned, as if he'd been hit flush on the jaw by Marciano's right fist. *Brother-in-law, dear friend, and family? What is he saying?* He kept his distance from Delgado but lowered his gun. Was he telling the truth? Hunter wiped the sweat from his face with his free hand, leery of being manipulated.

"You're going to have to say something more to convince me. If I sense a hint of a lie, it's over, and we go to the police." Hunter sat down, maintaining his distance in case Delgado tried to rush him. "Start talking."

Delgado raised his head and looked at Hunter. He ran his tongue over his lips. "Are you familiar with Argentina—the politics, I mean?"

"A little. What's that got to do with it?"

"A year and a half ago, there was a military coup."

"That much I know. Go on."

"That was when General Eduardo Lonardi came to power. A few months later, General Pedro Eugenio Aramburu overthrew him, and Argentina descended into hell. But instead of hell, they called it the Revolución Libertadora. The military government rounded up all who were loyal to Juan Perón—all of the Peronists. They either killed them or put them in prison. But some escaped and are now living abroad. My wife, Ignacio's sister, was murdered during the coup, as well as my two children."

"What were their names?" Hunter asked, snapping his fingers. "Quick!"

"Alejandra was my wife; Sophie and Juan Pablo were my children." He paused briefly. "You want the dates of their birth? I wish I were lying to you. I wish they were still alive."

"Go on."

"There was nothing we could do, so Ignacio and I fled to Spain, where Perón himself was staying. I didn't stay long. I came here to Cuba to organize an armed struggle to overthrow the Aramburu government. Ignacio came here recently to talk me into going to America with him."

"Why?"

"Because he thought we could get more resources there and have more support for the cause. He felt we'd be safer."

"Go on. What about the jewels?"

"The government, from the onset, started to eliminate all traces of Peronism. They sent their secret service agents overseas— especially to Spain, because that was where most of them had fled— to assassinate anyone they found and to take anything associated with Perón. Understand that in Argentina, you can be arrested for just having a picture of Perón or his wife, Evita. Or even for just speaking their names." He stopped talking and ran his tongue across his lips again. "I need some water. My mouth is dry."

"Get up, and get some, but be careful." Hunter lifted the gun so Delgado could see it.

Delgado got some water from the tap and drank two glasses full. He then sat down again and continued. "The agents came looking for Ignacio in Madrid. We had no idea how they knew he was there, but they belonged to the Secretaría de Inteligencia, which works with the CIA, so they have long arms. They knew he had been Eva Perón's secretary and that he had inherited some of her jewels. They wanted Ignacio, and they wanted the jewels. After the coup, the bastards even stole Eva's body. No one knows where it's at.

"The agents followed Ignacio here to Havana, hoping to first find the jewels. After they stole them, they then poisoned Ignacio. I am sure of that. When I saw you staking out my apartment, I thought you were one of the agents, looking for me. I knew Ignacio was dead; I thought I was going to be next. When you came into my apartment just now and I heard you speak, I then thought you were CIA, assisting the agents. Your Spanish is good, but you speak with an American accent. I too worked in the Perón government but at a much lower level than Ignacio."

The story sounded reasonable to Hunter; the pieces fit together. Delgado knew too much to be winging it. However, what he had just told Hunter could have been devised ahead of time as a cover story for one of the agents in case he found himself in just this position, but Hunter doubted it. Besides, Navarro had said the name Santiago Delgado; it was unlikely he had known the name of one of the agents following him.

Hunter decided to trust him. "What are you going to do now?" he asked.

"I will stay here and organize, just as I have been doing. My family has been murdered; Ignacio's gone. I have nothing left— except revenge."

"Those two agents—they could still be looking for you."

"Anything is possible, but they have the jewels, and they killed Ignacio. That's why they were here. I'm a small catch. Besides, I really don't think they know I'm here. As far as the military government is concerned, I'm still in Spain. If they did know, I wouldn't be talking to you now; I'd be dead myself. No, they're probably gone now, back to Argentina."

Hunter felt pity for the man. His losing his family under those conditions made Hunter's problems seem small by comparison. The only decent thing to do was to let him go. Yet there was a chance that Delgado was lying to him and that Delgado himself was one of the agents sent to hunt down Navarro. Intelligence operatives of all nations were experts at deception and misdirection, which had been practiced by humans since they first walked the earth. Hunter himself functioned as an investigator by using his brain rather than his heart—but his heart was telling him that Delgado was telling the truth. Yes, the only decent thing he could do now was let him go.

Hunter crossed Avenida de Belgica and went to the remnants of Havana's seventeenth-century fortified city wall. Under the direction of the Spanish crown, African slaves had labored for twenty-three years to construct the wall as protection from British artillery and from English and French pirates. Over the years, it had been damaged and rebuilt many times. As the city had grown beyond the wall, the colonial government had ordered its destruction, and 123 years after the wall had gone up, it had come down. African slave convicts had demolished what their forefathers had built. Now only traces of the wall existed. Hunter sat down on the edge of a crumbling stone and felt the presence of ghosts.

It was relatively dark, with a waxing crescent moon above. Hunter gazed upward. He wasn't superstitious, but ever since he was a kid, he'd enjoyed entertaining himself with the zodiac and how the moon moved through the heavens. He had memorized the signs and what they meant, and in a certain way, he felt he was guided by them. The moon sign that night—and for the last two nights—was Pisces. What did that mean for Hunter, who'd been born under that sign? He remembered descriptions he'd read in the past.

Pisces are friendly by nature, so they often find themselves in the company of different people. They are selfless and always willing to help others without hoping to get anything in return. A Pisces is characterized by empathy and compassion.

Hunter was conflicted. Those characteristics were supposed to be his strengths. They might have been fine for most people, but in his work as a private investigator, they could lead him into trouble. It was true that he always had the desire to help people out of deplorable situations. Maria Sanchez had been one of them. He had helped her escape from her crazed husband. But he had had only Maria's word to go on. Yes, there had been marks on her body to substantiate her abuse, but could they have been inflicted by other means? He hadn't bothered to find out. Instead, he had taken her word for it.

Now there was Santiago Delgado.

He had listened to his story and empathized with him, and compassion had led Hunter to release the man instead of taking him to the police, who most surely would have tortured him for a confession. Had he ignored his gut feelings and freed the killer of Navarro? He would never know.

Hunter remembered the weaknesses of Pisces. *They're overly trusting. Prone to depression. Possess a desire to escape reality. Might become a victim or a martyr for a cause.*

Hunter had fought with depression, a side effect of the war, ever since Italy. Maybe that was the real reason he had never sought out a permanent relationship with a woman, excluding Angie, preferring instead to go from one woman to the next. He didn't want to inflict his malady on someone else. It was his way to escape reality. Trusting someone fully had always brought on a certain amount of depression, for which he usually sought the bottle for a remedy. But he never thought himself a victim of anything. He always explored consequences before he acted.

Or did he? Now, with Delgado, he didn't know. Compassion was certainly good, but it was a difficult thing to harness.

He looked up at the crescent moon a second time and wondered about his life. Maybe he was too trusting to be an investigator. Maybe he should do something else; he was still young enough. Making chairs for a living wasn't a bad idea—good-quality ones with fancy inlay work. He already had the skills; he'd just have to refine them somewhat.

"Hey, amigo! You got a few pesos for an old man?"

Hunter looked over his shoulder and saw a man wearing tattered clothes and a straw hat. He looked to be in his sixties. In the dim light, Hunter could see that the man's black face was full of deep creases. His hands were large, calloused and hard from manual labor. His sandals were rubber and homemade. Could he have been an ancestor of one of the slaves who built or destroyed the wall, a piece of which Hunter was now sitting on, the only reminder? Perhaps the old man himself was one of the ghosts the local people claimed haunted the area on which the wall once stood, looking for some sort of justice for the inequities committed against him.

Hunter reached into his pocket and gave him all the change he had.

"Jesus will be kind to you, mi amigo," the old man said. "You will find what you seek. Muchas gracias."

Then he disappeared as fast as he'd come.

26

All Hell Broke Loose

The next morning, Ash Hunter was up earlier than usual. He hadn't slept well, tossing and turning for most of the night. He passed Babs at the front desk without stopping. He groaned something that sounded like either a greeting to her or a warning to the universe that he wasn't quite ready yet for whatever it was going to throw at him that day. Babs lifted a hand without looking up and fluttered her fingers at him, continuing to work without skipping a beat. Hunter grabbed a cup of coffee at the beverage nook and sat down at one of the tables.

He filled his pipe and lit up, feeling out of sorts, and then sipped his coffee. It was hot and strong. Santiago Delgado was still on his mind—the lost opportunity. He'd failed to find Navarro's killer, and he'd failed to find the Perón jewels. He hated failure about as much as the average schmuck did. As a kid in Saint Paul, he'd brooded for days whenever he failed to accomplish something. It was no different now, in spite of the fact that finding either one had been a long shot. He puffed on his pipe and gulped down more coffee. Failure was part of life, but he didn't like it. Maybe he'd have to consult the resident philosopher at the Paradise Inn and get some cheap advice.

He heard the phone ring at the front desk, and a few seconds later, he heard Babs's voice.

"Ash! You've got a call. The man says it's urgent."

Hunter got up and went to the front desk. He picked up the receiver off the counter. "Hunter here."

"It's Val. Can you speak freely?"

"Yeah, go ahead. What's up?"

"What's up? I'll tell you what's up. Two men showed up at my shop this morning. I'm not even open yet, but I let them in. They got my name by asking around town. They wanted to know if I was interested in buying some jewels. They described what they had, and they most definitely are the jewels you're looking for. They said they're worth over a million dollars. They want two hundred thousand in cash for them in US dollars."

Hunter was floored.

"Are you there, Ashton?"

"Yeah, I'm here. What did you tell them?"

"I told them to meet me back here after I close tonight at nine o'clock. I said I'd assess the jewels first and would have the cash ready for them, if I decided to buy. Did I do good?"

"You did good, Val. I'll be there at eight."

"Ashton?"

"What?"

"The two men. They looked very mean—dangerous. I don't keep guns here."

"I can look mean too, Val. You ever see me look mean?"

"No, Ashton. Never."

"It ain't a pretty sight." He put the receiver down on the cradle, walked past Babs, and went to the safe in the back room.

Babs looked over her shoulder at him. "The gun again? Jeez, this feels more and more like the Wild West."

219

Later that night, Hunter took a taxi to Miramar, to the Hotel Comodoro. He walked in and went directly to the Hollywood Jewelers. Valenzuela was at the counter, waiting for him. It was precisely eight o'clock. Valentino and Hunter went into the back room.

"I sent Alicia home," Valenzuela said, "so we can talk freely."

Hunter thought his friend looked a bit nervous, but that was to be expected. "Don't be upset, Val. I'll take care of the whole thing."

"I am not upset, but I am very concerned about my involvement."

"Listen, you're getting twenty percent of what I get."

"I understand that, Ashton, yes. But I had something else in mind. These men—if they escape, they will come after me. And you. You yourself said that you cannot take them to the police, because you don't have enough evidence that they poisoned—what was the man's name?"

"Navarro."

"Yes, Navarro," he said, crossing himself. "And you do not wish to tell them about the jewels, because they might decide to keep them themselves and say they were stolen from the police station. So there is no motive for these men to kill Navarro, and there is no evidence of them stealing anything." He stopped for a moment to collect his thoughts. "If you take the jewels from the men at gunpoint—did you bring your gun?"

"Of course."

"If you take the jewels from the men at gunpoint and let them go, surely they will come after us."

Valenzuela was right. Hunter hadn't thought this through. In theory, he wouldn't have minded shooting the two Argentinians and then burying the bodies. But he wasn't a killer. As an alternative, he could wait until the two men drew their guns and then shoot them both dead. But this wasn't the Wild West, in spite of what Babs thought, and besides, it would still be premediated murder. Hunter faced a dilemma.

"I see on your face that you are at a crossroads, not unlike the ancient Greeks, not knowing which direction to go," Valenzuela said. "Do you go left? Do you go right? Which road will successfully lead you toward your goal? Most people face such roads once in their lifetime; some do many times. The choices they have to make are not always fair and can lead one to despair. Oftentimes—"

"Val! Do you have an idea?"

"I was just leading up to that. After I talked to you this morning, I did some research. That is the key to life: to do your research. I then contacted some people I know."

"If you have a plan, just tell me, please." Hunter had never known another person who could take so long to make a point. *Circuitous* should be his middle name.

"I have, and it's this. These two men are very bad. You Americans have an expression: bad apples. We have a metaphor too, but we do not use apples. I won't go into that right now, but it is quite interesting. I'll share that with you another time. Anyway, I did my research and discovered that these bad apples are agents of the Argentine government."

"Yes, I know that."

"You did? Then you know they are killers. Navarro"—he crossed himself again—"wasn't the first man they killed, and if we let them go, he won't be the last. Professional killers—that is what they are. In Argentina, they make people who are against the government disappear. These people are called *los desaparecidos*. Just like that, they're gone!" He snapped his fingers. "I know people here in Havana who do the same thing—make people disappear. And their fees are most reasonable. I will pay them myself, but you may contribute if you so desire."

Hunter didn't like what he was hearing, but he told Valenzuela to continue.

"I took the opportunity to enlist their services. They are here now, waiting outside in the shadows. You don't have to do a thing. Five minutes after the two Argentinians come in, they will enter as if it were a robbery. But they will put hoods over the heads of these two bad apples and take them away. They will disappear Cuban-style. Out the back door. Our problems will be solved." After a moment, he added, "Their fees are definitely within my budget."

Hunter was tired of thinking about it. He didn't like Valenzuela's plan, but he didn't have a better one to offer. He didn't look forward to looking over his shoulder for the next week or month, and he certainly didn't like the idea of putting Valenzuela in harm's way if he allowed the Argentinians to walk away. The plan was already in motion; he wasn't going to stop it.

"Let's do it," Hunter said.

"It's almost nine now. Stay here in the back. I will go out to the showroom."

Hunter peeked through the curtains and had a clear view. He looked at his watch. It was five minutes after nine. The front door opened, and two men walked in; one was thin, one was much larger, and both had mustaches. They fit the description.

"Gentlemen! Good evening to both of you," Valenzuela said. "I trust you brought the jewels with you for my assessment."

The larger of the two men opened a wooden box and set it on the counter. Valenzuela picked up one of the earrings, leaned over, put a handheld 4.2-inch ×20 magnifying loupe to his eye, and examined the diamonds. After about two minutes, he raised his head.

"Excellent, gentlemen. Excellent! We can most surely do business. Let me examine the rest first."

Then the front door burst open, and all hell broke loose.

27

The New Client

The sun had peered over the horizon several hours earlier, sending rays of light fanning outward like long shards of glimmering glass being thrust forth by some Mephistophelian beast that sought to make war or to collect the souls of the damned; it didn't much matter. Already the day was a scorcher, and one could have sliced through the humidity with a steak knife. Things moved slowly in Havana, especially people. And why not? What was the rush? Rushing only wore a person out, and then what damn use was he or she to anyone?

Hannigan and Babs were in the café, having their morning coffee with Hunter before the breakfast rush began, filling him in on Margot Reed and the statue. When they finished, Hannigan brought up a serious issue that needed to be dealt with. The air conditioner hummed away as Hannigan narrowed his eyes at Hunter.

"We stayed up, Ash," Hannigan said. "Stayed up until we couldn't keep our doggone eyes open any longer." He hoped Babs would keep the rhythm flowing to see how much guilt they could levy on their friend.

She did. "Stayed up until three twenty-two in the morning," she said. "Three twenty-two is late even by Cuban standards."

"Stayed up because we were worried about you. Stayed up because you left here with a loaded gun in your paw and didn't tell us where you were going." Hannigan raised his voice one octave higher. "Stayed up because you were too much of a nitwit to pick up a phone and call us to let us know you were all right!"

There was a pause while Babs decided if there was anything else she could sling at Hunter. Having decided in the affirmative, she let loose.

"Stayed up until we heard the little birdies chirping outside in the trees," she finally said.

"I should have called. I know," Hunter said with his hands up shoulder high, palms outward, in unconditional surrender. "Sorry— won't happen again."

"So cough it up, man," Hannigan said. "Speak to us! What was so damn important that required a forty-five-caliber semiautomatic?"

Hunter explained to them what had happened on Monday night with Santiago Delgado, leaving no details out. When he finished, he downed the rest of his coffee.

"So the jewels are gone," Hannigan said, dejected. "Gone for good."

"And gone is the ten percent cut for finding them," Babs added.

"I'm not done," Hunter said. "There's more." He got up for more coffee. When he sat down again, he filled his pipe and lit it. Looking at the bowl, he tamped the ash down and then relit the pipe. He puffed on it a few times, and after that, he sipped his coffee.

"You planning on telling us the rest sometime this year?" Hannigan asked.

"We need to know so we can schedule it in," Babs added.

Hunter chuckled and blew smoke up into the air. He finally told them what had happened the night before with the two Argentinians at Hollywood Jewelers. "It wouldn't have happened without Valentino."

"So where are the jewels?" Babs asked. "I'm dying to see them!"

"I didn't want to walk around with a million dollars' worth of jewels, so I brought them to Gomez at the Tropicana. He was happy to see me, to say the least. We'll work out the details later, but we're going to be rolling in money, minus the twenty percent cut for Val. I stayed on to play a little blackjack and won fifty bucks. That's why I was so late."

Hannigan and Babs praised Hunter and slapped him on the back several times. Hannigan knew Hunter didn't like attention drawn to himself. *He'll change the subject*, Hannigan thought.

Sure enough, after the third slap on the back, Hunter asked them how Margot Reed was doing, diverting their adulation from him.

"Babs gave her a makeover—dyed and cut her hair and told her to put on a uniform. We put her to work cleaning rooms. You might not recognize her. She should be fine and dandy if Trafficante's men come here looking for her."

The bell over the entrance sounded, and soon Sammy appeared in the café.

"Whaddaya doing here, Sammy?" Hannigan asked. "It's your day off. You should be out chasing women!"

"Oh, Mr. Slane, just this morning, one woman was chasing me!"

"And did she catch you, Sammy?" Babs asked. "We'd like all the gory details, if you don't mind."

"Yes, she did, Miss Babs!" He went on to tell them about his old girlfriend back in Port-au-Prince.

Ten years before, Sammy had left Haiti for Havana for adventure and to find work, but he also had left because the woman he had been having a serious relationship with left him for another man. The man hadn't been rich by any means, but he'd been older, had a government job, been stable, and owned his own house. He'd died from malaria recently, leaving the woman a widow. Having no children, she'd decided to go to Havana to seek employment because the economy was better there than in Port-au-Prince. To their surprise, she and Sammy had met each other that morning in a park nearby, where he took his morning walks three or four times a week.

"I came back to change my clothes and spiffy up; we are going to spend the day together. I will show her the sights of Havana and maybe help her find some work. I am very happy today—very happy indeed!"

"Love and romance rekindled in the tropics!" Babs said. "What more could a body want?"

"Be sure to bring her back here, Sammy, when she gets settled in," Hannigan said. "We'll treat the lovely couple to the best chow in Havana!"

"He means the best dining in Havana," Babs said, "but you get the point."

"I don't know if we are a couple yet, but I can always hope!"

"We'll hope with you, Sammy," Babs said. "Spiffy away!"

A few minutes later, the bell over the entrance rang again. Babs got up and walked to the lobby. Maybe someone was looking for a room. They had one available as of that morning. A few seconds later, Babs peeked her head into the café.

"You're being summoned, Mr. Ashton Hunter!" she said.

Hunter rose from his chair and went into the lobby. Babs introduced him to the woman who was doing the summoning. She was a long-legged blonde, possibly in her early thirties, dressed as if she were going out nightclubbing for the evening. She was possibly the most gorgeous woman south of Key West. Babs hated her.

"I'm Julie Manning, Mr. Hunter," she said. "I'd like to hire you."

Hunter invited her into the café, and they took a seat at the far end, where the view of the Malecón was the best.

"Would you like something to drink, Miss Manning?"

"It's missus, and no, I'm fine. Please call me Julie."

Hunter was suspicious whenever a complete stranger sought out his services. "How'd you get my name, if I can ask?"

"You can ask." She paused. "But I guess you just did. A little mouse told me."

"Does this little mouse have a name?"

"I suppose he does, but he never told me." She grinned a long grin. Her lips were painted red, and she had a porcelain complexion. Her blue eyes were spaced apart at the right distance. Her nose was thin but not too thin.

Hunter stared at her for a moment. Everything in his brain told him to get up and show the lady the door. *Find an investigator to hire. The little mouse was wrong; I'm not in the business. I'm not an investigator.* But at the moment, his brain wasn't working properly. It was overshadowed by his hormones. He decided the little mouse wasn't worth pursuing.

"How can I help you?" he said.

"Maybe a little coffee isn't such a bad idea after all."

Hunter excused himself, got two cups of coffee, and returned to the blonde.

"As I said, I want to hire you." She paused for a moment to sip her coffee. "I'm from Miami. My husband is a businessman and comes to Havana often on business. I want you to find out whether it's just business he's after and not something else."

"You think he's having an affair?"

"The idea has crossed my mind."

He took out his notebook, opened it to a clean page, and took out a pen. For a second, he wondered why any husband would cheat on his wife when the wife was a veritable blonde bombshell. Husbands did—he knew that for certain—but he could never figure out why. Often, the other woman wasn't nearly as good looking as the wife the man was cheating on. But it happened all the time, and because it did, it kept Hunter in business.

"His name?" Hunter asked, looking at her sympathetically.

"Crawford Manning. He's an executive at a major Miami import-export liquor distributor."

"Do you have a picture of him?"

"I thought you might want one, so I brought it with me." She reached into her pursue and gave him a five-by-three.

Hunter looked it over. It showed a clear shot of his face and body. He looked to be twenty years older than his wife. Usually, when older men cheated on their wives, they did so with younger women. That didn't seem to be the case with the Mannings, unless he was simply bored and wanted some spiced-up tropical excitement he wasn't getting at home—a little change in the routine. Anything was possible.

"What makes you think he's having an affair?"

"He travels a lot worldwide. Several times, when he was supposed to be in Europe, I called his hotel in Havana—he always stays in the same one—and the front desk man said he had checked in. If he's having an affair, I want to know about it, and I want the evidence."

"Yes, of course, Mrs. Manning."

"Please, just Julie."

"I assume Mr. Manning is in town now."

"Yes, at the Hotel Nacional."

"And where are you staying, so I know where to get a hold of you?"

"The Hilton. Room 301."

"Tell me a little about your husband. I'd like an idea of what to expect. Does he frequent nightclubs? Does he like to gamble? Play the horses? Those sorts of things."

"Actually, Ashton—"

"Just Ash is fine."

"Actually, Ash, my husband is quite boring. Do you know what he finds exciting?"

"No."

"Of course not. How could you? For one thing, he likes stamp collecting. He spends a fortune on his little hobby. Every time he goes abroad, he brings home a box full of new stamps. He goes into his office, and I don't see him for a week. He wants to have stamps from every damn country in the world. That's what excites him. Do you know what else he likes?"

"No."

"He likes playing horseshoes with his buddies. He says he finds it relaxing, as if he needed anything more to relax him."

"What else does he do in his spare time?"

"You mean besides watching *The Ed Sullivan Show* and *Gunsmoke*? Not a lot. He's what is known as a homebody. He says the traveling takes all the spunk out of him, as if he had any to begin with."

Hunter made a mental note of the cynicism in her voice and the resentment. "Do you have any children?"

"No, thank God."

"How long have you been married to him?"

"Two years. Why?"

"I just want to get a clear picture of your husband. Anything I know about him could help. Has he ever cheated on you before that you know of and that you've confronted him about?"

"No, not that I know of."

Hunter took a sip of his coffee and reflected for a moment. Then he said, "Frankly, Julie, he doesn't seem to be the kind of guy who'd cheat on his wife. Can you think of any other reason besides business he'd be in Havana for and not tell you?"

She seemed to take offense at the question. "Listen, just because he might not have cheated on me in the past doesn't mean he's not doing it now. I can't think of a single reason why he'd lie to me about being in Havana when he's supposed to be in London, Paris, or a dozen other cities in Europe. If you don't want to take this case, just tell me now, and I'll find someone who does."

A second opportunity. This was Hunter's way out. All he had to do was tell her to find someone else. It would be that simple. Instead, he looked into her big blues eyes.

"No, no, no. I'll take the case, Julie. I just wanted you to consider that your husband may have another reason for not telling you the truth. This is just a standard procedure I use with all my clients who think their husbands are cheating on them. I have to tell you—most of them are cheating. Wives seem to know when they are."

Julie Manning was reassured. She calmed down again. "Are you married, Ash?" she asked after sipping her coffee, looking over the rim of the cup at him, hiding most of her face except for her eyes.

"Almost once. But that was a long time ago."

She lowered the cup and stared at him for a long time with a straight face, until her lips spread and turned up at the corners.

Hunter didn't expect to spend too much time on her case. It was straightforward. He'd have to shadow the husband around town for a couple of days—maybe three. If Crawford Manning was cheating on Julie, he'd know by then. Manning wasn't traveling all the way to Havana without making the most of it, even if he had business to conduct in between the lovemaking sessions. In spite of everything, Hunter was confident the husband was hiding something. If it wasn't an affair, then it was something else. Now it was his job to find out what it was.

He gave Julie a flat fee of $300, plus expenses. She could afford it. He promised he'd be in touch with her in two days for an update.

"Thank you very much, Ash," she said. "I look forward to talking to you soon."

She paid him in cash and left.

Hannigan came over and sat down in her chair, which was still warm. "What was that all about? If I wasn't a happily married man, I'd go gaga over her."

Hunter told him she was a new client and gave him the bare details.

"Three hundred smackers!" Hannigan said. "Yes indeedy, the tourist season is starting off with a bang!"

It was, but at the moment, Hunter could think only of Julie Manning's nice little smile and big blue eyes.

Crawford Manning was a free man.

At least for the day. He had deliberately cleared his schedule so he'd have time to think this through. He had a major decision to make in his personal life, and by golly, this time he would make it. Enough with the subterfuge and the deliberate dishonesty. He couldn't take it any longer. This time, on this trip, right there in Havana, he would make the decision and let the chips fall where they may.

Crawford was a wealthy man, but he was dreadfully unhappy. He had been for most of his life. His parents had had oodles of money, so he'd grown up in Miami privileged, never in want. By the time he'd turned thirty, he and his business partner had owned a liquor distribution company, and he had gone through two marriages with women of the same standing. He'd vowed never to marry again, and for the next sixteen years, he hadn't. Until he had met Julie. They'd met at an exclusive country club he belonged to, and it had been love at first sight for him. Astonishingly, she'd shown interest in him as well. She'd been a new hire—a waitress twenty-two years his junior. But the age difference hadn't mattered one whit to either of them, and they'd struck up a relationship. With two failed marriages behind him and sixteen years of breathing space, Crawford had decided to give it another go. Three months after meeting, they'd married.

Crawford ordered another daiquiri at the bar of the Montmartre. He always came there whenever he was in town. There he could be free. He could drink and gamble all he wanted—although the truth was, he didn't do much of either; he just liked the idea that he could—and he greatly enjoyed the floor shows. Dorothy Lamour was on at nine. He'd stay to see the show, but it was still early, and he had something more important to do. He was meeting someone in a few hours—a rendezvous with someone special who always brought him joy and happiness in his otherwise empty life. Before that, he had to see a particular person who would cleanse him of his sins.

Again.

After two years of marriage to Julie, now forty-eight, Crawford was as miserable as ever. He had everything a man could want, including money and a beautiful young wife, but still, happiness eluded him, except when he came to Havana.

The bartender brought him the daiquiri. Crawford put the glass to his lips and held it there for a few seconds to savor the liquor before swallowing it.

He had discovered a new sensation of happiness there in Havana during the previous year, and it had been so powerful and life-changing that he couldn't ignore it. Soon he'd started taking more and more trips to Havana and lying about it to Julie. How could he tell her? How could she understand him? He was being deliberately disloyal to her. For all intents and purposes, he had a good marriage. However, he was, in fact, cheating on her. It had taken him quite some time to finally acknowledge that to himself. She'd be devastated if he ever brought up the subject.

He took a long swallow of his drink.

But this time, he would. The deception had gone on long enough. He was at a crossroads, and he knew it. This time, he would finally make the break. There was too much at stake. He wasn't getting any younger, and Julie would have her whole life ahead of her. The person of his dreams was right there in Havana—the person who brought him true happiness, the person he wanted to spend the rest of his life with, the person he made frequent trips to see and spend glorious nights making passionate love to. He would finally rid himself of guilt and deception once and for all and begin the remainder of his life with something he had never known before.

He looked at his watch, downed the rest of his drink, and left the Montmartre. He walked two blocks south and five blocks west to Saint Francis Church. He was going to confession, and for the last time, the priest would rid him of his sins.

El Encanto department store was open late that night. Hunter needed a couple of new shirts, and as he was passing by, he decided to buy them there. El Encanto was an upscale store. He usually bought his clothes at La Epoca or Woolworth's, but he decided to treat himself to something special.

The store was crowded with shoppers who looked more like models wearing fashionable clothes, both male and female. He made his way to the men's department. He felt out of place, but he didn't care. After examining the shirts for about fifteen minutes, he chose a white one and a blue one and added a striped tie to boot. *Why not? You only live once.*

He paid the lady behind the counter, grabbed the bag, and made his way to the exit. As he was approaching the door, he glanced back over his shoulder toward the ladies' department and saw Maria Sanchez.

He stopped dead in his tracks and turned fully in that direction. Shoppers were walking back and forth, blocking his view, but he was sure he had seen Maria. Or was he? She was in London. He had walked her to the plane himself. He'd watched her climb aboard and watched the plane take off.

He walked back to the ladies' department, shouldering people out of the way. He couldn't see her, so he wandered around the entire ground level, going from one department to another. After twenty minutes or so, he felt foolish, so he decided to leave. The idea of checking the other floors occurred to him, but he might have been at it for the next several hours.

Out on the street again, he decided he simply had seen someone who looked like her, at least like her in disguise. That was all. It happened to others all the time. Some guy saw a woman walking down the street and thought he knew her. He rushed up to her, but up close, he realized she was a complete stranger. Notwithstanding, the clothes, blonde hair, and snap-brim hat had been exactly the same. He shrugged.

Maria Sanchez was gone. He would never see her again.

He didn't give it another thought.

28

The Jig is Up

"Okay," Hannigan said to his wife. "Are you ready for this one?"

"I hope it's better than the last."

"You just don't have an appreciation for jokes. Like I said last week, you've become a cynic."

"I like jokes just fine, dear. It's how they're told that puts me off. You always start laughing long before the punch line. I ask you—where does that leave me?"

"Okay, this one is really funny. Jake the barber opens up his shop."

"Where is it located?"

"It doesn't matter where. Let's say Hoboken. Now, don't interrupt. He opens up his shop. A minute later, this priest he's never seen before walks in. 'How 'bout a haircut?' the priest says. 'No problem, Father. Have a seat,' Jake says back to him. When Jake finishes, the good Father asks, 'How much?' Jake says, 'Nothing, because you're a man of the cloth.' So the priest leaves.

"The next morning, before Jake opens up his shop, he finds an envelope stuck in the door with a hundred-dollar bill in it. A minute later, a Methodist minister he's never seen before walks in. 'How 'bout a haircut?' the minister says. 'No problem, Reverend. Have a seat,' Jake says back to him. When Jake finishes, the good reverend asks, 'How much?' Jake says, 'Nothing, because you're a man of the cloth.' So the reverend leaves.

"The next morning, before Jake opens up his shop, he finds an envelope stuck in the door with a hundred-dollar bill in it. Okay, Babs, are you ready for this? It's going to be a gas!" Hannigan said, trying to suppress his laughter.

"Stop giggling, Hannigan. You haven't said the punch line yet!"

"Okay, okay, here it comes. A minute later, a rabbi he's never seen before walks in. 'How 'bout a haircut?' the rabbi says. 'No problem, Rabbi. Have a seat,' Jake says back to him. When Jake finishes, the good rabbi asks, 'How much?' Jake says, 'Nothing, because you're a man of the cloth.' So the rabbi leaves. The next morning—get ready, Babs, because here it comes."

Babs rolled her eyes.

"The next morning, before Jake opens up his shop, he finds a long line of rabbis at his door that twists around the corner for two blocks." Hannigan burst out laughing.

"That wasn't funny, Hannigan. Worse than the first one."

"You don't get it. That's why it wasn't funny for you."

"I got it. You think the rabbi was cheap, so he told all his cheap rabbi friends."

"No, he wasn't cheap. He was just economical. He wasn't rich, and neither were the other rabbis, so he spread the word. They were just being economical. You see? They watched their money is all. If something's free, it's free. That's the point. There's a lesson in that."

"Like I said, it wasn't funny."

"Okay, how about this one? There was an old farmer from Oklahoma who—"

Just then, the bell over the entrance rang, and two men came into the Paradise.

"Good morning, gentlemen," Hannigan said with a wide grin. His grin disappeared when he recognized who they were. *Mutt and Jeff. Trafficante's men.*

235

"The boss wants to know if you found out anything on that Chinese statue yet," the short one said.

"Tell your boss I'll call him if I do. Tell him there's no need to send you two guys around here. Tell him it's bad for my business. Tell him I run a respectable inn for respectable guests."

This time, the taller one spoke. "Our boss told us to be nice, so we're being nice. Otherwise, we might take offense by what you said."

"Take it whatever way you want. Tell Trafficante I'll call—"

Just then, Margot Reed came up to Hannigan.

"I'm done with the east wing, Mr. Hannigan. Do you want me to start cleaning the guest rooms in the west wing?"

"No, that's fine," Hannigan said. "Take a break. Have some coffee." He noticed the two men eyeballing her as she left.

The short one spoke. "That's Margot Reed, isn't it?"

Hannigan was stunned. How had he recognized her with her hair cut short and dyed? "You've got the wrong girl. She's hired help. She's got a name, but it isn't Margot Reed."

"Listen. We're being nice about this. The girl is Margot Reed. She was Armstrong's lady friend. She's wearing a necklace Armstrong gave her. How do I know? Because I helped him pick it out for her. He couldn't decide, so I looked hard and picked a real nice one for her and suggested he buy it. He did, and she's wearing it right now."

Hannigan stared at the men, not knowing what to do. He was caught in a cul-de-sac with no way out. Babs was standing beside him. She put a hand on his shoulder.

"Santo really does want the statue," the short one said. "Maybe Margot knows something about where it's at. No one's going to get hurt, but we should take the girl to see him."

Hannigan had run out of excuses. He had no choice but to cough it up. "I've got the statue but only because I didn't want the girl killed. I'll give it to you if you keep the girl out of it."

"Listen, Santo doesn't want to hurt the girl," the short one said with a little chuckle. He threw his arms out to either side.

"He doesn't want to hurt nobody." He put his fingers and thumb together as if squeezing something and shook his hand several times in Hannigan's face. "He just wants the statue. So where is it?"

Hannigan told them he'd buried it in the back. Ten minutes later, he was back with it.

"Okay, this is good," the taller one said, holding on to the statue. "We want to take you and the girl back to Mr. Trafficante so you can tell him about it and answer any questions he has. Know what I mean? Otherwise, we'll be going back and forth like some loonies, trying to get straight answers. You can clear the air nice-like. Okay?"

"All I saw was the dame standing there in the glare of the headlights, waving her arms like a huge puppet, and the curse I spit out filled the car and my own ears."

Hunter liked that—the first sentence. It made him want to read more. Hunter admired Mike Hammer for no other reason than Hammer could do things Hunter couldn't, like turn some wise guy's brains into pulp. He closed *Kiss Me, Deadly*. As much as he wanted to, he knew he couldn't start the book. About the time he really got into the novel, Crawford Manning would come down in the elevator and fade away into the Havana sun, and Hunter wouldn't even be aware that he'd missed him. He'd brought the book with him nonetheless, on the off chance an opportunity arose where he could read and keep an eye on Manning at the same time. But right now wasn't the time. He'd be following him for the entire day, late into the night, so maybe he'd have a chance to read a chapter or two somewhere along the line.

Surveillance work was godawful boring, and Hunter hated it. That was the reason he'd charged Julie Manning so much. If he was going to subject himself to boredom, there had to be something interesting in it for him—namely, money—and she looked as if she could afford to write a few checks without them bouncing like a basketball.

For the last half hour, Hunter had been sitting in the lobby of the Hotel Nacional, where he had a good view of the elevators. He craved some coffee. He had forgone having a cup before he left the Paradise early that morning because the more he drank, the more trips to the can he'd make and the more opportunities Manning would have to squeeze by him. There was another reason he hated surveillance: shadowing someone seemed intriguing in novels, but it was actually a giant pain in the ass.

The morning was mild, with no rain in the forecast. At least that was in his favor. He slid Manning's picture out of the book; he was using it as a bookmark. He looked at it for the umpteenth time. Manning didn't look like the type who'd cheat on his wife, but what cheater did? Cheaters came in all sizes and shapes. But his profile didn't suggest it either. Manning spent his time pasting stamps into a stamp book and watching *Gunsmoke*. He rarely took his wife out, and according to her, he never received any suspicious phone calls. Cheaters usually had some questionable behaviors; Manning had none, except for lying to his wife about being in Havana when he should have been in Europe. Like now. Maybe he was cheating on his wife or maybe not, but he was definitely hiding something. Hunter would find out what it was in the next few days.

Another hour went by while Hunter watched people get off and on the elevators. No sign of Manning yet. The craving for coffee intensified, and Hunter did his best to ignore it. He heard the bell ping and saw the light go on over one of the elevators. Several people got off, tourists probably, followed by a well-dressed man in a business suit, carrying a briefcase. Hunter glanced at the picture and then stared at the man. Crawford Manning finally had made his appearance. He walked through the lobby and out the front door. Hunter got up and followed him at a safe distance.

Outside, Hunter watched Manning get into a taxi. Hunter got into the one behind him and told the driver to follow the car.

Manning's taxi followed the road parallel to the Malecón and then took a right into Old Havana. Five minutes later, it pulled into the front entrance of a tall building. Hunter knew it was the tallest building in Havana, but he'd never been inside it. The Bacardi Building was known to all. It was an eight-story art deco building with a striking tower in the front. He watched Manning get out of the taxi and go inside. Manning was a liquor distributor, so he was there for business, Hunter assumed. Hunter told the driver to park in the parking area where he could see the entrance.

There he waited. And waited.

Hunter was tempted to read his book, but he didn't; instead, he had a long chat with the gregarious taxi driver. The driver was a Habanero and knew the city like the back of his hand. He was uneducated but well read, so they talked about many things. The driver said he would one day like to see Miami and New York and listed all the things he'd like to do in the two cities. For Hunter, his company was a welcome distraction, and the time flew by as the two men chatted away, with Hunter keeping an eye on the entrance of the building.

Soon more than three hours had gone by, when Crawford Manning appeared at the front doors. Instead of hailing a taxi, he began walking. Hunter thanked the driver and paid him, giving him more than enough to compensate him for his time. Thanks to his expense account, Julie Manning would be paying for the taxi. He got out and jogged a little to catch up with Manning, staying half a block behind him.

Fifteen minutes later, they were in Chinatown. Manning went into a restaurant called Great Wall of China. Hunter waited outside and, after ten minutes, decided to peek in the window. Manning was eating alone, reading some papers, presumably taken from his briefcase, that lay open on the chair next to him. If he'd planned to meet someone there, he probably would have waited to order. After a half hour, Manning exited the restaurant and walked west. Hunter continued to follow behind him.

That afternoon, Hunter followed him around Chinatown and a great part of Havana Centro. Manning stopped at various shops, mostly looking but occasionally buying things. By late afternoon, Hunter was dead tired. Manning hadn't gone into any bars to meet anyone, and he hadn't acted suspiciously in any way.

Julie Manning was right; her husband was a boring guy.

Hannigan and Margot entered Trafficante's office after Jacopo and Stefono had filled Trafficante in on what had happened at the Paradise.

"Margot," Trafficante said, clearly happy and surprised by her appearance.

"Hello, Uncle Santo," she said.

"I nearly didn't recognize you! You cut and dyed your hair."

"Do you like it?" she asked, fluffing it up.

"It changes your looks so much, but yes, yes, I really like it!"

"It's called a bob," she said, twirling around for him.

"Lovely," Trafficante said.

For the next ten minutes, Trafficante and Margot sat on the couch and reminisced about their time in Tampa. Hannigan sat across from them with his mouth hanging open.

"Well now, Margot, tell me all about this statue," Trafficante said. "I've never been angry at you, and I don't intend to start now."

"Yes, well, Shaw did steal the statue, but I had no idea it belonged to you. He never told me the truth," she said, confident her lie would go undetected. The only person who would have known she was lying was dead. She explained that Armstrong had had a copy made and kept the original one for himself. He'd given the copy to Trafficante. "When I found him dead in his apartment, I panicked. Shaw told me the statue was valuable, so I took it with me before the police came. If I had known it was yours, I would have told you right away. I'm really sorry, Uncle Santo."

"No need to be, Margot. It wasn't your fault, and I assure you I had nothing to do with his death. Now, on a happier note, do you want to see why the statue is so valuable?"

"Oh yes, Uncle Santo!"

Trafficante went to his desk, where the statue was. Margot followed behind. Hannigan remained seated. Trafficante grabbed the hammer he had used on the first one.

"Here it goes," he said.

He raised the hammer and then brought it down, hitting the statue flush on the top. He then began chipping away at it until there was nothing left but a heap of plaster on his desk.

Just like the first one.

No one said anything. There was silence in the office. Hannigan and Margot were shocked and fearful about what might come next.

Trafficante was steaming, and it took all his willpower not to explode in anger. "Well, I guess we have another little surprise."

"What was supposed to be in there, Uncle Santo?"

"Something that made it valuable." He thought for a moment and then asked, "How many copies did Shaw make?"

"Just one."

"Do you know where he had it made?"

"No, Uncle Santo."

Trafficante knew of only one place in Havana that could possibly have made a replica of that quality and on short notice: Wong's gift shop. He knew Wong personally. He knew him to be the head of the tong in Havana and a complete scoundrel and unscrupulous swine. That said, he also liked the man. They'd done business together many times over the years. It had all been honest and above board.

Trafficante apologized to Hannigan and Margot for any inconvenience he had caused them. He'd promised Hannigan $10,000 if he found the statue. It wasn't the right statue, but he wrote Hannigan a check for $1,000 for his trouble anyway. He then asked his men to drive Hannigan and Margot back to the Paradise and apologized once again before they left, this time for cutting the meeting short. He gave Margot a big hug, told her he was delighted she was in Havana, and said they should get together soon. "Just like old times!"

But right now, he had an important errand to do that couldn't wait.

Yat-Sen Wong and Santo Trafficante knew each other well. Trafficante had bought many pieces of artwork from him for his hotels, nightclubs, and casinos. Trafficante thought Wong looked a little nervous as he stood in front of him now, and that made him suspicious. He stared at Wong with a friendly smile on his face, but the message was clear: he wanted the truth.

"Tell me again what happened, just so I don't misunderstand you."

"Of course, Santo, as many times as you want. This man—Mr. Smith. I had not seen him before. This man came in and wanted me to make him a statue like the one he had with him. A Chinese statue. The Guan Yin, the goddess of mercy. I've made it many times before. I said, 'No problem.' So I made the statue. I gave him both statues the next day. He picked them up and left. That's it. I'm sorry I cannot be of more help to you."

"And you made only one statue? One duplicate?"

"That's right—only one. He left with both of them. I only saw this Mr. Smith those two times. I did not know the statue belonged to you, or I certainly would have called you to verify that it was okay to make."

"Okay, I've got it now. I understand. No hard feelings, Yat-Sen. I'll be back next week. I need a few things to spruce up one of my clubs."

"It will be my honor, Santo. And please tell Mr. Raft that my wife and I saw one of his older films last night. It was *Manpower*. He was most excellent in his performance."

"I'll do that."

Outside, Trafficante relit his cigar. *Goddamn it*, he thought. *That son-of-a-bitchin' Corsican in Saigon did me in!*

He wasn't going to let the Corsican get away with this, not on his life. There was only one thing for Trafficante to do. He'd phone his associates in Saigon. They wouldn't mind a contract if the price was right. He'd make sure it was.

Money! he thought. *More fucking money!*

He'd just chalk it up as a business expense.

By six o'clock, Manning and Hunter were back at the hotel. Manning went into the elevator, and Hunter sat down once again in the lobby. He had to wait for Manning to either go out again or turn in for the night. He had to wait it out; there was nothing else he could do. He was tired and hungry, but he didn't feel sorry for himself; he was being well compensated for his time.

At midnight, he decided to hang it up. It was unlikely Manning would go out at that point. For any other person, he would have waited longer, but in this case, he was certain the man was snoring away by then. It was safe for him to leave. Yes, Crawford Manning was indeed one boring guy.

But what the hell was he hiding?

29

I Know What You Did

The next day turned out to be about as lousy as the day before.

Once again, Hunter waited in the lobby of the Hotel Nacional for Crawford Manning to appear. When he did, Hunter followed him by taxi to a liquor distillery and waited outside for an hour. Then Manning walked to the Presidential Palace in Old Havana for a tour of the neoclassical building. There was a large group of American tourists, so Hunter paid for a ticket and fell in with them. The tour lasted for two hours, upon which Manning walked to the National Museum of Fine Arts, which showcased national works by Cuban artists. Hunter shadowed him, stopping every so often to look at the paintings.

The only time during the course of the day when Hunter thought Manning was going to have a romantic rendezvous was when he went to the Montmartre. But Hunter was disappointed. Manning had a drink alone and left. There was no rendezvous, not even a healthy flirting with the girls there.

After Manning went to a small rare stamp and coin shop in Havana Centro and stayed there for three hours while Hunter waited across the street, he went to the Taquechel Pharmacy Museum. At that point, Hunter was tired, hungry, dying for a cup of coffee, and completely bored and frustrated. The money wasn't worth the agony he was going through. Hunter tailed Manning back to the Nacional and decided he needed to see Julia Manning. Maybe the guy wasn't hiding anything after all.

He took a taxi to the Hilton, where she was staying. He phoned her from the lobby and asked her to come down. She wanted him to come up to her room, but he thought that was a bad idea. During his previous interview with her, Hunter had sensed she was being flirtatious. He didn't want any part of that. She was gorgeous, but he was there on business, and business he would conduct.

"Julie, I know you think your husband is having an affair with someone here in Havana, but by what you've told me about him and by what I've seen in the last two days, I just don't see that he's doing that."

He took out his notebook and went over each day, including the places her husband had been and the things he'd done. She listened patiently.

"He was in before dark and stayed in his room. There's absolutely no indication he was doing anything suspicious. I would have noticed. You're wasting your money. I'm okay with refunding you half of it." If she asked him for all of it back, he would be more than willing to write her a check or give her cash for the full amount, either way she wanted to take it. He just wanted an end to the case.

His conclusion should have been good news for Julia Manning—her husband wasn't having an affair—but it wasn't.

"He's supposed to be leaving soon. He told me he'd be back in Miami sometime during the weekend. Today's Friday. Please stay on him, will you? I'll give you another three hundred dollars."

Hunter's heart nearly stopped. He couldn't bear to think of following Crawford Manning around the lobby of his hotel, let alone around the city, for another minute.

"I'm telling you: you'd be wasting your money. I don't think you have any—"

"Ash, dear, please do this for me, will you? This might be my only chance to catch him." She lowered her head in a pout, pushing her bottom lip forward slightly, and looked up at him with those beautiful blue eyes.

Dear? he thought. "I just don't think—"

"Please?" She hung on to the word for all it was worth. "I'll get down on my hands and knees and beg if you want me to, right here in the lobby."

Three hundred bucks. Maybe he shouldn't look a gift horse in the mouth.

"Okay, but I'm telling you that you're wasting your money."

"But it's mine to waste, isn't it? Besides, he's got another day here or maybe two—plenty of time to hook up with his little lover and then scoot back to Miami for supper on Sunday evening."

Hunter supposed it was. "I'll do my best."

"You do that, Ash. You do that."

There were plenty of taxis outside the Hilton, but Hunter needed some fresh air and time to think, so he decided to walk at least part of the way back to the Paradise. He crossed Calzada de Infanta into Havana Centro. *Six hundred bucks and expenses!* It wasn't as if he'd stolen the money from her. He'd warned Julie Manning that it was unlikely her husband was cheating on her. He no longer thought Manning was hiding something, other than perhaps a rare stamp from another collector. The guy seemed normal—more than a little boring but otherwise normal. Hunter continued walking.

The streets were crowded and noisy. Street musicians were playing away on their guitars, accordions, and maracas, and fruit sellers were hawking their wares: "Pineapples! Bananas!" Hunter was hungry and would eat at the Paradise later, but he stopped and bought a banana to fill the gap. He proceeded on, peeling the banana and taking a generous bite from it.

On his second bite, he stopped dead in his tracks. There she was again—the woman he'd seen at El Encanto department store last Wednesday, two days ago. She had the same clothes, same blonde hair, and same snap-brim hat. He decided to follow her and maybe get a closer look.

He stayed behind her about ten feet. There were plenty of people between them, so he had little chance of being seen. He followed her for about three blocks, when he noticed her stop at a bar with outdoor seating. He stopped and watched her sit down. He couldn't be certain, because the woman was wearing large sunglasses, but she was a dead ringer for Maria Sanchez in disguise.

A waiter came out, and the woman ordered something. A few minutes later, he brought her what looked like a brandy. Her mannerisms—the way she sat with one leg crossed over the other, the way she held her drink—were identical to Maria's. Should Hunter approach her? The worst that could happen would be that he made a fool of himself. He'd done it before, and most assuredly, he'd do it again, so it was no big deal.

He approached and stopped directly in front of her but didn't say anything. She looked up at him. He saw her flinch, but it was subtle. If she was shocked to see him, her surprise was hidden behind the sunglasses. Slowly and cautiously, the woman removed her glasses.

"Hola, Ash," she said.

It was Maria Sanchez. He sat down on the chair opposite her.

"Too much smog for you in London?" he asked.

"Oh, Ash," she said, "I hated every minute there."

"You weren't there long enough to know."

"You're right; I wasn't, but the second I stepped off the plane, I knew I couldn't live away from Havana." She grabbed the arms of her chair and scooted herself forward a little. "I knew I had done the wrong thing. Please don't be angry at me."

"Maria, it was your money. The passport, the paperwork, the ticket to London—they cost you dearly. I was only trying to help."

"I know. Your heart was in the right place. And for that, I will be eternally grateful."

Hunter didn't know what to say. He wasn't angry, but he felt let down. She had been in danger. He had gone out of his way to help her out of that danger, and now she'd placed herself right back in it.

"I'm not looking for gratitude, Maria. Just a little honesty." He stared at her for a long moment. She looked a bit nervous, perhaps from seeing him so abruptly, yet she seemed amazingly composed. "Were you ever going to contact me?"

"I was, yes, in a few days. I needed some time to figure things out."

"What about your husband? If I could find you, surely it wouldn't be a problem for your husband, especially if he has his thugs out looking for you."

"But you knew my disguise; they don't."

"If he finds you, he'll kill you. You said that yourself. It's dangerous for you to be walking around Havana like this, disguise or no disguise. You're a beautiful woman; you draw attention to yourself. Where are you staying?"

"I rented a small room in Marianao, not far from Oriental Park Racetrack. Just far enough away from the center of the city."

"And yet here you are, in the center of the city."

"I know. It was foolish of me."

"I saw you last Wednesday at El Encanto while I was buying some shirts. You're not being very careful."

"You saw me there? Why didn't you say anything?"

"I tried catching up to you, but you disappeared."

She took a piece of paper and a pen from her purse and wrote something down. "Here's my address and phone number. There's a restaurant right next door. It's the only one on the block. Can you meet me there tomorrow at six for dinner?"

Hunter would be shadowing Crawford Manning around the city all day and maybe into the evening tomorrow, but if there wasn't much happening, he could break free.

"Sure. If I can't, I'll call you. But right now, you'd better take a taxi to your room and stay away from town."

She finished her drink and stood.

Hunter raised an arm, and a taxi pulled up. He opened the door for her, and she got in.

He bent down and put his head into the window. "I can't say I'm sorry to see you here. You look great, even in your disguise."

"You look great without a disguise." She leaned up and kissed him hard on the lips.

The taxi pulled away, leaving Hunter on the curb with his hands in his pockets and mixed feelings in his heart.

The Sans Souci was one of Havana's sensational nightclubs, rivaling the internationally recognized Tropicana, complete with indoor and outdoor entertainment, luscious cuisines, booze, gorgeous women, and gambling. The one-story hacienda-style Spanish building had arched openings, low-slung red-tiled roofs, and a stage with multilevel circular platforms, each with ornately costumed singers and dancers gyrating to the sounds of a live orchestra. Its brochure invited guests to "stroll in the starlit night through the sweet-scented, romantic gardens. Dance outdoors beneath a Latin moon to the languid music of two top orchestras. Enjoy the sheer luxury of perfect, potent cocktails and a delicious dinner in this magic atmosphere."

Indeed, it was magical. Santo Trafficante made sure it was, because he owned it.

That night, he was entertaining two of his out-of-town guests in the outdoor area. Tony Bennett had just finished singing and was starting his break. The orchestra began playing again, and the dancers moved with the music.

"It's wonderful to see you again," Trafficante said to the lady across from him. "It's been a long time."

"We couldn't travel all the way to Havana and not stop in for a visit," Lizzy Maddox said.

"That's right," Bradford said, chewing his steak. "Lizzy has told me so much about you that I just had to meet you."

Trafficante looked at him for a moment. He didn't know him at all. He'd known Lizzy for years because she'd lived next door to him in Tampa when married to Travis Reed. Reed had been gunned down in a burglary gone wrong, and Trafficante had heard she remarried shortly after. He'd been in Havana when both events— the murder and the marriage—happened.

"Is that right?" Trafficante said. "And just what did Lizzy tell you about me?"

"That you were an okay guy," Bradford said, smiling.

"An okay guy," repeated Trafficante, chuckling to himself.

"Oh, Bradford, I didn't say such a thing," Lizzy said, slapping her husband's shoulder playfully. "I said he was a sterling gentleman with impeccable taste."

Trafficante threw his head back and laughed, and then he pushed his plate forward. "I can't eat another morsel, or I'll bust!"

Lizzy and Bradford kept eating.

Trafficante lit a cigar and then said, "You probably heard about what happened to Shaw, hmm?"

"Terrible. Just terrible," Lizzy said. "Did the authorities find his killer?"

"I don't think so. Haven't read anything in the papers."

"We were going to look him up while we were here and have him show us around Havana—you know, his favorite places. Then we found out what happened. Such a shame."

"Yeah, a shame," Trafficante said. He eyed them while they ate. He didn't especially like Lizzy's husband, but he didn't know exactly why. It was just a gut feeling. Something was off, though. He sensed it. He was good at picking up on people when they tried to hide something from him. The vibes weren't strong, but they were there nonetheless. "So how's Margot doing these days?"

"I wish I knew," Lizzy said. "She took off—only God knows where she went—when Travis was murdered. She took it hard. We all did but especially her. I guess losing a father is hard. Husbands can be replaced, but you can't replace a father."

Trafficante puffed on his cigar and looked at Bradford, who continued to eat as if he weren't listening. "I'm sure she'll pop up one of these days," he said to Lizzy. "She can't mourn for the rest of her life."

"No," Lizzy said, "she can't very well do that, now, can she?"

Their conversation was interrupted by thunderous applause at the reappearance of Tony Bennett onstage. Lizzy, Bradford, and Trafficante looked toward the stage and joined in. Bennett took the mic off the stand and walked around, greeting a few people sitting up front.

"I have to tell you a little secret," Tony said as a signal to stop clapping. Then he whispered into the mic, "I love Havana!" Another round of booming applause erupted as the audience stood up. After a few minutes, everyone took his or her seat again, and it became quiet.

Tony continued. "Thank you, thank you, especially to John and Anna Benedetto, my parents. They made this possible. You know, they emigrated from Reggio Calabria—for those who don't know, that's in Italy, at the tip of the boot." There was laughter here and there. "They emigrated from Reggio Calabria and landed in America without a pot to piss in—excuse my French. And here I am, their son, entertaining folks here in Havana, Cuba."

There was yet another round of applause.

"I'd like to dedicate this next song to them and to you—that you get what you want in life and always follow your dreams." The orchestra played the introduction, and Bennett began singing: "I know. I know what you've done for me."

Trafficante leaned across the table and whispered, "I know what you did," and then he winked. He sat back in his seat and directed his attention to the stage.

Lizzy and Bradford looked at each other. Bradford grimaced, as if to say, "What the hell was that all about?"

Tony sang, "Without you, I would have wandered through life. Without you, the sun would never appear. Without you, I would go through life in fear."

Trafficante leaned across the table again and this time spoke in a normal voice. "He might have deserved what he got, but he worked for me. It wasn't your decision to make."

The song broke in again. "So I will take your dream and make it my own. And I will follow it wherever it may go."

"I want you out of Havana tomorrow. Return to Tampa, clean your house, and put it up for sale. Whenever I return to Tampa, I want to see you gone."

"And the stars high above in the sky," Tony sang, "will always show me the glory. And until the day that I die, I will always know what you have done, what you have done for me."

"Your ambition makes you reckless. If I see you again, I'll shoot both of you myself."

With that, Trafficante smiled, got up, and left.

Three Centavos Gets You a Song

Early Saturday morning, a medium-sized delivery truck pulled up outside the Paradise Inn. Two men in tan uniforms got out and went to the rear.

"It's here, just like they said it would be!" Hannigan shouted, looking out a window. "By golly, these Cubans are efficient. They say what they mean, and they do what they say! Sammy, go open the door for them."

Babs and Hunter were in the café, having coffee.

"What did he buy this time?" Hunter asked.

"I'll never tell," Babs said. "He swore me to secrecy. Wait a few minutes, and you'll see for yourself."

The two men had their cargo on a dolly and were maneuvering it through the doorway with Sammy guiding them. Sammy looked around it to the left and right so they wouldn't scrape the doorframe. So far so good. They were squeezing it through without a nick.

"Where would you like it, senor?" one of the men asked.

"Bring it right through here, and put it against this wall," Hannigan said, indicating the café.

"My God, it's a jukebox," Hunter said.

253

"Technically, it's a Wurlitzer," Hannigan said, proud of himself, "complete with the latest American and Cuban records! Can you beat that?"

"How much is that going to set us back?" Hunter asked.

"We're leasing it for six months with an option to buy," Babs said.

"That'll give us time to see if it's worth having," Hannigan said. "Doesn't it look great there?"

Babs and Hunter looked at each other.

"He was so excited about it," Babs whispered. "I couldn't say no."

Hannigan signed the delivery papers, and the men left. He then plugged it in. "Okay, who's got some centavos? Three gets you a song!" He reached into his pocket. "Never mind. I've got some." He put three centavos into the slot and then pushed B12. After a few seconds, the record was in place, the arm dropped, and the song began playing on its maiden voyage.

"Ah, 'In the Still of the Night,'" Babs said.

"Fred Parris and the Satins," Hunter said. "At least he's got good taste."

"I wonder if they know they're the headliner at the Paradise Inn, Havana, Cuba."

"Doesn't it sound great?" Hannigan said, grabbing Babs's hand. They began dancing slowly around the tables. Babs was tickled and giggled.

Hunter chuckled to himself, clapped his hands several times in appreciation for the entertainment, and then finished his coffee. When the song ended, he got up. "Slane, you did it again. It's going to be a hit with the guests."

"We should have done it years ago!" Hannigan said. "Where're you going? I was just gonna play another song."

"Business. Someone's got to work to pay for the lease."

"Before you leave, I've got two ringside tickets to the fights tonight. Our old buddy from Saint Paul is fighting Kid Gavilan at nine. Babs doesn't like violence like we do. Wanna go?"

"You mean Del Flanagan? Del's in town? Sure. We haven't seen him in years."

"We'll have a beer with him after the fight."

"I might be a little late, but I'll be sure to be there for the main bout."

"You do that," Hannigan said, giving him the ticket. "Del will be happy to see us!"

Hunter left, and Hannigan put three more centavos into the slot, pressed E2, and looked at Babs. "Shall we?" he asked, bowing.

"We shall!"

Soon they were dancing to Benny Moré singing "Bonito y Sabroso." After the song ended, they laughed like giddy teenagers.

"I think this is going to be great, Hannigan," Babs said. "We may have to rearrange the tables a little for some space. Our guests are definitely going to want to dance."

"If we decide to go with it permanently, we could expand the café and put a small dance floor in."

Babs was just about to say something, when the bell over the entrance sounded. They looked toward the door as a well-dressed man who must have been in his late sixties came in. He was wearing a white suit and a straw fedora and had a long gray beard. It was Clarence Tolliver, better known as the Poet. But that was a misnomer; he didn't actually write poetry. He was a retired university professor from Cleveland who had decided to spend his golden years in the tropics. Whenever the spirit summoned, he would recite poems wherever he happened to be—often right there at the café in the Paradise Inn.

"Hello, Clarence," Hannigan and Babs said. The Poet went to a table and sat down while Babs fetched him his usual.

"How's life?" Babs asked, setting his coffee and a shot of brandy on the table.

"Life? What can I say about that? The goddamn guerrillas are up in the mountains. If they decide to come down, they'll ruin everything, and I'll have to move to Bermuda or some other god-awful place. Life is dismal at best, Mrs. Hannigan. Dismal indeed."

"Well," Babs said, not knowing what else to say to that. "In the meantime, enjoy your coffee and brandy. I don't think the guerrillas are coming down this morning. If they do, I'll be sure to send them right back up, at least until you finish your drinks."

"You jest, but just wait and see. Mark my words!"

She went over to Hannigan at the front desk and gave him a wink.

"If he starts his nonsense," Hannigan whispered, "I swear I'm going to throw him out. I don't care if he is a paying customer."

At that point, the nonsense began.

"*The Waste Land* by Thomas Stearns Eliot. Part one, 'The Burial of the Dead,'" said the Poet in a loud, deep baritone voice. He cleared his throat and continued: "April is the cruellest month, breeding lilacs out of the dead land, mixing memory and desire, stirring dull roots with spring rain."

Hannigan gritted his teeth.

"No, don't," Babs said. "Leave him be."

Hannigan darted into the café, stopped in front of the jukebox with his arms akimbo, and glared at Clarence.

"Summer surprised us, coming over the Starnbergersee with a shower of rain."

He didn't throw the Poet out. Instead, he reached into his pocket for three centavos, turned to the jukebox, put the money in the slot, and pressed E2 again. He stretched an arm behind the Wurlitzer and turned up the volume. In no time, Benny Moré was once again singing—very loudly.

By late afternoon, Hunter was tired and discouraged. He had shadowed Crawford Manning around town all day and come up with nothing. Manning had gone to two appointments with liquor wholesalers, a museum, a public art show, and another rare stamp and coin shop and ended up at Parque Central, feeding the pigeons for two hours. For a time, Hunter had thought he was going to be meeting up with a love interest at the park, but no such luck.

He looked at his watch. It was 5:20. He could stay with Manning for the rest of the day and night, but he knew it would be worthless. He'd end up sitting in the lobby of the Nacional until eleven o'clock that night, having missed dinner with Maria and the fight with Hannigan. He decided Manning could do what he wanted, though Hunter guessed he would eat dinner somewhere and then turn in for the night. He, on the other hand, would be enjoying the evening.

He grabbed a taxi to Marianao and found Maria waiting for him at their table.

They spent the next few hours chatting away about this and that. Both avoided talking about the obvious: what she was going to do about her husband. She seemed amazingly calm for someone whose husband was hunting her and might even kill her if he found her. The least she could expect was a thorough beating.

Hunter was interested in her—there was no mistake about that—and he sensed the feeling was mutual, but he wasn't a fool. It wasn't healthy for him to be attracted to the wife, albeit estranged wife, of a captain on the National Police force. As he left, he wished her well and expected he wouldn't see her again. Nevertheless, he leaned down and kissed her on the lips.

An hour later, he was ringside at the Gran Estadio de La Habana, sitting beside Hannigan. The last preliminary fight had ended in the middle of the first round, the house lights had come on, and everyone was waiting for the main bout of the evening to begin. The boxers would come out of their dressing rooms and enter the arena from the other side of the ring, so Hunter and Hannigan wouldn't see Del Flanagan until he ducked under the ropes and entered the ring.

Sure enough, Flanagan appeared and began his long walk down the aisle.

The Saint Paul fighter stepped into the ring to the cries of "Boo!" He ignored the crowd as he jumped up and down, swinging his arms to loosen up. He threw a fast combination—a left jab followed by a right cross and a left uppercut—and the booing got louder. Hunter and Hannigan hadn't seen Del in a donkey's age; he was older, of course, but as fit as ever.

The boos turned into cheers as Kid Gavilan came down the aisle, ducked under the ropes, and climbed into the ring. The official odds were in the Kid's favor but not by much. He had something going for him that Flanagan didn't: the hometown crowd. Sometimes that made all the difference.

"Fifty bucks says Del wins by a knockout in the sixth," Hannigan said.

"You're on," Hunter said. "It's going the distance. Del wins by unanimous decision."

"Let's up it to a hundred smackers, if you're so sure of yourself."

"How 'bout one fifty?"

"You're on," Hannigan said, smiling. "Easy money tonight."

"We'll see."

After the announcer made the introductions, the referee gave his instructions to the two fighters. Then the trainers for both fighters stepped outside the ring. The fighters continued to loosen up as the timekeeper rang the bell for round one.

Both men entered the center of the ring, circling each other, trying to get accustomed to each other's style. They had never fought each other before. They danced around for a time, flicking the occasional jab at each other. Flanagan was the more aggressive of the two, and soon he was throwing lefts and rights into the face and body of the Kid. Gavilan blocked most of them and danced away, continuously throwing jabs at his opponent.

Hunter looked to his right and saw Rita Hayworth, Gary Cooper, and Montgomery Cliff sitting together with their eyes glued to the fighters. He pointed them out to Hannigan, who only shrugged, as if to say, "So what?"

Hollywood stars were a dime a dozen in Havana.

The next four rounds were uneventful, but in the sixth, Flanagan had the Kid on the ropes and unleashed a series of combinations that nearly dropped him.

"You want to up the bet to three hundred?" Hannigan asked Hunter, who ignored him.

In the tenth and final round, Hannigan noticed Santo Trafficante sitting to his far left. He was smoking a cigar and cheering on one of the fighters. On the other side of him was Margo Reed. They looked chummy, having a great time. He nudged Hunter.

"They look like old pals," he said. "And to think I felt sorry for her."

This time, Hunter did the shrugging.

The round ended, and both fighters looked tired. After five minutes, the announcer read the scorecards of the two judges and the referee. Del Flanagan won by a unanimous decision.

Boos flooded the auditorium and echoed in the rafters.

"I'll take cash—no check," Hunter said. "I don't trust that it won't bounce."

Hannigan snorted several times and then grunted something, but the surrounding noise was too loud for Hunter to hear the words. Whatever he said, Hunter was certain it wasn't fit for Babs's ears.

Their conversation dried up.

31

A Transformation

Ash Hunter felt like shit.

It was seven o'clock on Sunday morning. He should have been curled up in bed in a deep sleep, but he wasn't. Instead, he was sitting in the lobby of the Hotel Nacional with a hangover, waiting patiently to see what thrills lay ahead of him for the day. His head hurt. If he'd been a thumb-twiddler, he'd have been doing that right now.

He'd had enough of Crawford Manning. If he never saw another museum and rare stamp and coin shop again, it would be too soon. Notwithstanding, what a person had done yesterday and the day before yesterday was calculatingly predictive of what that person was going to do today and tomorrow, so Hunter knew what he had to look forward to.

The pain in his head intensified.

Last night, after the fight, he and Hannigan had gone to Del Flanagan's dressing room and reunited with their old buddy from Saint Paul. Flanagan had never been in Havana before, so they showed him the sights, which, of course, at night meant going nightclub hopping. Flanagan had insisted his trainer go with them to keep an eye on him, as he was still in training and had another fight coming up the following week back in Minnesota. They'd said their goodbyes at four o'clock, and Hunter and Hannigan had gotten back to the Paradise at four thirty. Hunter had managed to get an hour and a half of sleep before he got up and shaved and showered.

Now, without the benefit of coffee, he sat in the lobby with the morning paper folded on his lap, nursing a headache. He cursed Crawford Manning. When he finished, he cursed Julie Manning for hiring him, and then he cursed himself for accepting the job. But he'd taken on the case and had to follow through on it. Thank God this was going to be the last day. Or maybe tomorrow would be—he couldn't remember.

If that day was indeed going to be like the previous days, Manning wouldn't be coming down for another hour or maybe longer. God, what Hunter wouldn't have done for a cup of strong Cuban coffee right then. He unfolded the paper and read the headline: "Police Captain Assassinated." He looked up and gazed across the lobby toward the front desk, focusing on nothing in particular. He was unsure whether he wanted to read the full article. His eyes were glassy; there was a throbbing pain in his temples.

Maria, he thought.

Reluctantly, he lowered his head and read the first line of the article: "Captain Ricardo Manuel Raul Sanchez of the National Police was shot dead last night at seven o'clock in front of his home in Vedado."

He looked up again. *Seven o'clock last night*, he thought. He'd been having dinner with Maria at that time in Marianao. *Could she have*—

He shook his head; he didn't want to think about that possibility. Maybe it was just a coincidence. As much as his muddled mind would allow him, he went over the sequence of events: she had been beaten by her husband; Hunter had helped her flee the country in fear of her life; a few days later, she'd returned; her husband, not knowing where she was, had had his men out looking for her; and unfazed by that, she'd appeared peaceful and calm last night. But as they'd chatted away while eating their pork chops and black beans and rice and drinking their daiquiris, as they'd laughed and shared some stories of their childhood, her husband had been lying outside their home, shot to death. Suddenly, her problem was magically solved.

Was that just a convenient coincidence?

If he'd been a praying man, he would have prayed it was nothing more than that—that she hadn't hired someone to kill her husband while she sat with Hunter, who could later testify in court—if it came to that—that she had been miles away at the time of the murder, having supper with him.

As much as he wanted to, he didn't buy that it was simply a coincidence.

Hunter broke out in a cold sweat. Maria had returned from London for the express purpose of hiring someone to get rid of her problem, and—maybe as an afterthought—she had used Hunter to establish her whereabouts at the time of the shooting. That was the only thing that made sense to him.

The question now was whether the killing was premediated murder or an act of justifiable self-defense.

Hunter had no doubt her husband would have one day killed her. If she had hired someone to kill him first, then she would have been acting rationally, defending herself from the inevitable. However, a clever prosecuting attorney would point out that she'd gone to London, out of harm's way. Deliberately returning to Havana and hiring someone to kill her husband was premeditated murder and required the death penalty.

His temples felt as if they were going to explode. He decided to pare down the situation to the essentials. *Maria Sanchez*, he thought, *was a battered woman who was in danger of being killed by her abusive husband. She acted to save herself before her husband had the chance to unleash his fury for what would be, in all likelihood, inexorably the last time. Case closed.*

There was no need to finish the article.

He sat still, barely breathing, for the next hour, trying to clear his mind, when the elevator doors opened, and Crawford Manning stepped out. Something was different. He was dressed more casually, wearing a sports jacket and no tie. But of course, it was Sunday, so he wouldn't have any business appointments.

Manning walked through the lobby, waving at the young man at the front desk as he went by. Hunter followed him out the door, keeping distance between them. The streets weren't crowded, so Hunter had to be more careful than he usually was. Manning walked west for a couple of blocks and then turned into a building and disappeared. When Hunter caught up to him, he discovered it was a restaurant that catered to American tourists. They served meals one could find in any restaurant across America. Hamburgers, hot dogs, french fries, and pizza were their specialties, as well as the great American breakfast.

The restaurant was large and only half full of customers. Hunter went to the opposite side and sat down at a table where he had a clear view of Manning. He ordered toast and coffee. He would eat the toast but nurse the coffee to avoid later stopping to use the lavatory. Manning had ordered off the menu and was now wolfing down a hearty breakfast consisting of eggs, bacon, hash brown potatoes, toast, and coffee.

After he finished, he lit up a cigarette and drank his coffee. Hunter pretended to read the newspaper, looking up every so often at Manning. His mind, however, was still half on Maria.

A tall, well-built man with a dark complexion, maybe in his midforties, wearing a guayabera shirt, entered the restaurant. He saw Manning, went over to him, and sat down at his table. The men appeared to be extremely happy to see each other. They obviously knew one another well. This was the first time Hunter had seen Manning interact with anyone on such a personal level and the first time he'd seen any genuine emotion in the man's face.

This piqued Hunter's interest.

Hunter watched them for a half hour or so, even though he was too far away to hear anything they were saying. By the expressions on their faces, though, the conversation ran the gamut from serious, bordering on sad, to animated to the point that they intermittently gained the attention of those around them. Their laughter, at times, was very loud.

This was a different Crawford Manning from the one Hunter had followed around the previous days. He was much more alive and vibrant. He seemed genuinely happy.

Who was this man sitting next to him? Obviously, he had an enormous effect on Manning. Hunter continued watching them as they scooted their chairs closer to the table and leaned into one another, lowering their voices, gesticulating with their hands as they spoke. He could detect a near glow in Manning's eyes as he talked. It was strange, but Hunter could imagine Manning sitting there with some sexy young Cuban chick, planning some kind of romantic rendezvous, and acting the same way instead of being there with a hulk of a man.

Hunter was so amazed that he nearly forgot the pain in his head. If Julie had pulled him off the case right now, he still would have stayed with it. He rarely saw anyone transform so abruptly, and he was bound and determined to find out what had caused it.

He changed his mind again; Crawford Manning was hiding something.

He pulled his notebook out of his jacket pocket and jotted some things down. When he looked up, Manning was paying the check. The two men got up and left the restaurant. Hunter replaced his notebook, left some money on the table, and watched them through the large plate-glass window. It was too early for him to leave, as the men were right outside. Manning stuck his hand out, and within seconds, a taxi pulled up. The two men got inside. Hunter hurried outside as the taxi sped way. He hailed a taxi, which came right away, and told the driver to follow the cab ahead of them.

The taxi crossed Havana Centro and went into Old Havana, to the area around the port, not far from the Dos Hermanos bar. The neighborhood was derelict; the buildings were dilapidated. Hunter, still in his taxi, watched from a distance as the other taxi pulled up to the curb. Manning and his friend got out and went to the door of a ground-floor apartment.

They kissed each other on the lips and held hands as they went inside.

32

None of His Business

Invertido, Hunter thought.

That was the word Hunter had heard the locals use. It meant "reversed," but it was also used to mean something else. Now it was clear to him: Crawford Manning was a homosexual.

He'd known Manning was keeping a secret. This discovery accounted for the deception and all the trips to Havana. Hunter never in a million years would have thought this was the secret. How was Julie Manning going to take this news? Her husband had been cheating on her with a man. She was going to be devastated.

Hunter got out of the taxi and sat on a stool outside a small shop that sold a variety of everyday items, such as soap, cigarettes, pop, and beer. He bought a bottle of beer and took a swig from it, looking across the street at the apartment, wondering what to do next. Did he have enough information to go to Julie with? It was none of his business what Crawford Manning did with his life, but he did have an obligation to Manning's wife to get as much information as possible. He decided to hang on for a bit longer; maybe something more would come up—something relevant he could tell her besides that her husband was a queer. After all, she was paying for it.

Manning's homosexuality had caught him completely off guard. It was the last thing he would have considered. It never even had come up on his radar. No wonder Manning was hiding it. Cubans were no more tolerant of queers than Americans were. To Cubans, homosexuality was *el pecado nefando*, or the abominable sin of sodomy. *Invertido* was a neutral term, if there was such a thing when it came to homosexuality, but *maricas* and *mitad hombres* certainly weren't. They meant "faggots" and "half men," respectively, terms that were all too common there. Cuban heterosexual men were macho; homosexuals were reversed. Manning, as an American, would have been looked at in the same way as any Cuban homosexual would have been: as a marica.

For the next hour, Hunter sat there nursing a beer and watching people walk back and forth. Several times, couples or small groups of people went into the apartment Manning and his friend had gone into, but by the side entrance instead, which Hunter had seen while in the taxi. He had only a partial view at the moment, however, because of the huge jagüey tree near the building. The trees were common throughout Cuba. They had strong, wide trunks, with aerial roots and abundant foliage on large branches that appeared like arms reaching upward into the heavens. They produced small figs approximately the size of the ones on a fig tree. The jagüey trees had become a symbol for Cubans of ingratitude and betrayal, because they sought support early in their existence from other plants. When they no longer needed that support, they overpowered the plants until they died.

Hunter watched another group of five people go to the side entrance; one was carrying a rooster by its legs. The people who had gone into the apartment were both black and white, male and female, and dressed in common, everyday clothes. He waited for another fifteen minutes; no one else arrived. His interest piqued, he decided he'd have a look for himself. Something was obviously happening inside the apartment. Maybe a celebration of sorts.

He crossed the street and went around the jagüey to the side door. The closer he got, the more he could hear drumming and singing from inside. He tried the doorknob, which turned freely, so he slowly opened the door, which led directly into the kitchen. If someone inside saw him, he'd say he had the wrong apartment and excuse himself.

Once he was fully inside, the drumming and singing became louder. No one was in the kitchen. Opposite the door, on the other side of the room, was a colorful cloth that separated the kitchen from another room. He walked through the kitchen, carefully making his way to the cloth. There he separated the cloth from the doorframe with his index finger just enough to peek through it. No one noticed him; they all seemed to be in some kind of trance.

Including Crawford Manning.

Three black men were sitting on low stools, pounding on batá drums, their fingertips tapping both ends of the drums. Their eyes were closed, their heads swung from side to side to the beat, and sweat dripped down their faces. Fifteen to twenty people, male and female, some wearing white and others wearing colorful shirts or dresses but nothing out of the ordinary, were dancing to the drums with eyes closed and arms flailing in all directions, as if they were possessed by some demon. Some of them smoked cigars as they danced, both male and female. Hunter thought they looked absurd.

To the right of them was an altar with half coconut shells on the floor in front of it; some contained a clear liquid, some contained honey, and one contained cowry shells. Around the shells were freshly picked sunflowers, pineapples, guavas, and bananas. On the altar was an image of the Virgin Mary holding baby Jesus, surrounded by candles. Around her were statues of saints. All of them, including Mary and Jesus, had black faces.

Hunter watched intently for the next half hour. He knew he was seeing a Santería ceremony of some sort. He had seen them before, and the ceremonies differed greatly. What amazed him was that Crawford Manning was participating in it. Hunter's eyes were glued to him as Manning danced to the rhythm of the beating drums. Manning's eyes were closed like those of the others; they seemed to be possessed by something powerful.

An old woman with a cloth wrapped around her head, wearing a loose-fitting white cloth dress down to her ankles, danced her way to the altar and began spreading salt around the Virgin Mary and the saints.

The black man Manning had come there with suddenly broke free of the group and disappeared into another room. A minute later, he returned with a rooster, holding it by its feet upside down. He went to the altar and began swinging the rooster left and right, plucking feathers from it and spreading them around. All the time, he was singing in a high-pitched voice that made him stand out among the others.

Manning went to him and took out a knife. His companion twisted the neck of the rooster, and Manning made a small slit in it with the knife, killing it. His companion then began squeezing the neck until drops of blood came out. He dripped the blood over the altar and into one of the coconut shells filled with clear liquid. The drumming intensified as the people continued to dance even more fervently.

Hunter had seen enough; he went outside, crossed the street again, and got another beer. He sat down where he had been before.

So this was Crawford Manning's secret world. The boring guy who watched *Gunsmoke* on TV and collected stamps back in Miami was a homosexual who participated in Santería in Havana. No wonder he had hidden this from his wife. It would have been much easier for Hunter to tell Julie Manning that her husband had been shacking up with some gorgeous redhead. He didn't look forward to the conversation he had to have with her. Would she even believe him? He took a long swig from his bottle. What in the hell was he going to tell her?

After weighing his options, he decided he'd talk to Crawford Manning first. Normally, he had little or no contact with the person he was shadowing. Hunter was under no obligation to him; it was Julie who'd hired him. But this was an extraordinary situation that required something extraordinary from him. From the information Julie had given him and from his observations of her husband over the last few days, Hunter concluded that Manning wasn't a bad person. It wasn't as if he was a murderer who chopped up little children. Granted, it wasn't every day Hunter came across a queer who practiced Santería. It was a delicate situation, and Hunter didn't want Julie Manning to have a heart attack when he told her the news. Manning was what he was, and frankly, Hunter couldn't have cared less whom he slept with or what religion he practiced. But Manning needed to come clean with his wife; that much was clear. Manning himself needed to have a heart-to-heart talk with his wife. Hunter wasn't a psychotherapist, and besides, it wasn't any of his business. He was simply a gatherer of information.

So why was Hunter willing to make it his business?

He didn't know, except he felt that if the deception continued on much longer, it wouldn't end well for either Crawford or Julie. If Hunter could make a difference, he was willing to try. So he waited for Manning to come out of the apartment.

He drank another bottle of beer and felt his bladder fill, but he didn't care. He was going to have a talk with Crawford Manning, come hell or high water.

An hour and a half later, he finished his fourth bottle of beer. He asked the owner of the shop to tell him if anyone came out of the apartment, and he hurried into the back to relieve himself. Upon returning, he noticed that the people who had come for the ceremony were leaving, individually and in small groups, as they had come. Crawford Manning was not among them.

It was quiet all of a sudden.

The night was hot and humid, as usual, but there was a pleasant breeze blowing. After a few minutes, Manning appeared at the front door with his companion. Hunter watched them kiss each other on the sidewalk.

Hunter's eyes caught movement to his left. A man wearing a straw hat was approaching them. The couple must have sensed that, because Manning's companion went inside the apartment and closed the door, and Manning turned around and proceeded down the street. Hunter stood up and was about to cross the street and approach Manning, when he heard the man in the straw hat yell, "Marica!" He knew that meant "faggot" in Spanish.

There was going to be trouble.

The man drew a blade from his ankle and rushed at Manning, who was about ten feet in front of him. Manning kept walking, ignoring the man, who was steadily gaining on him.

Hunter darted across the street. From behind, he grabbed the wrist of the attacker with one hand and wrapped his other hand around the man's face. He was a small man, so Hunter had little problem lifting him off the ground while taking the knife from him.

The attacker twisted his body loose from Hunter, fell to the ground, and then got up and yelled, "*¡Eres una marica! ¡La concha de tu madre!*" as he ran away. He slurred his words, so Hunter couldn't fully understand him, but he knew the comment wasn't nice. Hunter threw the knife into a nearby bush.

Manning rushed over to Hunter and asked him if he was all right.

"I'm fine," Hunter said. "I think you were about to be robbed. Tourists are easy marks in this part of town, especially at night."

Both of them knew Manning nearly had been attacked because he was *reversed*.

"Thanks," Manning said. "I'm not really a tourist. I'm here on business." He paused for a moment and then said, "You risked your life for me. The guy had a knife. You could have been hurt."

"Like I said, I'm fine. My training in the army came back to me. I just acted."

"I owe you something for that."

"No, that's okay. You don't owe me anything. I'm just glad I was here to help."

"Can I at least buy you a drink?"

Hunter thought for a moment. This would be a good opportunity to talk to him. "Yeah, I think we both could use one. Dos Hermanos isn't far from here."

"Okay, let's go."

Manning ordered a daiquiri, and Hunter continued with another beer, even though he had had enough already. They took their drinks to the only empty table available. The bar was crowded and noisy, with a conjunto playing in the background, so they could talk without fear of being heard by anyone nearby. A bar filled mostly with inebriated seamen and longshoremen wasn't the ideal place for a queer to be, but Hunter thought it was safe enough.

Manning was talkative. He told Hunter what business he was in and about the countries he traveled to. He went on and on about the museums he'd visited in Havana and how they compared to the ones in Europe. At some point, there was a long pause. Hunter thought that was a sign it was his turn to tell Manning something about himself. After listening to the guy, Hunter was confident in his belief that Manning was just a decent guy caught up in a bad situation that he didn't know how to deal with.

Hunter decided now was the time for him to come clean. "I have a confession to make," he said.

"I'm not a priest, but I'll listen if you want me to."

Manning wasn't cracking wise; he was as sincere as it got, and Hunter was impressed, which made what he was about to say even more difficult. "I'm a private detective. Julie hired me."

"Julie? You know her? You know my wife?" His stunned look was undeniable and genuine.

"She thinks you're having an affair. She hired me to find out."

"She's here in Havana?"

"She is."

There was a long moment of silence. Hunter could see the wheels spinning in Manning's head. Some men would have felt trapped and acted spontaneously with violence under such circumstances. Taking a swing at him or overturning the table wasn't out of the question. He didn't think that would be the case with Manning, or he would have found another way to tell him.

"I take it you've been following me around," Manning finally said.

"I have."

"Today?"

"Today and for the last few days."

There was another long moment of silence. Manning's eyes were fixed on the table in front of him. Slowly, he looked up at Hunter. "Then you know."

"Yes, I know."

"Let me explain," he said. He briefly paused. "All my life—"

"Listen, Crawford," Hunter said, interrupting him. "You don't have to explain anything to me. I'm not judging you, and it's none of my business."

"Thank you for that," he said. "You said you were following me. Were you there at the ceremony tonight? I thought I saw someone looking through the curtains, but I couldn't make out who. Was that you?"

"I'm afraid it was."

"Then let me just explain something to you, because it might not make sense otherwise." He took a sip of his drink. "The person I care

273

about—his name is Enrique—is a high priest in Santería. He's called a *babalawo*, or father of mysteries. The ceremony you witnessed was a cleansing ritual to help me get rid of the guilt I feel and to help me accept myself for who I am. You see, homo—" He stopped and looked around him before continuing. "You know, it's accepted in Santería. As paradoxical as it may sound, it provides a space for people like me in society. I've never known peace and acceptance in life as much as I have here. I hope I'm making some sense."

"You are, and I'm glad you've found it, but to be blunt about it, that's not my concern. My concern is with your wife. I work for her. I shouldn't even be talking to you, but I'm afraid if I give her the news, she either won't believe me or will have a stroke. I'm exaggerating a little, but I think you get my point. She's concerned you're having an affair."

"I see what you mean. I've already decided to tell her. As long as she's in Havana, I'll do it here rather than waiting to get back to Miami. Where's she staying?"

"She's at the Hilton."

Hunter sensed that Manning wanted to talk some more, so he kept his mouth shut. A moment later, Manning continued.

"I've had these feelings ever since I can remember. I ignored them, but it cost me two marriages, because the feelings never went away. Nearly sixteen years went by, and I thought I was over them. But I know now that I was only fooling myself. Then I met Julie. I have to say, she was pretty aggressive in going after me. I was very attracted to her as well, so we started to date, and a few months later, we got married. I thought it was a new start. But almost immediately, the feelings came back. I started to withdraw from her. Since then, we pretty much have led separate lives. I'm not surprised she thinks I'm having an affair. What else could she think? What are you going to tell her?"

"Nothing, except that I talked to you and that you'll see her before she leaves Havana. The rest is up to you."

"Yeah, up to me. To tell you the truth, I don't think she'll be heartbroken. We've had a bad marriage too long for that. More likely, she'll be relieved. She's young, with her whole life ahead of her. I'll see that she's taken care of financially. That's something, hmm?"

A bell rang in Hunter's head; the pieces suddenly fit into place.

Like Crawford, Hunter couldn't help but think that Julie Manning was going to be relieved. There was never any sense of warmth or love when she talked about her husband. There was never any sense of wanting to repair their marriage or sense of compassion—but there was plenty of resentment, hatred, and contempt. Sitting there across from Crawford, Hunter realized that all Julie ever had wanted was a divorce from her husband, but she'd needed evidence of infidelity, and to get that, she'd needed Ashton Hunter. She hadn't given up and had been willing to beg on her hands and knees for Hunter to continue the case. He hadn't taken her literally then, but now he did. It had been a scam from day one.

She had told him how they met, but she'd been after his money from the time she first served him dinner as a waitress at the fancy country club two years before. He was an older man, single, and loaded with cash. He had become her means to the good life.

Hunter hoped that Crawford would fight it out in court and that all she'd get was the change in his pocket—sort of a final tip.

He doubted that would happen. Crawford was too decent of a guy.

But it was none of his business.

"Yeah, that's something," Hunter said.

33

The Dilemma

On Monday morning, Hunter met Maria in the park across the street from where she was staying in Marianao.

She was every bit Maria Sanchez again; the blonde wig was gone, as was the name Luciana Ruiz. She really never had been Luciana to him, yet he didn't know who this Maria was, not really. He had known her for only a few days before she went to London. Last Saturday night, they had had dinner and talked for a few hours—nothing of much substance, but it had been pleasant. Actually, it had been more than pleasant. They had both been attracted to each other, but that had not been the time to pursue it. Maria seemingly had understood that as well.

Now Hunter was sitting on a park bench beside her, not knowing what to say. She appeared to be emotionally intact, much as she'd been when they had dinner two nights before. At that time, he had found it bizarre, considering she'd been in danger from her husband. But now it all made sense to him.

He had to ask himself, *Why am I even here?*

Yesterday he'd thought about it a lot. There was no doubt in his mind Maria had returned from London and hired someone to kill her husband. That was crystal clear. My God, if she was capable of doing that, what else was she capable of doing? She had been justified in protecting herself, but she had done what few other women in her position ever did: she had taken one more step forward, deliberately and with premeditation. With that one step, she had become a murderer.

Hunter had spent the night before trying to rationalize it. If a woman were being attacked by her husband and felt her life was in danger, any court in the world would conclude she was justified to use deadly force to protect herself. But that had not been the case with Maria. Hunter had helped her remove herself from that situation—temporarily, as it turned out, through no fault of his own, rather than permanently, as he had intended—so she wouldn't be in immediate danger. In London, she had been out of harm's way. She would have been free to create a new life for herself, away from her husband's punches and whatever else he'd done to her. Instead, she intentionally and calculatedly had returned to Havana, placing herself back in danger for the sole purpose of hiring someone to murder her abuser. She had taken the step from being safe of further abuse to committing homicide.

The kicker was, Hunter knew about it. That was, he'd put the pieces together after her husband was murdered. In law, both in the States and in Cuba, he would be considered an accessory after the fact if he withheld that information from the authorities. In Cuba, that would mean a long prison term. As for Maria, her hiring someone to kill another person was treated the same as if she had put a gun to her husband's head and pulled the trigger herself. It meant the death penalty.

So what was he going to do?

Hunter wondered if he was being unnecessarily harsh with Maria. Had he underestimated the effects that his planning and implementation of her escape to London would have on her? Asking her to change her identity, leave her own country, and go somewhere else to live for the rest of her life, away from family and friends, carried extraordinary consequences that no person should have to be subjected to. Yet he'd done it. Was he himself culpable in what had happened in the aftermath?

He remembered the first time he'd met Maria in Los Bohemios and their first conversation. She had made it clear from the onset that she wanted him to find someone to kill her husband. His plan then had been to circumvent that. Maria hadn't had many options. But Hunter had given her a way out. It hadn't been the ideal solution, but it might have been the only one, and it was better than murder. Or was it? Maria apparently hadn't thought so, or she wouldn't have returned.

So what was he left with?

Should he go to the police and lay the whole rotten story out for them? That would certainly get him off the hook from prosecution. But would Maria—a woman who had been physically and mentally abused and tormented for five years, constantly had feared for her life from the very man who should have been protecting her, had been unable to seek help from the agencies that existed for that purpose, and had gone through hell and had the marks on her body to prove it—be deserving of the death penalty?

Hunter was ashamed to think he was facing a moral dilemma. There shouldn't have been one. The answer should have been right there for him to see. There should have been no dilemma whatsoever, but there was. Little was clear to him.

Again, he asked himself, *What am I going to do?*

He had to decide now, while sitting next to Maria on that bench in the park, because if he waited too long—an hour, a day, or even a decade or more—the problem facing him would become a different problem, a more serious one.

He swayed between the sharp horns of the dilemma. The thought occurred to him briefly to end the dilemma by chopping off one of the horns—an easy task he was unable to perform. He realized that to resolve the dilemma, he had to use the same mind he had used when he created it, and that was a terrible realization.

If he did not risk making a mistake now, he would be risking even more later.

The problem with dilemmas, as he'd found out during the war, was that there was a tendency to forever argue the positions rather than to make a decision. Ironically, below the surface, where it could be hidden from public view, there was something comforting in never resolving an issue. But the avoidance never lasted. Sooner or later, the dilemma had to be resolved, or one would face a new dilemma. Hunter felt like a prisoner in a tiny cell or, more accurately, a swimmer among drowning men. If he reached out a hand or a leg for them to grab on to, they would take him down with them. Being left to drift forever seemed like a better option. But being out in the high seas with no sign of rescue, he would also be in terrible peril.

Notwithstanding, he'd created the dilemma and the rules, and only he could abide by them or break them. Only he could choose.

Hunter always had striven to live a moral and compassionate life, but how could he do that with the knowledge of blood and horror, with the knowledge of the darkness of existence that he'd discovered was also inside him? In Italy, when killing people he didn't know, he had been challenged by that for the first time in his life and had failed. He had decided not to confront that dilemma, and now, a little more than a decade later, he faced another one, no less serious. Everything around him had failed; he had nowhere else to turn. He was faced once again with making a decision that he had cowardly eluded before.

The real moral dilemmas facing the human spirit never involved right and wrong. Most people sorted through those dilemmas with ease and speed if they were grounded in some sort of acceptable moral code of humanity instead of an ethical wasteland of despair. The only authentic dilemmas that mattered were the ones that declared war against themselves: right versus right. With those dilemmas, you got to hold the soul of another person in your hand and make a decision that would forever change the landscape of not only that person's soul but also yours. If you procrastinated, if you hesitated, if you succumbed, the dilemma would evaporate and then rear its horns once again sometime in the future when you thought life was grand, taking on a new, more terrible form that, unlike the previous one, you could not escape.

That was precisely where Hunter now found himself.

He knew that ultimately, whichever way he went, whichever horn he was gored by, he'd have to make peace with the intolerable consequences of not doing something he should have done or doing something he shouldn't have done.

He turned his head toward Maria, who was gazing silently at a tree in front of them, as he had been. She was calm and peaceful, as he was not.

"Had you read any of the papers yesterday—the headlines?" he asked her. He had seen only the *Havana Post*, but all the daily newspapers had carried the murder of the police captain on the front page. All of Havana was talking about it. The news agencies would have follow-ups for the next week at least, or until something else more newsworthy came along.

She didn't answer right away; instead, she continued to look steadily at the tree in front of them. It was a Caribbean pine. Several birds fluttered in and out of its branches. The tree was common, nothing special, and wasn't particularly beautiful, but she continued to stare at it.

"You know, Ash," she finally said, "this is the first time I can remember feeling this peaceful. I see this tree and the birds and feel the sun on my face as if for the first time."

That was all she said.

He sat there with her in silence for a while longer. Then he got up, leaned down, kissed her on the top of her head, and walked away.

Later that night, Hannigan, Babs, and Sammy all pitched in and cleaned the café after the dinner rush was over. There was only one guest left, a little old lady who made an annual pilgrimage to Havana for the sun. She was a seventy-three-year-old retired schoolteacher from North Dakota who felt she deserved a midwinter break from all the snow and ice. She was sitting off by herself, reading a book. Her name was Mrs. McGillicuddy, and she'd been a widow for the last five years. Hannigan and Babs sat at a table, sorting out the receipts of the day, and Sammy was sitting on a stool beside the jukebox, cleaning his guitar. This was their downtime.

"I wonder where Ash is," Babs said. "He left early this morning, and I haven't seen him since."

"He's probably on one of his cases, as usual," Hannigan said, writing some numbers down in a ledger. "He's a big boy. He can take care of himself." He looked up at Babs. "I taught him everything he's knows. He'll be fine."

"You taught him everything he knows?" Babs repeated skeptically. "Like what, Mr. Philosopher? Do tell."

"Like how the world works. Like how to shove the pieces in place so that everything fits nicely. That's how you avoid problems—knowing where everything goes. Right, Sammy?"

"If you say so, Mr. Slane," Sammy said dejectedly, running a rag down the guitar strings.

"That's the key to life—knowing where to put things," Hannigan said. "Sammy knows."

"How come you never taught me that?" Babs asked sarcastically.

"Women are different. They don't have to know that stuff. All they have to do is marry someone who does."

Overhearing the conversation, the little old lady looked up from her book and grimaced.

"Hannigan," Babs said, "if I weren't so tired, I'd get up and punch you a good one."

"So would I," Mrs. McGillicuddy said, throwing in her two cents.

"Well then, let's be thankful you're both tired."

Babs reached down for one of her shoes and threw it at him.

"Ouch! Let's not resort to violence now," he said. "I thought you didn't like violence." He picked the shoe up and tossed it in her general direction.

"If you make another comment about what women should or shouldn't know, I'll resort to more than violence!"

"Cool it, Babs! You're making Sammy upset."

"What's wrong, Sammy?" Babs asked. "You've been moping around all night."

"It's the woman I told you about. The one who came here from Port-au-Prince."

"Your love interest," Babs said. "Did you have a lovers' tiff?"

"More than that, I'm afraid to tell you. It's better I should sing than tell."

"Sing away, Sammy," Hannigan said. "You have three pairs of sympathetic ears."

Sammy dropped the rag to the floor, strummed the guitar a few times, and then began singing.

One morning in the park, I was greatly surprised
by a woman who'd taken my love and then vaporized.
She threw me over for another man,
threw me out the door like a used bedpan.
Now she came all the way from Port-au-Prince to sunny Havana.
But I have to admit that it was not as far as snowy Montana.

Everyone threw his or her head back and clapped at the clever rhyme, including Mrs. McGillicuddy. She always said Sammy's calypso music was the highlight of her trip.

She came to say that she was so very sorry for treating me wrong;
I was her only true man, whom she greatly loved for so very long.
She hungered and suffered being apart from me all these years.

282

She ached and grieved and harbored so many fears
that living without me was an unbearable thought.
A life away from me would bring her absolutely naught.
But last night on a romantic beach,
where we talked and laughed and shared a juicy peach,
I told her Sammy was not a rich man; he has so little money.
I looked at her with passion and called her my honey.
"But we have each other, and we could start anew."
At which point she stood up and simply bade me adieu.

"The story is longer and sadder than that," Sammy said, "but I do not have the heart or energy for any more."

"Well, that's a downright shame," Hannigan said. "To think all she wanted was money."

"Maybe it'll turn out for the best," Babs added. "Better that you find out now rather than marry the woman and have children with her."

"That's a good point, Miss Babs," Sammy said, no less dejected. "I will take that thought with me to bed. Good night to all. Good night to you, Mrs. McGillicuddy. I hope you have a restful sleep."

"Thank you, Sammy. You do the same," the old lady said. "Sorry about your romantic misadventure."

"Try to sleep well, Sammy," Babs said. "Tomorrow's a new day."

"See you in the morning," Hannigan said.

At that point, they heard the door open and saw Hunter come in. He turned right and went down the hallway toward the guest rooms without saying anything, which was uncharacteristic of him.

"Wonder what's wrong with him," Hannigan said. "Think I'll go find out."

"Leave him be," Babs said. "If he wants us to know, he'll tell us."

"Oh yeah? It took him over a decade to tell us about Angie. If there's something bothering him, I don't want to have to wait until I retire to find out."

"Go over to the jukebox. Drop some coins in. We should be happy tonight that all's going well. Instead, I'm on the verge of despair." She winked at Mrs. McGillicuddy, who returned the wink.

"Don't exaggerate, Babs. It's not good for the digestion. But the jukebox is a good idea!"

Hannigan went over to the machine, put three coins into the slot, and pushed D5. Babs got up and walked over to him.

Hannigan took her hand and then went over to the retired schoolteacher and grabbed her hand. "C'mon, Mrs. McGillicuddy. I'll show you how this is done. It's all copacetic!"

The record spun on the turntable, the arm rotated above it and then lowered the needle into the grooves, and the music began playing.

> One, two, three o'clock, four o'clock rock.
> Five, six, seven o'clock, eight o'clock rock.
> Nine, ten, eleven o'clock, twelve o'clock rock.
> We're gonna rock around the clock tonight.

The three of them danced away, kicking up their heels like teenagers, as if there were no tomorrow.

34

A Grain of Sand

It was Chunhua's birthday. Her name meant "Spring Flowers."

Yat-Sen Wong placed a bouquet of pink peonies in a vase and set the vase in the middle of the table. They were artificial rather than fresh, because it was not yet the blooming season. Nevertheless, they were Chunhua's favorite flowers, and because they were silk and nearly indistinguishable from real ones, he decided to honor her in the best way he could. Peonies symbolized riches and prosperity and were appropriate for the gift he had secured for her, which he'd wrapped in colorful, festive Chinese paper and tied with a yellow ribbon. Instead of placing the gift beside the flowers on the table, as one might expect, he set it under the table. When they finished their meal, he would reach below him and surprise her with it.

Wong had closed his gift shop at noon and spent the rest of the day preparing for his wife's birthday. He had requested Chunhua spend the day at a friend's house so that when she came home, everything would be a surprise. Tomorrow night he would throw a big party for her and invite all the tong members, but that night, he wanted something special for her, a celebration with just the two of them. He could hardly wait to see her eyes light up when she unwrapped her gift.

Wong's parents and extended family had left China to seek their fortune in New York City in the late 1800s. Among them had been Sai Wing Mock, his uncle, the younger brother of his mother. Sai Wing Mock, better known as Mock Duck, had wasted no time in forming a criminal organization. He'd called it the Hip Sing Tong.

As there had been other more proven criminal gangs in Chinatown, Mock Duck's new gang had presented a problem. The problem soon had escalated into all-out war. The Hip Sing Tong soon had established dominance, but that dominance had been challenged by another immigrant by the name of Tom Lee. By 1910, the war between Mock Duck's Hip Sing Tong and Tom Lee's On Leong Tong had become too much for Wong's parents, so they'd packed their bags and moved to Havana, where economic opportunities were plentiful. An added benefit had been an established, flourishing Chinatown in the city to help them better adjust to life in the tropics.

Wong had been only one year old at the time.

In Cuba, as he'd grown older, he'd excelled in school and acquired a love for learning, but as he'd discovered in his teens, academic life wasn't for him. His interests lay elsewhere. By the time he'd turned twenty, he had made several trips to New York to visit his uncle Mock Duck. There in New York he had sown the seeds of his future. His mission in life had been clear, given to him by his uncle: Yat-Sen would extend the New York Hip Sing Tong and create a branch in Havana. He would be its leader.

And that was what he had done.

Moreover, it was the only tong in Cuba. Ostensibly, a tong was a social hall or gathering place for the Chinese diaspora. Celebrations and other cultural events were commonly held at a tong. It also provided essential services to the Chinatown community, such as finding jobs for its members and teaching the language of the country—in this case, Spanish.

In fact, the Hip Sing Tong provided an essential cover for Yat-Sen's greater, more lucrative enterprise: his criminal activities. Within ten years, he had established his tong in racketeering, prostitution, counterfeiting, robbery, extortion, illegal gambling, arms trafficking, money laundering, and drug smuggling, much to the delight of his uncle back in New York, who had received a monthly cut in the operation. Although Yat-Sen didn't have another Chinese tong to compete with, which in itself was exceptional, he did have a big problem that plagued him: the Italian mob and the Jewish gangsters.

Exponentially, the problem had gotten worse over the years. The mob and the gangsters had been moving into Havana more and more over the last five years, increasing the numbers of their legal casinos and all the underground illegal activities that went with them, strong-arming their way into Wong's territories without regard for common decency. More and more, Yat-Sen was left with just a few grains of sand on the huge beach that was Havana. One errant grain of sand in particular had worked its way into his shoe and caused him a great deal of irritation: Santo Trafficante.

Then, one day recently, through a fluke, something extraordinary had happened. It wouldn't change much for his tong; that much he knew for certain. But it would bring him great satisfaction—greater satisfaction than anything else ever had given him in the past, save, of course, his marriage to Chunhua.

The table in their small apartment above the gift shop on Calle Cuchillo was set with food. He had cooked his wife's favorite meal: roasted Peking duck. Created during the Ming Dynasty, it had become the national dish of China. Chunhua, who was now seated at the table, was normally a reserved woman, but she became emotional when she saw the meal, nearly tearing up.

Yat-Sen thinly carved the mahogany-colored duck. He was pleased they could hear the crispy skin as he sliced into it, as that was a sign the duck had been properly roasted. He laid the slices in two neat rows on a plate. Then they both took a Mandarin pancake in one hand and used the other hand to pick up a slice of duck with chopsticks and dip it into the plum sauce. They spread the sauce onto the pancake using the slice of duck and then added some more slices as well as some cucumbers and green onions. Finally, they rolled up the pancake and ate.

The first bite brought a symphony of flavors to their palates, melding the scrumptious duck with the light sweetness and tartness of the sauce, the crunchiness of the skin, the contrasting coolness of the cucumber, and the piquant excitement of the green onions. The second time around, they added garlic paste and sugar, and of course, there was rice—plenty of it.

Yat-Sen had created something magnificent for Chunhua. They ate until they no longer could eat another bite. But the best was yet to come.

He looked into the eyes of his wife and could see she was greatly pleased. She was beautiful in her red-and-gold cheongsam. Yat-Sen had decided to wear a Western suit and tie for the occasion rather than his changshan, which he wore nearly every day for the tourists.

He poured another merlot for them. He'd chosen that wine because it was soft, sensual, and approachable, just like his wife.

"And now," Yat-Sen said, "for the pièce de résistance, if you'll allow me to use the French."

Chunhua put her hand to her mouth and giggled. Yat-Sen was not beyond showing off once in a while if the occasion warranted it.

He reached below the table, picked up a hammer he had placed there earlier, and gave it to his wife. She cocked her head to the side, looking at it. Then, confused, she looked at her husband.

He smiled and reached below the table again, and this time, he picked up the gift and set it before her. He motioned with his hands for her to unwrap it.

She did.

In all its splendor, there sat the Guan Yin statue.

"Take the hammer, and hit it solidly on the top. You'll want to break it. Go ahead; give it a good whack! Trust me." He knew that would seem like a bizarre thing for her to do, so he gave her a little more encouragement. "Trust me," he said again. "Smash it to pieces!"

She did.

That was precisely what he had done after Harry Smith left the statue with him. After he'd made not one but two copies of the statue, he'd smashed to pieces the original one out of curiosity—and who could have blamed him? Through the grapevine, he'd heard that a special Guan Yin was coming into the country from Saigon. Not only had the rumor been true, but the statue had landed in his little gift shop on Calle Cuchillo. Using one of the two statues he'd made as a mold, he'd recast the original. How could he not have taken advantage of that once-in-a-lifetime opportunity, especially when it involved Santo Trafficante?

When the plaster fell away, a solid-gold Guan Yin was revealed, worth in excess of a million dollars. Chunhua's eyes widened in disbelief.

"Happy birthday, my love," he said.

Yat-Sen reached down and took off one of his shoes. He held it upside down, and a single grain of sand dropped to the floor, never to get on his nerves again.

Printed in the United States
By Bookmasters